CROOKED PLOW

Itamar Vieira Junior (b. 1979) was born in Salvador, Bahia, Brazil. He received his master's degree in Geography from the Universidade Federal da Bahia, and from the same institution he received his PhD in Ethnic and African Studies. His doctoral research focused on the ongoing struggles of *quilombos*, the Afro-Brazilian communities organized by escaped slaves and their descendants. In 2018, his novel *Torto arado* (*Crooked Plow*) won the Prémio Leya, a prestigious Portuguese literary prize awarded to unpublished fiction. In 2020, the book won the Jabuti, Brazil's most important literary prize, for Best Novel, as well as the Oceanos Prize for any literary work written in the Portuguese language. He has published collections of short stories, including *Dias* (2012) and *Doramar ou a odisseia* (2021), and a second novel, *Salvar o fogo* (2023).

Johnny Lorenz, son of Brazilian immigrants to the United States, is a professor of English at Montclair State University. He translated Clarice Lispector's *A Breath of Life* and *The Besieged City* (New Directions). His book of poetry, *Education by Windows*, was published by Poets & Traitors Press. His research has appeared in *Luso-Brazilian Review*, *Modern Fiction Studies*, and *Latin American Literary Review*. He has received a Fulbright and a PEN / Heim Translation Fund Grant. His translation of Itamar Vieira Junior's *Crooked Plow* received generous support from the National Endowment for the Arts.

CROOKED PLOW

Itamar Vieira Junior

Translated by Johnny Lorenz

VERSO

London • New York

The translation of this novel from Brazilian Portuguese received
generous support from the National Endowment for the Arts (NEA),
for which both the author and the translator are deeply grateful.

This English-language edition published by Verso 2023
Originally published as *Torto arado*
© Itamar Vieira Junior and Leya S.A. 2018
Translation © Johnny Lorenz 2023

3 5 7 9 10 8 6 4 2

Verso
UK: 6 Meard Street, London W1F 0EG
US: 388 Atlantic Avenue, Brooklyn, NY 11217
versobooks.com

Verso is the imprint of New Left Books

ISBN-13: 978-1-83976-640-4
ISBN-13: 978-1-83976-641-1 (UK EBK)
ISBN-13: 978-1-83976-642-8 (US EBK)

British Library Cataloguing in Publication Data
A catalogue record for this book is available from the British Library

Library of Congress Cataloging-in-Publication Data

Names: Vieira Junior, Itamar, 1979– author. | Lorenz, Johnny, translator.
Title: Crooked plow : a novel / Itamar Vieira Junior ; translated by Johnny
    Lorenz.
Other titles: Torto arado. English
Description: London ; New York : Verso, 2023.
Identifiers: LCCN 2023003661 (print) | LCCN 2023003662 (ebook) | ISBN
    9781839766404 (paperback) | ISBN 9781839766411 (UK ebook) | ISBN
    9781839766428 (US ebook)
Subjects: LCGFT: Novels.
Classification: LCC PQ9698.432.I5357 T6713 2023 (print) | LCC
    PQ9698.432.I5357 (ebook) | DDC 869.3/5 — dc23/eng/20230201
LC record available at https://lccn.loc.gov/2023003661
LC ebook record available at https://lccn.loc.gov/2023003662

Typeset in Electra LT by Hewer Text UK Ltd, Edinburgh
Printed and bound by CPI Group (UK) Ltd, Croydon CR0 4YY

For my father

The land, the wheat, the bread, our table, our family (the land); within this cycle, father would say in his sermons, there is love, labor and time.

Raduan Nassar

CONTENTS

I. EDGE OF THE BLADE

1.

When I opened the suitcase and took out the knife, wrapped in a grimy old rag tied with a knot and covered in dark stains, I was just over seven years old. My sister Belonísia, at my side, was about a year younger than me. We'd been playing outside of our old house with dolls we'd fashioned from corn harvested the previous week. We'd transform the yellowing husks around the cobs into dresses, pretending the dolls were our daughters, the daughters of Bibiana and Belonísia. When we noticed Grandma Donana in the backyard, walking away from the house, we turned toward each other to give the nod: all clear. It was time to find out what she'd been hiding in her leather suitcase, among threadbare clothes that smelled like rancid lard. It wasn't lost on Grandma how quickly we were growing up; curious girls, we'd push into her bedroom and interrogate her about conversations we'd overheard and things that piqued our interest, such as the objects buried in her suitcase. Our parents would reprimand us constantly, but Grandma only needed to give that firm look of hers, and we'd shiver and blush as if we'd drawn too close to the fire.

So when I saw her walking through the backyard, I immediately looked over at Belonísia. Determined to rifle through Grandma's things, I decided I'd tiptoe over to her room and open the suitcase, its worn leather tarnished and covered in a layer of dirt. That suitcase had been hidden beneath her bed for as long as we could remember. From the doorway I spied Grandma making her way toward the woods past the orchard and vegetable garden, beyond the old roosts of the chicken coop. In those days we were already accustomed to the way Grandma would talk to herself, muttering the strangest things, like when she'd ask someone—someone we couldn't see—to stay away from Carmelita, the aunt we'd never met. Grandma would tell that ghost dwelling in her memory to leave her girls alone. She'd utter a jumble of random, disconnected phrases. She'd talk about beings we couldn't see—spirits—or people we didn't know, distant relatives and comadres. We were used to hearing Grandma ramble on like that in the house, at the front door, on her way out to the fields, and in the backyard, as though in deep conversation with the chickens or withered trees. Belonísia and I would glance over at each other, laugh under our breath, and draw closer without her noticing. We'd pretend to play with whatever was at hand just to eavesdrop on her, and later, in the company of our dolls and the plants and animals, we'd repeat what Grandma had said with great seriousness. We'd repeat, too, what our mother whispered to our father in the kitchen: "She was talking up a storm today, she's been talking to herself more and more." Our father was reluctant to admit that Grandma had been showing signs of dementia, claiming she'd always talked to herself, she'd always recited her prayers and incantations aloud with that same distracted air.

On that day, we heard Grandma's voice fading into the distance amid all the clucking and birdsong, as though her prayers and chants, meaningless to us, had been chased off by our own excited panting, triggered by the wicked thing we were about to do. Belonísia squeezed herself under the bed and pulled out the suitcase. The peccary hide covering the rough, earthen floor bunched up beneath her body. I opened the suitcase now lying before our eyes. I pulled out a few pieces of old clothing, mostly threadbare, and others still quite vibrant and made brighter by the sunlight of that dry day, a light I could never accurately describe. Among the disordered clothes lay something mysterious, covered with a filthy rag, and it attracted us like a precious stone. I was the one who undid the knot, listening for Grandma's voice. I saw Belonísia's eyes catch the metal's radiance, as though she'd been presented with a gift still glowing from the forge. I picked up the knife, which was neither particularly large nor small, and my sister asked if she could hold it. I wouldn't let her; I wanted to examine it first. I sniffed the blade. It didn't have the rank odor of the other objects in my grandmother's suitcase; it wasn't stained or scratched. At that moment, what I wanted was to study my grandmother's secret in depth, not squander the chance to discover the meaning of the gleaming blade in my hands. I saw part of my face reflected back at me, as if in a mirror, and I saw the reflection of my sister's face behind mine. Belonísia tried to wrench the knife from my hand, but I jerked it backward. "Let me hold it, Bibiana." "Just wait," I said. It was then that I put the metal in my mouth, so intense was my desire to taste it, and just a moment later the knife was snatched violently away. My puzzled eyes locked on those of Belonísia, who was slipping the blade into her own mouth. Along with the lingering taste of metal came the flavor of the hot blood that began to run from a corner of my half-opened lips and drip from my chin. The blood further darkened the grimy, blotted cloth that had covered the knife.

Belonísia pulled the blade from her mouth, too, then brought her other hand up, as if trying to hold something in. Her lips reddened, and I wasn't sure if it was from the excitement of tasting the silver blade or from wounding herself, for she was also bleeding. I swallowed as much blood as I could. My sister was wiping her mouth frantically with her hand, her eyes squinting with tears as she tried to stand the pain. I heard my grandmother's slow steps approach, then she called out to me, to Zezé, Domingas, and Belonísia. "Bibiana, can't you see the potatoes are burning?" I became aware of a smell of burnt potatoes mingling with the smell of metal and the blood wetting our dresses.

There was a curtain separating Grandma Donana's room from the kitchen, and when she opened it, I'd already picked up the knife from the floor and wrapped it haphazardly with the soggy cloth, but I'd not yet pushed the leather suit-case back under the bed. I saw my grandmother's startled eyes, before her heavy hand struck the side of my head and Belonísia's in turn. I heard her ask what we were doing there, why her suitcase was out from under the bed, where did all that blood come from? "Say something!" she demanded, threatening to tear out our tongues. Little did she know that one of us was holding her tongue in her hand.

2.

Our parents returned from the fields to find Grandma out of her mind, plunging our heads into a large bucket of water and screaming: "She lost her tongue, she sliced her tongue!" She kept screaming it over and over so that the first thing Zeca Chapéu Grande and Salustiana Nicolau must have thought was that their two daughters had deliberately muti-lated themselves in some obscure ritual. The bucket was a red well. The two of us were crying our eyes out, and the more we sobbed, embraced by our parents and wanting to plead for their forgiveness, the more difficult it became to figure out which of us had lost her tongue and urgently needed to be taken to the hospital, many miles from Água Negra. The manager of the plantation showed up in the Ford Rural, green and white, to drive us there. The land-owners used the Rural when visiting the plantation, and Sutério, the manager, would drive it to town or around the vast fields when he wasn't on horseback.

My mother grabbed blankets and towels from various rooms to soak up the blood. She shouted impatiently at my father, who was gathering herbs from the garden with trembling hands. Her bulging eyes and shrill voice betrayed mounting despair. The herbs my father picked would be used during the ride, with prayers and incantations. Belonísia's eyes were red from weeping; as for my eyes, I couldn't tell, and my mother, bewildered, kept asking us what had happened, what had we been playing with, but we'd only answer in long moans impossible to decipher. My father was holding the tongue, wrapped in one of the few shirts he owned. Even then, what I feared was that the tongue would cry out on its own to tell on us. That it would turn us in for our meddling, our stubbornness, our transgression, our lack of concern and respect for Grandma and her things. And, worse, our irresponsibility in putting a knife in our mouths, knowing very well that knives bleed the beasts we hunt and the animals in the pen, and they kill men.

My father dressed the tongue with the herbs he'd collected. From the car window, I saw my siblings gathered around our grandmother while Dona Tonha, our neighbor, took her by the arm to lead her back into the house. Years later I'd come to regret what I did to leave my grandmother in tears, with a mind so confused, thinking herself incapable of looking after anyone. On our way to the hospital we could hear my mother's anguish in her whispered prayers, and her calloused hands, usually so warm, felt as though they'd been soaked in a bucket of water left out in the cool evening air.

At the hospital, we sat waiting for someone to attend to us. Our parents huddled in a corner of the room. I looked at my father's pants, caked with soil, which he hadn't had time to change. My mother was wearing a brightly colored kerchief around her head, the same one she'd wear in the fields under a hat to protect her from the sun. She wiped our faces with random items of clothing, constantly pulling out some musty article I couldn't identify. My father was still holding the tongue, wrapped in the shirt. He hid the herbs in the pockets of his pants, afraid, perhaps, of being singled out as a witch doctor in those unfamiliar surroundings. It was the first place I'd ever been where I saw more White faces than Black. I noticed people looking at us with curiosity but without drawing near.

When the doctor led us to the consulting room and my father showed him the tongue, like a wilted flower in his hands, I saw the doctor shake his head. He gave a long sigh when we opened our mouths for him almost in unison. This one's much worse. She'll have difficulty speaking and swallowing. There's no way we can reattach it. Now I have the words to explain what was happening, but, at the time, none of it made sense to me; it could hardly have made sense to my mother and father. While the doctor was speaking, Belonísia wouldn't look at me, but I knew we remained united.

Our wounds were sutured, and we spent two more days at the hospital. We left with an assortment of antibiotics and painkillers. We'd need to return in a couple of weeks for the stitches to be removed. We'd eat only porridge and purées, various kinds of mashed food. My mother would abandon her work in the fields for weeks and devote her time to caring for us. Only one of her girls would have serious problems with speaking and swallowing. Nevertheless, both of us grew silent.

Before the accident, we'd never ventured beyond the plantation. We'd never seen such a wide road, with cars traveling in both directions. A road leading to the most distant places on earth, that's what Sutério said. On the way to the hospital, we were overwhelmed by our own suffering, by the smell of clotting blood and the prayers of our stunned parents. Sutério just laughed, telling our parents that kids are like cats; one minute they're here, the next they're off somewhere else getting into all sorts of trouble, giving their parents headaches. He had children, he explained, so he knew all about it. On the ride home, the two of us were still in terrible pain, one even more than the other, both of us exhausted, though our injuries were different. One of us had cut off her tongue completely; the other had a deep wound but wasn't in danger of losing her tongue.

We'd never ridden in the Rural before, or in any automobile. How different it all was, the world beyond Água Negra! How different it was, the city with its houses pressed one against the other, sharing the same walls. And the roads paved with stones. The roads around the plantation and even the floors of our houses were just flattened earth. Made of mud, nothing else, the same mud we'd use to make pies for our corncob dolls, the same mud from which the plants would grow, the plants that fed us. The same mud in which

10

we'd bury the placenta and umbilical cord of each newborn child. The same mud in which we'd bury the mortal remains of our dead. The same mud into which we'd all descend one day. No one escapes. We only noticed that new world outside our window on the way back home, sitting on separate ends of the back seat, our mother between us absorbed in thought after the mess we'd made of things.

When we arrived at the house, Zezé and Domingas, the little ones, were there with Dona Tonha. My father asked where Grandma was, while my mother stood at the doorway holding our hands. Tonha said it had been a couple of hours since Grandma headed down to the river. By herself? Yes, and carrying a small bundle.

3.

My mother, Salu, once told me I was the eldest of four living children and just as many who didn't survive. Belonísia arrived shortly after me when my mother was still breastfeeding, disproving the theory that a woman couldn't get pregnant while nursing. My mother gave birth to me and then to my sister without any stillbirths in between, unlike what would happen later. After Belonísia, my mother was delivered of one dead child, then another, and then, two years later, my brother Zezé arrived, and Domingas was last. But between Zezé and Domingas my mother had two babies who didn't make it. Grandma Donana assisted my mother each time she went into labor. She was a midwife, or what folks around here

11

call "a mother who catches babies." In a sense, Donana was both grandmother and mother to us. On leaving the womb of Salustiana Nicolau, all of us—the living children, the dead ones, and those who would soon die—were welcomed by Donana's small hands, the first space we occupied outside of Salu's body, those cupped hands I've so often seen filled with earth, with shelled corn and picked-over beans. Small hands with clipped nails, just what a midwife's hands should be, Dona Tonha would say. Hands small enough to enter a womb and skillfully turn a baby who was breech or otherwise facing the wrong way. Grandma assisted the pregnant women on the plantation when it was time, and she continued to deliver babies until she was quite old.

When we were born, our parents were already working in the fields of the Fazenda Água Negra. My father had gone to fetch Grandma Donana weeks before my birth. I grew up listening to Grandma grumble about being so far from the plantation that had been her home, betraying a longing she half suppressed. She would never demand to go back, she understood her role at her son's side, but she'd continue muttering her lament. The day my father went to get her, back at the place where he was born, Grandma was alone in that old house. Her children, one by one, had left in search of work. My father was the first to leave, then Carmelita. She ran away one day without telling anyone where she was going, just after Grandma had become a widow for the third time. Grandma wouldn't have tried to stop her.

By then, the fields of the Fazenda Caxangá, so abundant in fruit trees, had been carved up by ambitious men who took possession of large tracts of land. The long-established tenants were being evicted, and more recent arrivals had also been told to pack their bags. The big shots, accompanied by armed thugs, would show up bearing obscure documents and announce that they'd bought a section of Caxangá. Some of these transactions were confirmed by the foremen; some weren't. After my father had arrived at Água Negra, he'd occasionally go back to visit his mother. Salu told us these stories as we grew up. They'd allowed Grandma Donana to stick around the plantation out of respect for her advanced age; they'd grown used to her presence. But there was another reason: word had traveled from house to house, from tongue to tongue, about the strange powers of the old witch, her cycles of marriage and widowhood, the cross she'd had to bear in life, along with rumors about her son, the boy who'd lost his mind and hidden for weeks in the woods, in the company of a jaguar.

Belonísia and I were the closest of Salu's children, and maybe for that reason we quarreled the most. We were almost the same age. We used to wander together around the backyard of the house, gathering flowers and scooping mud, picking up stones to build our stove, collecting branches to make our jirau—a sort of outdoor kitchen counter, very primitive—and tools to till our imaginary fields, imitating the movements our parents and ancestors had handed down to us. We'd argue about what went where, what we were going to plant or cook. We'd squabble over the shoes we made from wide, green leaves gathered in the surrounding forest. We'd straddle wooden sticks, pretending they were horses. We'd collect the extra firewood to make our furniture. When our disagreements turned into full-fledged fights, our mother, who didn't have time for foolishness, would intervene, refusing to let us out of the house unless we behaved. We'd promise not to fight, then go back outside and start playing our games again, inevitably scuffling and scratching and pulling each other's hair for good measure.

But during those first few months while we healed from our wounds, we felt a powerful bond between us, impervious to quarrels and infantile squabbling. A great sadness had descended upon our home. Our neighbors and godparents often visited, wishing for our speedy recovery. The women in the community looked after our younger siblings while my mother made a special porridge for us, or a salve to help with scarring, as well as purées of yam, sweet potato, manioc. Our father continued going to the fields at daybreak. He'd leave with his farm tools, but first he'd put his hand on our heads, whispering prayers to the encantados, the spirit beings. When eventually we went back to our children's games, we forgot all about our past quarrels, because one of us would have to speak for the other. One would be the other's voice. From then on, when we interacted, one of us would need to become more perceptive, read more attentively a sister's eyes and gestures. We'd become one. The sister who lent her voice studied the body language of the sister who was mute. The sister who was mute transmitted, through elaborate gestures and subtle movements, what she wanted to communicate.

For this symbiosis to occur and endure, our differences had to be put aside. We devoted our time to gaining a new understanding of each other's bodies. At first, it was hard for both of us, very hard—the constant repetition of words, picking up objects, pointing here and there so that one sister might grasp the other's intention. As the years passed, this shared body language became an extension of our individual expressions until each of us almost became the other, but without losing herself. Sometimes one of us would get annoyed with the other, but the pressing need for one sister to communicate something, and for the other to translate it, made it so that we'd both forget what had annoyed us in the first place.

That's how I became a part of Belonísia, just as she became a part of me. In the meantime, we were growing into young women, learning to cultivate the fields, studying the prayers of our parents, caring for our younger siblings. And so the years went by, and we felt like Siamese twins, sharing the same tongue to make the words that revealed what we needed to become.

4.

Grandma Donana came home with the hem of her dress soaked. She said she'd gone to the riverbank to leave the wickedness there. I understood "the wickedness" to mean the knife with the ivory handle, and even from a distance its radiance blinded me to what had just happened. Grandma returned downcast and pale, her eyelids drooping, swollen. She came toward us to pet our heads with the same hand with which she'd struck us. After her knobby fingers had caressed our faces, she went to her room without a word. She didn't come out until the next day.

My father headed to the room where he kept the saints, and lit a candle. My mother led us into her bedroom, asking us to lie still in her bed. She tied up the curtain at the entrance to the room so she could keep an eye on us, wary that we might try something else. She told us she was going to wash the pile of clothes, soaked with blood, that she'd taken to the hospital. From the bedroom I heard Tonha asking for the clothes so she could wash them herself. My mother was a tall woman, taller than our father, with strong limbs and large hands. There was something distinctive about her that people admired, that endeared her to them. But that day, slouching and exhausted, my mother seemed to have lost her noble demeanor.

Belonísia reached her hand toward mine and held it tightly. Unable to talk, we began learning, in an instinctive way, that our gestures could communicate what couldn't be said. We fell asleep in that position.

Grandma Donana never recovered from the events of that day. She hardly left the house to go outside. She'd sit on the edge of her bed, packing her old leather suitcase and then unpacking it. She'd take out all her things, her clothes, an empty perfume bottle, a small mirror, an old hairbrush, a missal, sheets of paper, documents of some sort. She regretted not having a single portrait of her children. It no longer annoyed Grandma when we entered her room, even during those private moments when she was packing and unpacking her suitcase. It was her way of killing time. It had been a while since she'd gone out to the fields; she limited herself to puttering around the vegetable garden. But she showed little enthusiasm even for the garden that had been one of her few pleasures in later life. She lost all interest in her plants, in the root tinctures she used to prepare for us and for the neighbors. My mother took charge of these domestic tasks Grandma had once considered her responsibility. She tried to stir Grandma's interest, calling her into the back-yard to see how big and strong a certain plant had grown, to check if the umbu tree had blossomed yet or if any pests had appeared amid the chaos of greenery. Grandma, indifferent, would glance at the garden and mutter something under her breath, then return to her room, picking up where she left off, removing things from her suitcase, putting them back in, as though at any moment an invitation might arrive asking her to return to the plantation where she was born, the only place that held any interest for her.

In the months that followed, while the two of us were recovering from our wounds, as one learned to express the desires of the other, and the other made those desires legible through her facial expressions, only one thing could draw Grandma Donana away from the realm of memory and from her daily ritual of packing and unpacking: a crippled dog that Belonísia had found by the roadside. The dog would wag his tail like the frond of a palm tree and hop around on three legs because one of his hind paws was fractured. It was heart-rending, watching the dog hold one leg off the ground and struggle to walk. Something about this creature broke through the silence that had, for months, enveloped our family. We noticed how often Grandma would call one of us over to point out any slight change in the dog's movements. For a time, she forgot all about her suitcase and spent her days gazing out the window at Fusco. She was the one who named the dog, and it was only Fusco's company she seemed to want.

Soon after, however, she asked Belonísia and me to sleep in her small room, so she wouldn't be alone. We agreed. Grandma would tell us stories that never ended. She'd fall asleep somewhere in the middle. Knowing that no story would reach a conclusion, I'd sometimes fall asleep before Grandma did. In the early morning, I'd hear her get out of bed and open the back door while it was still dark, and she'd go and talk to Fusco, almost whispering, but I could make out her voice. Grandma had never raised her hand against us—except on that day when we'd violated what she considered sacred, intruding into her past, bringing back what she didn't wish to remember. She didn't want our innocent hands touching the source of her anguish; at the same time, she didn't want to let go of her memories completely— they were keeping her alive. Those memories gave meaning to the days she had left to her; by the same token, they reminded her that she had never surrendered to the difficulties life had put in her way.

One morning, Grandma Donana awoke and started calling me Carmelita, explaining that she'd come up with a solution and I shouldn't worry, I wouldn't have to leave. I was twelve years old at the time; Belonísia would've been almost eleven. Later, I'd sometimes hear Grandma call Belonísia, too, by Carmelita's name. My sister would just laugh at the mix-up. We'd glance at one another and make fun of the confusion that had overtaken her mind. In Grandma Donana's eyes, Fusco had changed into a jaguar; she advised us to be careful. She kept asking us to walk the trails with her in search of my father, who could be found, she'd heard, at the foot of a jatoba tree, sleeping beside the tame jaguar into which it seemed our dog had been transformed. We knew our father labored in the fields every day, so the things my grandmother was saying didn't make sense. Even so, my mother asked us to go with her, to keep an eye on her so she wouldn't get hurt or lost in the woods. "Don't let your grandmother step into the stream. Watch out for snakes. And don't laugh at your grandmother." We'd walk beside her and then, as it was already December, we'd stop here and there to collect ripe fruit. We'd end up forgetting about Grandma, sometimes we'd lose sight of her completely; but then we'd keep quiet, and soon her voice would ring out from the middle of the woods calling for Carmelita and her other kids to help find Zeca, and we'd run to meet her.

When my father returned home from the fields and we tried to explain to Grandma that Zeca was standing right there in front of her, she always said it wasn't him, and that the only thing she wanted from that man was his hat.

One afternoon in February, while we were nodding off in the summer heat, Grandma slipped out. When my mother, farming a plot of land closer to the house, came back home to drink some water, she noticed that her mother-in-law wasn't there. She told me to find her. I wanted Belonísia to go with me, but I didn't know where she was. I went down the path Grandma usually took with her other "kids" when searching for my father. Along the way there stood a large buriti palm, and the ground was covered with fallen fruit. Before resuming my search for Grandma, who should have arrived by then at her usual spot, I gathered all the fruit I could carry by lifting the skirt of my dress and improvising a basket. The copper-colored globes had thick, scaly skin; you would never guess at the succulent flesh whose juices stained the bodies of the women carrying the fresh pulp to sell in town. The money it brought in allowed us to buy necessities when our crops were destroyed by drought or floods. Carrying the buriti fruit in the fold of my skirt, I arrived at the shallow part of the Utinga River where it fed into a marsh near the path to the fields, and there in the shallows I found Grandma, floating face down like an animal. Her white hair, like a luminous loofa sponge, reflected the sunlight in the clear water. I recognized her faded dress; it was so old, it might have been the same dress Grandma was wearing when she first arrived at our house in the back of a truck, my father at her side, just before I was born. Terrified by the vision before me, likely the first time I'd seen death up close, I let all the fruit fall and roll into the shallows. I shook my grandmother—might she wake up?—and turned her small, frail body over, then tried to pull her out of the water, but I wasn't able.

I ran home for help, suffocated by what I'd seen. Along the way I found Belonísia crouching by the same buriti tree where I'd stopped just minutes before. She was gathering the fruit I'd been unable to carry with me to the river. She looked up and saw the terror on my face. One of us would tell the others what had happened.

5.

No one touched the suitcase Grandma Donana had spent the final months of her life packing and unpacking day after day. We were by then familiar with every item of clothing, every object, having watched Grandma conduct her endless ritual. My mother suggested that perhaps some passing traveler, in search of work and needing clothing for his family, might accept the suitcase as a gift. But my father didn't have the stomach to give away what had belonged to his mother, so Salu didn't bring it up again. No one mentioned the knife; no one had any idea what happened to it or why there was so much mystery around it. No one ever got out of Grandma why the knife had been wrapped in that bloodstained rag, or why such a handsome blade had not been sold when we were facing financial hardship. My father, with the knowledge he'd acquired on his travels, had judged the pearly-white handle to be real ivory.

My father embarked on a long period of mourning. He suspended the festive rituals he'd always organized at our house to honor the encantados. He continued attending to people who'd arrive at our door with their afflictions, in need of help, or a prayer, or a root tincture. Zeca Chapéu Grande only revealed his grief in subtle gestures, for people like my father didn't have the luxury of shutting themselves away to mourn. His eyes turned misty; he didn't speak much. And he kept on tramping out to the fields to work.

A few weeks after the burial, I noticed my mother standing in the doorway, her face turning suddenly pale as she looked out at the road. I went to her side; Belonísia and Domingas were in the front yard running around with Fusco, our crippled dog who, when playing with us, seemed to forget his infirmity. Something my mother saw made her say, "Lord have mercy." Belonísia, Domingas, and even the dog stopped what they were doing, alerted now by the strange howls that had reached their ears. A man was leading a woman by a rope down the road, the two of them accompanied by another woman. They were still some distance away, but I could see they were struggling as they headed toward us. The woman being pulled along was screaming the most disturbing and venomous words I'd ever heard.

"Isn't that Crispiniana I see there? Or is it Crispina?" my mother asked, referring to Saturnino's daughters, the twins. They were our neighbors at Água Negra. Saturnino was walking in front of the crazed daughter who was tied up with rope, crying out across earth and sky things we couldn't make sense of. The other twin, either Crispina or Crispiniana, was walking behind her, helping her father on the journey, pushing her mad sister and no doubt suffering from the harsh blows she dealt her, her sister's wild body lassoed as though she were an animal, her arms bound by knotted rope. Another piece of rope had been tied around

22

her wrists. She was barefoot, and her disheveled hair wasn't tucked as usual beneath her kerchief.

My mother asked us where our brother Zezé was. "He's with Papa," Domingas responded. "So go, you and Belonísia, go find your father and bring him back. Tell him compadre Saturnino is here with his two girls. It's something for your father." My sisters ran off while I drew closer to my mother's powerful body, dewy with sweat like the fields at dawn. From the doorway we could see the young woman's red eyes, her contorted face, spit foaming at the corners of her mouth. The sight transfixed me with curiosity and dread. As the three figures approached, my mother asked Saturnino what had happened, and, again, which sister this was. He looked spent, exhausted from dragging his daughter along the banks of the Santo Antônio to our house, near the Utinga. Taking off his hat respectfully, he replied, "It's Crispina."

"Ah, so you found her?" My mother's voice was trembling.

"She was hiding in the cemetery, they found her there asleep," Saturnino said as he stepped into our front yard.

Just the previous week, Crispina's father and siblings, including Crispiniana, had gone out searching for her. Many years earlier, their family had been welcomed at Água Negra; in fact, the first men who arrived at the plantation looking for work were Saturnino, Damião, and my father Zeca. Crispina and Crispiniana were the only twins in our community, the only identical twins I'd ever met. There was something mysterious about the sight of these two young women, little girls no longer. Mirrors were rare in those parts. Grandma Donana owned just a shard of mirror, and once in a while we'd get the chance to marvel at it as she packed and unpacked her suitcase in that ritual of her delirium. But a real mirror, something we could see ourselves in? All we had was the calm surface of the ferrous river where we saw ourselves, Black in a mirror also black, a mirror brought into being, perhaps, so that we could find ourselves. I'd not forgotten, after all that had happened, the shimmering mirror of the knife with the ivory handle. I'd caught a glimpse of our faces in that unyielding blade that in a flash sliced off a tongue and all the words it was capable of producing. Often, Crispina and Crispiniana would walk together side by side, each the double of the other. Like a mirror but with depth, width, and height, and without the broken edges of Grandma's mirror, or the sand and trees that framed our image on the water's surface.

As they neared our front door, Crispina tumbled hard to the ground. She was dirty and emitted a foul smell of sweat, urine, and dead flowers. I saw the terror in my mother's eyes. It wasn't the first or second or even the third time someone with a troubled mind had arrived at our door. And Crispina certainly wouldn't be the last to take up residence in our house, a house like one of those hospitals in the city, or so I'd heard, that take in people who've lost their minds. These people were neither guests nor visitors; they hadn't been invited. They were those who'd been unfastened from their own "I," unrecognizable to family members and to themselves. Possessed by a pernicious spirit, they were at once familiar and strange. Their families placed their hopes in the powers of Zeca Chapéu Grande, the Jarê healer, whose

24

mission was to restore a person's body or mind when needed. We'd always had to live with this magical facet of our father's life. He was in most ways a father like any other we knew, but his paternal role was more expansive: he cared for the afflicted, the sick, those who required remedies that were not to be found at a hospital, who required a knowledge that medical doctors lacked, the doctors who besides didn't exist. At the same time that I was proud of my father for the respect people showed him, I suffered from having to share our home with strangers who were hardly discreet, given to bellows of anguish and bewilderment, while the house became filled with the scent of candles and incense, with colored bottles of tinctures, with good people and bad people, some who were humble, others who were a nuisance, all of whom would install themselves in our modest house for weeks on end. My mother was the one who suffered most, for she'd have to stay home, administering remedies at specific times, keeping company with the family member who would also take up residence with us—it was required, when someone was "admitted"—to help care for the disturbed relative.

The delicate order of our daily life was disrupted: you could see it in the way everyone involved became unbalanced, including us children, as we began fearing the nocturnal shadows of a house illuminated by kerosene lamps and candles. We'd avoid sleeping by ourselves and huddle close to protect one another from the terrors entering our room before dawn with a hoarse cry or a slight trembling of the ground, caused by dark forces we believed were invading our home.

To look at Crispina crumpled there at our feet, her eyes the color of fire, her kinky hair matted with dead leaves and flower petals—some of which still held a hint of color and a lingering perfume—her lips whitened with threads of saliva, her flesh exhaling a nauseating odor while her sister Crispiniana stood nearby, was to experience all over again the misfortune that devastated us the day we removed the knife from the suitcase and, eager to know the beauty of that strange, forbidden radiance, placed it in our mouths, feeling liberated, as though this were possible, from all the prohibitions of our parents' and neighbors' religious beliefs, from our own oppression as workers bound to the plantation. It was as if the broken piece of mirror in our grandmother's dusty suitcase had lost another shard, for in the mirror of that blade we discovered a part of ourselves. Taking advantage of my distraction, Crispina grabbed my foot with such strength that she knocked me off balance, and my mother couldn't prevent my nasty fall, though I wept for other reasons.

Saturnino lost patience and delivered a resounding slap to his daughter's face, but she didn't react. Crispiniana, who'd been watching, brought her hand to her own face as though she were the one her father's hand had struck.

Through my tears I caught sight of Belonísia and Domingas returning along the path that led to the fields. It didn't take long for my father to show up, too, carrying his satchel and hoe. Zeca Chapéu Grande was different from the rest of us; he knew how to handle situations like this. He responded with such tenderness to the unexpected problems that arrived at our door. He immediately ordered Saturnino to untie his daughter, which he did without hesitation or fear. My father helped the young woman to stand up. From his thick lips came ancient prayers that created a sense of calm, a calm transmitted by the power everyone felt in my father's presence. He asked my mother and Crispiniana to give the young woman a bath. Belonísia and Domingas stayed close beside me. My father headed toward the room where he kept the saints, and there he unfolded a straw mat. Beside it he placed a small bench of worn leather.

He set down a candle and lit it, and everyone's attention turned to the flame. If the candle remained lit, the disturbed woman could come into our home—but if, succumbing to the energy around it, the flame were to go out, it meant there was no cure.

6.

It took several weeks for Crispina to finally get a hold of herself. Meanwhile we had to endure her screaming and moaning, day and night. During the day, we could tolerate it. At night, however, we'd be startled from sleep, and the noises made our skin crawl. I'd catch sight of my father walking out of his room, my mother just behind him, to check on her. We could hear them from our small bedroom where all of us kids slept piled on top of one another, but their words, when they reached my ears, were just whispers I couldn't make sense of. My mother, carrying the lamp,

27

would come in and soothe us back to sleep. For weeks, this was our nightly routine.

One morning, after I'd watered the plants in the yard and returned to the house—Crispina was already responding well to my father's prayers and tinctures—I heard the two sisters talking, quietly at first, but they soon started raising their voices. They'd just returned from a walk out back, after my father had given his consent. I couldn't make out everything they were saying, but what I heard kept hammering in my mind for the rest of the day. "That's not true." "Yes, it is." "You're sick in the head, Crispina." "I'm not crazy, Crispiniana." "Don't talk nonsense in front of Papa." "You were in the woods with him." "Isidoro wasn't even around." "He promised we'd live together." "He didn't promise you a thing, you're making it up." "You say that because you want him, that's why you were alone with him in the woods." "You've lost your mind. Papa was right to drag you here."

I listened, breathing quietly, attentive to every word, and just as alertly I listened for my mother so she wouldn't catch me eavesdropping. I knew the scolding I'd get for listening in on a conversation between two people older than myself. Suddenly Crispina was screaming for her sister to go away, to leave her in peace, and from between the curtains I saw her eyes glow red as embers. She began drooling, a milky mucous in the corner of her lips. What followed was a commotion of screams and cries, total chaos. Both sisters were hollering and rolling around the floor, tearing the kerchiefs from each other's heads, yanking each other's hair.

That spectacle was a shock to me, but Belonísia was snickering as she joined me. My mother, washing the cookware with water I'd brought back from the river earlier that day, left the pans on the jirau outside and came running into the room. "What's all this?" she asked, charging forward to separate the sisters. "Get over here," glaring at Belonísia and me, "and help me out." We held on to Crispiniana's arms. Her eyes were swollen from tears; her hair was a disaster. My mother grabbed hold of Crispina, the disturbed one. Her eyes were glassy, and her mouth repeated the accusations she'd leveled earlier at her sister. My mother threatened to call Saturnino to take both of them back home, "and then there's nothing doing, we won't help you, and I won't allow you back here, Crispina." Shaken by the threat, Crispina broke down in her arms, resting her head on my mother's chest. Salustiana Nicolau ordered Crispiniana to take the two of us outside, so she could be alone with her sister.

Crispiniana straightened up her torn clothes and walked out into the backyard. She was weeping quietly, then, when she was done with tears, she picked up the utensils my mother had been washing and finished the chore for her. Belonísia and I remained in the center room, pretending to play in silence so we could listen to what Crispina told our mother. She continued saying what she'd said before, that she'd found her boyfriend lying down with her sister in the woods behind his house, that she was overcome by rage, a rage she'd never known before. She couldn't think straight, something evil had got into her; it was disturbing her mind. She'd only started thinking clearly again after spending those

29

few weeks at our house, and slowly it was all coming back to her, everything that had happened just before she ran away.

We were already familiar with the rest of the story from hearing Saturnino tell it when he arrived, but also from the gossip of neighbors, compadres, and comadres who spread the news up and down the paths that crisscrossed the plantation. After Crispina had vanished without a trace, her father, boyfriend, and siblings went searching for her in the fields, in the woods surrounding the Santo Antônio River and in the marshes and wetlands, without success. Crispina's father, tormented by her sudden disappearance, walked all the way into town to seek help from the police. Every day he'd hear a different story: that Crispina had been seen heading to a village not far from the plantation, or boarding a bus to the capital, or that someone had heard a madwoman shrieking in the night. Or even that she'd been spotted stealing fruit from someone's backyard and that compadre Domingos had fired his rifle at the thief, believing he'd seen a fox, and so Saturnino rushed over, but when he got there, his legs wobbly, he discovered the story wasn't true.

Eight days had passed when a gravedigger at the cemetery in town happened on Crispina sleeping among the tombs. She was unable to explain who she was, much less where she lived or what she was doing there. She was discovered just after All Souls' Day, surrounded by shriveled flowers retaining the scent of things wilted and diminished by their fugacity—wild angelicas, chrysanthemums and lilies left by well-off families, alongside flowers fashioned from wire and crêpe paper, shredded by the passing of time, the flowers left by families that couldn't afford real bouquets. Crispina had lost a lot of weight, abandoned to her own obliviousness, filthy from the earth that covered the dead, filthy from endless walking, her feet and hands wounded, her body reeking of sweat and urine. Compadre Saturnino, having surrendered to fate, accepting what could not be foreseen, went to find his daughter. He couldn't count on Sutério lending a hand and bringing her back home in the Ford Rural. In fact, Sutério had given him the excuse that he was too busy to drive out with the boss's truck, so Saturnino came up with the idea of lassoing her as if she were an animal or, indeed, a disturbed woman who needed the help of a Jarê healer. Accompanied by Crispina's sister, they walked for many hours until finally arriving at the door of Zeca Chapéu Grande, the man who could cure a daughter's madness.

My father knew all about madness, or so folks said, because Zeca himself had gone crazy when he was a young man. We'd been raised with the understanding that a Jarê healer was obligated to attend to the sick and restore the health of the body or of the spirit. What appeared most often at our door were maladies of the divided spirit—people who had somehow lost their stories, lost their memories, people separated from themselves, people you couldn't distinguish from wild beasts. Some thought madness was so common in that region because the first migrants had mining in their blood. They'd gone insane hunting for diamonds, seeking their radiance in the night, moving on from one hill to start digging in another, moving on from the land to go combing the river. People chasing fortunes who dreamed night and day of some good luck, but grew frustrated after enduring long periods of exhausting toil, breaking rocks and washing gravel, without the stone's radiance ever throwing a slender beam of light across their field of vision. But of those who got lucky, how many were able to free themselves from this delirium? How many found themselves unable to fall asleep, night after night, the stones tucked beneath them, protected from the envy of others? Unable even to bathe in the river, alert to deceivers on every side?

Crispina tried to convince my mother to send her sister back home and let her remain in our house by herself. My mother, speaking assertively, said to let bygones be bygones, they were sisters, and when Crispina had first arrived at our house, Crispiniana had cared for her with the devotion of a mother. "Who ever heard of sisters from the same belly acting like enemies?" she asked. She'd never seen such behavior. It could only bring bad luck to them both. The twins gradually started talking to each other again, getting along, at least well enough, during the rest of their time at our house. Though they stopped bickering, they weren't "fingers of the same hand," as my mother later explained to my father.

Crispina recovered her health, the color in her cheeks and the physical strength typical of our local women, women who worked on a plantation. Her eyes shone, and her face was once again a mirror reflecting the face of her sister Crispiniana. Soon it would be time for both to return to the banks of the Santo Antônio. The ties between us, between us all, had been strengthened: the hand of my father would rest upon Crispina's head for as long as she lived, and upon the heads of everyone in her family. Where we're from, "compadre" and "comadre" are what you call, respectively, the godfather and godmother of your child, just as a godparent would also refer to the father and mother of the godchild as "compadre" and "comadre." But folks referred to Zeca Chapéu Grande as compadre for a different reason: he was the spiritual father of the entire community at Água Negra.

When Crispina left our house she immediately got back together with Isidoro, against the wishes of her own father. They gathered their belongings and moved into the modest hut they'd built across the way, a typical dwelling with walls of dried mud. From the doorway of her father's house, Crispiniana would watch her sister with the man she loved so fiercely. We suspected this story wasn't going to end there.

7.

Years after the accident that had left one of his daughters mute, my father, with Sutério's encouragement, invited my mother's brother to join us at Água Negra. Sutério, the manager, wanted to bring in folks who "would put their shoulder to the wheel," who, as my father explained, "weren't afraid of hard work and would pour their sweat into the fields." They could build houses of mud, but not brick, nothing enduring to mark how long a family had been on the land. They could cultivate a small plot of squashes, beans, and okra, but nothing that would distract them from the owner's crops because, after all, working for him was what enabled them to live on this land. They could bring their women and children; the more the merrier, in fact, because eventually the children would grow up and replace whoever was too old to work. The owner of the plantation would have confidence in them, trust them; they'd be his godchildren. Money, there'd be none of that, but there'd be food on the table. The workers could make their home on the plantation with no problem, without being harassed. They just had to follow the rules. I heard my father tell my uncle that things were much worse during their grand-parents' time; you couldn't cultivate your own plot, you couldn't even have a house; everyone was piled up together in a single bunkhouse.

To convince his brother-in-law, my father explained how rewarding it was to work in the rice paddies, for the region received plenty of rain and the land was fertile. "Look around," and he threw his arms wide to show off the rows of crops, the lush backyard and the surrounding woods. "We got everything we need. And your kids, they can be real useful. See, round here there's this small, black bird, about so big"—his fingers indicated the approximate size of the pest—"that invades the rice paddy early in the morning. The kids can help scare the birds off. Here, everyone gets up early to scare them off; it's the only way to get a good harvest."

It was true. For the many years rice had been planted in the wetlands, along the edge of the marsh, we'd get out of bed before sunrise and head out to the paddies. We'd arm ourselves with sticks, stones, anything that could be used to scare off those small birds with feathers so black they shone blue in the morning light. If we weren't quick enough, strong beaks would break through the ripened grain and slender tongues would suck up everything inside. The adults went off to work, so it was left to us children to deal with the pests. The neighborhood boys would show up with slingshots in hand, and sometimes they'd even bring a bird down. Once it made Belonísia cry, and she only stopped when I suggested giving the bird a proper funeral, with the wildflowers we'd picked and an empty candle box for a coffin.

My uncle journeyed to Água Negra on the back of a donkey, his wife riding another, and the children on foot, but they all took turns riding and walking. They were allowed to stay for a while in a brick house that was kept empty to receive aspiring workers who'd just recently arrived. Candidates lived there during a probationary period in which to demonstrate their productivity and work ethic. If approved, they'd be given a parcel of land where they could build their longed-for house and keep a vegetable garden and small livestock.

And so Uncle Servó arrived with his wife, Hermelina, and their six children. It was the first time I'd met my cousins. My mother was thrilled, but, in that way peculiar to her, she preferred to hide her feelings. She killed two chickens and prepared a feast. We all sat on the ground with our plates. Our cousins, who were rather shy, hid behind their parents. Salu had never met her sister-in-law and was eager to know the names of her nieces and nephews. Hermelina said,

35

"This boy here's the one I waited for you to baptize." He was the eldest, my cousin Severo, nearly a young man, looking all grown-up but just as shy as the others. My mother rebuked her brother for his negligence: "Servó, you let the boy remain a pagan for this long?"

After lunch, my cousins, scampering around the backyard, got over their initial awkwardness. The house where they'd be staying was near the Santo Antônio River, on the opposite side from us. For that reason, we weren't in frequent contact at first. We'd get together for celebrations and holidays, or when we held one of our Jarê rituals. I couldn't watch them out in the rice paddies by the Santo Antônio to see if they scared off those gleaming cowbirds as well as we did. Still, Severo, my shy cousin, paid an occasional visit with his parents. On Jarê nights, we'd stay up until morning running around out back, sharing stories, screaming with laughter.

Strangely, Belonísia and I, though we'd been growing closer and closer, kept a slight distance on these occasions, unconsciously perhaps, as each tried to win Severo's attention. Domingas and Zezé occupied themselves playing games with their younger cousins, while Belonísia and I, almost adolescents, came to discover the interest that one boy could arouse in two girls whose breasts were becoming more visible against their dresses, whose hips were growing more defined and whose bodies gave off a strange, increasingly noticeable aroma. Two girls who were suddenly quite vain, who hankered for a mirror, who spent their free time styling their hair and trying out different combinations from their sparse wardrobes.

36

Severo eventually overcame his shyness and began talking to us more freely. At first, the one who was the other's voice, the sister who spoke for both, would try, maybe inadvertently, to show Severo how easy it was to understand the signs we'd developed without any formal instruction in order to communicate with each other. He quickly learned how to read these signs as well, and sometimes he proved better at it than anyone else in the house. Soon, one of us would grow not only jealous over her cousin's attention, but also envious of his ability to comprehend things so well and so easily. Our cousin seemed to understand us better than our own parents did.

Cowbirds everywhere, every day, at dawn. We headed out to the fields to scare them off with our weapons. But they'll fool you; they're crafty, and they're lazy. We have a saying: cowbirds want to eat, they just don't want to work for it. They let others take the strain. Out in the marshes, they might lay their eggs in the nest of a xanã or a sangue-de-boi, a tanager with feathers red as fire that sings "tiê-tiê" to the eggs it believes are its own. Cowbirds also leave their eggs in the nest of the carrega-madeira, an ovenbird that makes busy building a house for its future hatchlings — and for the hatchlings of that parasite bird. The cowbirds sneak their fertilized eggs into the nests of the xorró-d'água, cabeça-de-velho, sabiá-bosteira, sabiá-bico-de-osso, bem-te-vi, patu-d'água, and guachu. Their eggs develop beneath the beauty of the song of the sofrê, or even beneath the zabelê, which makes its nest on the ground. But I've never seen a cowbird's egg in a paturi nest, why is that? I still remember some of those conversations, when we'd meet at our house or at Uncle Servó's place in an arid stretch near the Santo Antônio.

My uncle's arrival also meant that we gained a musician, a fife player to enliven our rituals in honor of the saints, because the rituals for the encantados were dominated by atabaque drums. For many years, our uncle's fife would lead our celebrations and also those at distant locales, when we journeyed to honor Saint Francis and other saints held in high esteem in the villages of Remanso and Pau-de-Colher.

On the Feast of Saint Sebastian, a saint to whom my father was devoted, for that day also marked his birthday, we threw the biggest party of all—one that attracted folks from all over, including the Jarê faithful from beyond the plantation. Many traveled far for the ceremony, where they enjoyed all kinds of food and drink to celebrate the blessings they'd received from the encantados. We children didn't pay much attention to the main activities; the younger kids played games outside, while the parents kept a distracted eye on the adolescents. Belonísia and I were listening in on a conversation between the daughters of Dona Carmeniuza and Dona Tonha. They were discussing the plantation owners' recent visit. They wanted to know if the owners had arrived at our section, too, and if they'd seized potatoes from our garden as well. "But the potatoes from our plots don't belong to them," someone said. "They want to plant rice and sugarcane, but then they take our potatoes, and our beans and squashes, too. Even the herbs we use for tea. And if the potatoes we gather are too small, they make us dig up more so they can take the biggest"—it was Santa talking now, her eyes wide with outrage. "A bunch of thieves! They already keep all the profit from the rice and sugar we harvest." The owners could easily have bought potatoes and beans at the store or at the public market in town. We couldn't buy anything because we earned no salary, though sometimes we made a little money selling buriti fruit and palm oil, if we found time to sneak away from the fields. Someone replied to Santa in a tone between mockery and indignation: "But who owns the land? They do. If we don't give them what they want, they'll kick us out. They'll spit on the ground and tell us to beat it before the spit dries."

My cousin Severo was listening from a distance, carving something into the dry mud with a stick.

Later, well into the night, my mother asked if anyone had seen Belonísia and Domingas. Domingas was playing with Jandira's daughter by the side of the house, but I'd lost track of Belonísia. "Everyone's leaving," my mother said. She wanted me to put Domingas to bed, but I didn't exactly obey. I brought Domingas inside; she didn't seem the least bit sleepy. I went back out to look for Belonísia. Not far off, beneath the withered umbu tree, I noticed a shadow distinct from the darkness of the night. The air was cool, and some folks were bundling up as they started walking home, while others hugged themselves in an attempt to keep warm. I slowly approached the tree sheltering that shadow, but before I could get any closer, the shadow divided itself. Belonísia was walking away from the tree nonchalantly. She passed by me smiling, her head held high. Then I saw Severo moving away from the tree as well, heading back to find his parents who were ready to make the journey home, led by the trembling light of a kerosene lamp.

I went to bed but was unable to fall asleep, unable to even look at my sister's face. Disillusionment is what I felt, and bitter rivalry, feelings that were new to me.

8.

At dawn I went to see my mother and informed her that Belonísia had been alone with cousin Severo beneath the umbu tree. I wasn't sure of everything I'd seen but, trusting my intuition, I added this detail: the pair had been kissing. For the first time I saw my mother in a fury. Without waiting for an explanation and before the news could reach my father, she meted out punishment; she grabbed a sandal and gave my sister a beating. Every slap of the sandal that Belonísia received burned my skin. Though I'd been overwhelmed by a fierce desire for vengeance for what I considered her betrayal, at the same time her punishment hurt me, for I'd never seen my sister get such a thrashing before, and ever since the accident with the knife there'd been this feeling of mutual dependence between us, more intense than that of Saturnino's twins.

Up until that moment, Belonísia had been closer to our mother, while I'd felt a stronger connection to our father. But that beating had long-lasting repercussions, and what my sister felt inside was more significant than the stinging

40

pain of her flesh. Afraid of how our father might react, our mother said nothing of what had happened. I'm not sure, but she must have figured out a way to tell Uncle Servó about it, through a messenger or perhaps by sending a note, since she knew how to write. Because then, for a considerable period of time, our cousin Severo didn't visit. Not even for the festive Jarê rituals that continued to be a regular event at our home.

Belonísia didn't look me in the eye for weeks. She'd walk into the center room or out into the yard and engage with Zezé or Domingas, all the while ignoring me. My feeling of betrayal slowly dissipated before her enduring sorrow. I felt a sudden, terrible regret for having caused my mother to punish Belonísia and for unintentionally exiling Severo from our lives. I'd not considered the consequences. The house grew quieter, despite the mischief of Domingas as well as Zezé, when he wasn't out in the fields with our father, and despite the traffic of people who'd constantly show up seeking the help of the healer Zeca Chapéu Grande. I saw, too, the remorse on my mother's face for what she'd done. Salu was strong-willed, someone who spoke firmly and without hesitation, but she'd never hit one of her children, let alone with a sandal. She tried to make up for having lost her temper by offering Belonísia a cup of porridge before the rest of us, or by giving her the lighter chores around the house, like washing the dishes out at the jirau while I was made to fetch buckets of water from the well or the river.

If my sister became embittered by the way my mother had reacted, things between us were even worse. For weeks,

41

Belonísia directed toward me her contempt and scorn. She ignored any gesture of reconciliation on my part, which only increased my regret. My sister was very proud, and, despite her youth, she knew how to follow through with her decisions. I didn't know what had really happened that day, or what led her to be alone with Severo. We had always shared what we were feeling, but never broached how we felt about our cousin. Perhaps each of us was afraid to upset the other, since it was by now obvious that we were both under his spell. Perhaps it was easier to keep our rivalry veiled, trusting that neither of us would cross the imaginary line we'd traced in the sand.

Things began to change one afternoon following an unexpected storm, when my mother locked up the house and took us girls to the Santo Antônio River, tin cans and rods in hand, to catch the fish that came with the swollen current. Belonísia and I kept our distance, interacting with Domingas but without acknowledging one another. Since we had fallen out, when my mother gave a message to one of us to be communicated to the other, as she'd always done, we played dumb so that Domingas would have to be the intermediary. When my mother finally realized how bad things had become between us, she rebuked us both; she wouldn't tolerate such an attitude from two sisters living in the same house, sisters from the same womb who'd arrived in this world through the hands of the encantado Velho Nagô, the old African. Our mother had given birth to sisters, not enemies, and she wouldn't stand for our churlishness. We'd better start communicating; she would permit no more animosity between her daughters. We didn't protest, but neither did we make any sincere effort to reestablish our relationship. As time passed, however, we couldn't help but communicate with each other, pulled in by the smiles Domingas inspired and by her curiosity about all manner of things she'd discover along the paths we walked. Once, Domingas and Belonísia were arguing over a ripe tangerine, and Domingas tried to involve me in the dispute. In the end, Domingas divided the succulent wedges, claiming the largest and sweetest for herself.

The river's current was strong that day, and my mother led us to a small lake, really a tributary of the Santo Antônio. We started digging up worms from the wet earth for bait. Domingas announced that hers were the biggest, laughing at the worms Salu and I had dug up. My mother's capable hands transformed those poor earthworms, run through with hooks, into shrunken concertinas. "They're so full of holes now, they look like Saint Sebastian." We laughed at what Domingas had said, though my mother reproached her: "Don't make jokes about the saint. What are you thinking?"

The pond was muddy, its surface covered with green algae, but the flooded river brought us plenty of fish, quickly hooked by our lines. Helped by our mother, Domingas named the various types of fish. There was a lot of cascudo, or armored catfish. "You know catfish travel in schools, Domingas." "Not much fish on this fish," Domingas said, laughing, "you better catch something better." "You just take care of your own line," my mother replied, looking up at the sky, trying to guess if more rain was coming. "Something's nibbling,

Mama!" Domingas's eyes opened wide. I felt something bite on my line, too, then noticed Belonísia pulling hard on her rod as well. "It's an apanharí. Hold on tight, Belonísia," my mother said. "That one we'll have for lunch! Let me help you." And she ran over to my sister. My fish began thrashing in the water, struggling to get off the hook. "Girl, help your sister," my mother directed Domingas. When I finally lifted my fish up and out, it tried to wriggle free and get back in the water to breathe. I could see Salu's satisfaction; she said it was a molé, and she'd cook it in palm oil.

We spent another hour that morning hooking the travelers brought by the swollen rivers to the waters of Água Negra. On the way home, we had to cross the swampy stretch again barefoot because our sandals would get stuck in the heavy mud, preventing us from even lifting our feet. "Walk slowly," my mother said as we headed toward the road; she didn't want us getting hurt by the occasional rock or piece of splintered wood hidden in the mud. Just then, as I took a step, I felt something pierce the sole of my foot, and my face contracted in pain. I'd cut myself on something like the shard of a plate, and the gash was very deep. Belonísia, who was nearest, helped me lift my leg and make my way to the road. Salu, crossing the quagmire with some difficulty, shouted instructions: Belonísia was to pull the object out of my foot. "Didn't I tell you girls to be careful?" The object turned out to be an enormous snail shell, empty and broken, which had penetrated like a thorn deep into my flesh. I didn't have the courage to touch it; I was weeping from the pain. Belonísia held my foot and swiftly pulled it out. Domingas made her way over, pleading, "Let me see, let me see." We got to the edge of the river where we could wash our feet. The thick trail of my blood painted the land with the red of a bird's feather. Salu began gathering leaves, medicinal herbs, then crushed them in her hands and placed them on the wound. It would have to suffice until we got back home to find out what my father, the healer, would do.

9.

I made it home, hopping on one leg, helped along by my mother and Belonísia. For many days the deep wound prevented me from putting weight on that foot, but it was a relief to know that my sister was communicating with me again. Belonísia became my crutch, as well as Domingas, and for weeks they let me lean on them whenever I needed to get around.

It was hard for me after that injury, not being able to explore the yard or the fields or the riverbank. That had been my life with my sister, especially after the fateful day when Grandma Donana's knife had torn through our story, ever since that knife had sliced off a tongue, stopping the utterance of syllables, wounding the pride of a Mãe d'Água, a mermaid encantada and guide, and yet uniting two sisters who at different moments had left the same womb and, until recently, bringing us even closer together. What I felt for my cousin Severo was by no means stronger than what I felt for my sister, the protection I owed her, as well as the sense of security I felt in her presence. But for the injury to my foot, Belonísia and I might have remained estranged. Having turned our backs on the system of signs we'd developed, it was as if we'd silenced ourselves, silenced the deep intimacy between us. Not touching me, she couldn't feel the rhythm of my breath. Not touching her, I couldn't feel the velocity of the rivers of her blood. Her inner stirrings had been lost to me, and so, too, her secret moods, whether calm or troubled. Not looking at me directly, she could no longer divine what I was planning to do just by being attentive to my subtle movements.

We gradually surmounted the discord that had come between us, and as we drew closer we made sure to avoid discussing Severo. He became just another member of the family, and, by keeping him at a certain distance, the spell that had once mesmerized us seemed to have been broken. Time did what one expects of it: it calmed our impulsive passions and restored family harmony. My father, mysteriously, seemed completely unaware of what had happened, or, if he did know something, he preferred to keep it to himself for some reason we'd never discover, whether moral or mystical.

Cousin Severo began visiting again for the Jarê rituals, always very lively occasions. He'd arrive in the company of Uncle Servó, Aunt Hermelina, and our younger cousins, who were spending much of their own childhood scaring those cowbirds from the rice paddies. We greeted Severo with formality and emotional reserve, just as we had upon meeting him that first time he arrived at the plantation. We

were no longer little girls. Belonísia and I were already burying our menstrual blood out back with a handful of dirt. We
covered our breasts with a strip of cloth so they wouldn't
draw attention beneath the fabric of our dresses. The men
working in the fields began turning their eyes toward us more
and more. But they did no more than look, for we were the
daughters of the healer Zeca Chapéu Grande. My father
was respected by neighbors and devotees of the encantados.
He was respected by the landowners, by men with authority,
and by Sutério, the farm manager. My father was uniformly
praised as a model worker, who never complained, regard-
less of the burden. As difficult as it often was, my father
didn't shy away from taking charge of his fellow laborers,
making sure, with characteristic diligence, that the day's
work had been completed. When Sutério needed a field to
be irrigated, my father was the one to oversee the damming
of the river. He'd get the men together to cut down trees and
use his ingenuity to redirect one of the tributaries. He'd take
the cattle out to pasture, too, leading them where they'd find
grass. He was the worker the Peixoto family esteemed most
highly, and because they trusted him, my father was the one
they'd ask to recruit more hands for the fields of Água Negra.
They also had confidence in his ability to be persuasive and
resolve ongoing conflicts, over a fence, for example, or after
an animal had gotten loose and torn up someone's crops.

So, though forced to suffer the intrusive stares of men
who fantasized about deflowering us, we were untouchable,
for we were the healer's daughters. Unlike other girls our
age, we were largely spared from male harassment. Quite

47

a few girls had surrendered to some man's insistence, to his constant pressure, and with their parents' blessing had gotten married, even though their bodies were still maturing. They'd succumbed, for this was a man's world, to the domination of foremen and farmers.

The Peixoto family only cared about one thing: a profitable harvest. But they didn't live on the land, it wasn't in their blood. They sometimes traveled to the Fazenda Água Negra from the capital just to show their faces, so we wouldn't forget who the bosses were, then head straight back to the city. But there were increasing numbers of farmers and ranchers who relished the role of taskmaster; it appealed to those remote descendants of the colonizers. And then there was the occasional underling who got lucky mining diamonds and decided it was his turn to call the shots, lording it over those who had no choice but to submit.

One morning, my mother came home looking troubled; she sought out Dona Tonha. Unlike Belonísia, who seemed generally uninterested, I was curious about the world beyond our front door. I went out to the jirau to wash the dishes and eavesdrop on the two women.

They were talking about Crispiniana, whose belly was starting to show. She'd received a terrible beating from her father. They remarked on how difficult it must be for a widower to raise his children all by himself. Daughters are a lot of work. And when one of them comes home with a belly, what then? Who's going to raise the kid? They said Crispiniana had refused to reveal the name of the father. She had to spend a few nights away from home because

Saturnino looked fit to murder her. Gossip quickly traveled from mouth to mouth. Who was the dad? Someone from a nearby plantation or maybe from Água Negra? "If Saturnino beat her as bad as they say, comadre," Dona Tonha pondered, "could it be that the baby's father is her own brother-in-law, the one who'd been messing around with Crispiniana and made Crispina lose her marbles?" My mother squinted at her, incredulous. "Isidoro? You think so?"

Days later, Belonísia came looking for me to share what I'd already learned, mostly from eavesdropping on my mother and Dona Tonha: that Crispina and Crispiniana were no longer talking to each other. That Crispina was pregnant by her husband Isidoro, but Crispiniana was even farther along, and she wouldn't reveal the father's name. That Crispiniana got busted up worse than an old suitcase. That our mother felt offended because Saturnino said he'd cut out his daughter's tongue so she'd end up like Zeca's girl. And now the two sisters glared at each other from their doorways and exchanged insults with all the rancor that could exist between women, even though they'd once occupied the same womb together. They no longer recognized each other as sisters. And Saturnino, disgusted by it all, had started hitting the bottle.

I noticed something in my sister's expression, a resolute look. She'd taken a side in the conflict, that much was clear. No matter that Cousin Severo had stopped being a source of tension between us, no matter that our shared passion for him seemed to have faded, the look on Belonísia's face was a warning to me: even a sister could go too far.

10.

My mother had definitively assumed the role of midwife in our community. My father, who had been doing that work, transferred the responsibility to Salu. Such was the sense of decorum in this humble man, polite to a fault, that he'd become terribly awkward in the presence of the women, those wives and daughters of his compadres and followers, his filhos de santo, so he gladly delegated the job to my mother. When Grandma Donana was still alive and in good health, she'd performed the role of midwife with profound respect for the arrival of each new life. My grandmother would always say that she didn't deliver babies, the mothers were the ones who really delivered the babies; she was there just to help. And help is what she offered those girls, married so young, or made pregnant by one of the workers or a passing traveler, just as she'd help the heifers, mares, and bitches around the plantation.

When Donana was still the midwife for Água Negra and the nearby plantations, my mother used to act as her assistant. She'd study her movements, her prayers and prohibitions, what the women should or shouldn't do, what they should eat and drink. My mother learned when was the right time to wipe down the mother and child, when to handle the special scissors kept only for these occasions. She was aware of all the postpartum restrictions. When my grandmother could no longer do this work, my father, being a healer, provided the assistance those women required, and my mother accompanied him. I never saw my father actually performing, but my mother used to tell her comadres about my father's embarrassment, clearly written on his face, whenever he touched the body of a woman in labor. Sometimes he would direct the woman to lie on the ground with the help of a female relative or neighbor, then he'd press his right foot against her belly in order to interpret the baby's movements and decide if it was time to start pushing.

In a sense, it wasn't really my father standing there, embarrassed, ashamed to be so close to a woman in such a vulnerable position, a woman suffering stabbing pains, contorting her body abruptly, exposing a naked breast or her private parts. Often, the woman's clothing barely covered her body. But it wasn't my father standing there; it was the encantado Velho Nagô, an old acquaintance of the people of Água Negra. He was the master of my father's body and spirit, the giver of blessings and cures to the needy and to the land itself. And it was Velho Nagô, according to my father, who had assigned the role of midwife to Salustiana Nicolau. When a woman was in labor, the hands and even the mind of comadre Salu would be guided by Velho Nagô's power. At least, that's how my father explained it when a stranger once asked him.

Fusco was barking insistently in the yard. Belonísia led the messenger into our house and had him wait in the center room for our mother. One of Saturnino's twins, who'd been writhing in pain, was about to give birth at home, near the banks of the Santo Antônio. In all the excitement it wasn't clear which of the two daughters was about to give birth, but, according to my mother's estimate, it would have been

51

Crispiniana, who had accompanied Crispina to our house and had been responsible, in part, for Crispina's deranged mind.

Judging from the messenger's desperate face, the situation was urgent. Apparently, Saturnino had arrived in time to tie his daughter down, for she'd begun smashing everything in sight. She seemed possessed by some evil spirit. Her eyes were like live coals, her cries could be heard for miles. The strange sounds that had been traveling across the valley were in fact the frightening echoes of her screams, carried to our ears on the warm afternoon wind.

Belonísia was left in charge of the house. The situation was so urgent that my mother asked me to come along as she started down the road, troubled by what she'd learned of the young woman's condition. I still recall how upset my mother was when we reached the door and were met by the woman's roars, directed at our faces in a blast of hot, choleric air. "Mercy!" my mother cried out to Velho Nagô, breaking her own silent focus, the concentration she usually maintained during those moments when she served, just as my father had done, as a vehicle for the spirits.

The objects outside that house seemed to me somehow alive, involved in subtle processes of change. A tree had been chopped down; the woodpile would end up in Saturnino's stove and those of his children, whose dwellings had sprouted up around his own. There was a small heap of overripe jackfruit attracting a cloud of flies and even some bees. I noticed large, forked branches and piles of mud and some cans packed with dirt, evidence of one more house going up for Saturnino's growing throng of children and grandchildren. Stray missiles lay around the front door: a comb, an empty perfume bottle, enameled plates and mugs, a dented basin that, despite its age, had kept its shine.

My mother didn't have her mother-in-law's strength in the face of such spine-chilling events. It was as if Salu were more human, more fallible, than Donana. My grandmother was like some spiritual entity, almost superhuman. Even so, Salu stepped inside that house with the proud stature and authority bestowed by her standing as the wife of the healer Zeca Chapéu Grande.

I caught a glimpse of the young woman's disturbed countenance. Uncontainable, she broke free of the rope and came running toward Salu. At that moment, I could foresee somehow the beauty that awaited us. I'd spent my childhood amid the spiritual practices of my father, my grandmother, and now my mother. The sacred objects, the root tinctures, the prayers, the festive rituals, the encantados riding the bodies of their devotees, all were part of the landscape in which my siblings and I were raised. But the transformation of my timid mother—who'd come down the road pleading for Velho Nagô's mercy and help, but was now standing firm before a woman crazed by labor pains and perhaps by spirits unfamiliar to us—that transformation was a miracle in itself. Although I'd often observed Zeca's assertiveness, I'd never had the chance to see my mother take control of this kind of situation. I saw Salu raise her right hand and firmly grasp the woman's arm as it sliced through the air toward her face. That show of strength was enough to quell the woman's noisy rage, and a wave of serenity washed over the room.

It was, in fact, Crispiniana who was in labor. Distraught perhaps by her abandonment, by the loneliness of loving her sister's husband, she had surrendered to a torrent of anguish not unlike the anguish of her twin on the day she appeared, roped, at our front door. With the help of Aunt Hermelina, who'd joined us on the way over, my mother led Crispiniana back to her bed and made her lie down. A short time later, Crispiniana gave birth to a boy, and the cry of new life filled the room where his mother had been howling in pain and delirium just before. Exhausted, Crispiniana fell asleep with her child on her chest. She no longer wept for her future, or for her child's. The hand of Velho Nagô had pacified her raging body, and now her infant son was comforting her bruised heart.

Saturnino's face, smiling foolishly, bloomed with forgiveness as he gazed upon his grandson.

Crispina observed it all from her window across the way, unable to offer the reconciliation for which her father and even her sister were hoping. Ashamed of his misdeeds, perhaps, Isidoro had headed out to the fields rather than face either of the twins.

One lunar cycle passed, and my mother's services were required again, but now to attend to Crispina. And once again the moon was full. Belonísia accompanied my mother this time, but not long after they'd left, my sister rushed back home, terribly upset and looking for our father. There was something wrong with Crispina, and my mother thought it safer to fetch

Zeca. With his right foot pressed against the woman's belly, my father knew right away that the baby wasn't moving.

"An angel," my mother announced. Words no one wanted to hear.

11.

We all worried that Crispina might relapse into madness. She could simply disappear, as she'd done in the past; she might need to be brought back to our house to treat those maladies of her soul. Word went round that she'd sunk into a pitiful state of depression, refusing to eat or wash. Isidoro, preoccupied by his wife's sadness, cut back his hours in the fields to look after her. Crispina was constantly reminded of the source of her pain, for her sister remained in their father's house opposite, and she could see her little nephew growing healthy and strong—the nephew who was, perhaps, the son of her own husband.

Things wouldn't be resolved easily, but time played its part, and the intensity of the sisters' passions began to abate. We learned that despite the indifference Crispina had shown during Crispiniana's harrowing labor, Crispiniana didn't hesitate to seek out her twin, who was too despondent to respond one way or the other, allowing Crispiniana to look after her like their own departed mother. At first Crispiniana avoided bringing her baby boy along, afraid of provoking her sister, who might consider the child's presence an affront to her own bereavement. She feared, too, that Crispina might glimpse some trace of Isidoro in the boy's face.

But that innocent baby, with his tears and happy smiles, brought a sudden luster to the pallor of his aunt's condition. And then something happened, one of those things you can't explain or understand—Crispiniana's milk dried up. Who knows if what happened next was the mother's intention or one of those mystical events so common among the people of Água Negra. Crispiniana's sister, grieving over the loss of her child but moved by the wails of her distressed nephew, nestled the baby against her breast before anyone had asked her. No doubt it was instinctive, the way she let the infant's mouth find its way to the milk that, days after the emergence of her stillborn child, still poured from her breast like a natural spring in the mountain ranges of the Chapada Velha. It was the gesture that had been needed to reunite the sisters, at least for a while, until the next disagreement or fight, in that back-and-forth of affection and resentment that would characterize their relationship for the rest of their days.

I watched the boy taking his first steps and later running toward his aunt's breast during the many Jarê rituals in our home. The last time I saw him sucking at Crispina's breast, the two whispering to each other among the crowd, the boy was already almost two years old. He was strong and energetic, and he clearly resembled the twin sisters as well as his grandfather Saturnino; but in no way did he resemble Isidoro.

It was a December night, the Feast of Saint Barbara. My father, usually quite eager to fulfill his responsibilities regarding the Jarê ritual, had started the day in a cranky mood, replying curtly to any question put to him. Only we who were closest to him understood the reason for this agitation, evident in his every gesture. As the sun was setting, Dona Tonha brought over a battered box. It contained the paraphernalia of an encantada, the attire my father would be wearing that very night after the litany, when a spirit would arrive to take possession of his body and become manifest to everyone in the room. The garments of Saint Barbara, or Iansã, were in that box; it was her night. They had been washed and ironed and put away until the day came around for Zeca to don them again. His aversion to those accoutrements was such that he wouldn't even store them with the others in the saints' room; for safekeeping, he'd given them to Tonha, who was a "horse" ridden by the encantada on those nights of Jarê.

Zeca Chapéu Grande was embarrassed to take off his pants, clothing that honored his position of leadership on the plantation, his position as a spiritual father, and to put on a woman's skirt instead, loaning his body to a female spirit. He did it, however, because it was his obligation. He'd made a promise long ago, when he was cured of madness, and he made that promise in gratitude to the encantados in the house of João do Lajedo, in Andaraí. But it embarrassed him, nevertheless, for his audience would include compadres and neighbors, the very same men he'd take charge of when something needed to get done around the plantation.

During that night's ceremony I stood among the female devotees, the filhas de santo, who were helping my father to dress in the garments of Saint Barbara. The musicians warmed up their drums beside the bonfire.

After the litany and the explosion of fireworks, the first to arrive was Saint Barbara herself. The box brought by Dona Tonha contained all the appropriate items: a red skirt, Iansã's sword and her traditional adê, the crown and veil. The room of the saints, where the ladainha, or litany, was sung, was illuminated by candles and the brilliant colors glimmering from the sacred portraits and dolls. There were different-sized statues, too, both plaster and wooden, some in pristine condition, others rather shabby: Saint Sebastian, the Crucified Christ, the Bom Jesus, Saint Lazarus, Saint Roch, Saint Francis, and Padre Cícero. There were small portraits, some bright and others faded, of Saints Cosmas and Damian, Nossa Senhora Aparecida, and Saint Anthony. There were also photographs of my parents, of Grandma Donana, and many more, small ones, of various devotees. There were paper flowers, some newer, others already pale, as well as real flowers, sempre-vivas, that we'd find along the road or growing between rocks near our house.

It was a hot night. The devotees were dripping with sweat, wiping their faces with the backs or palms of their hands, their lips never faltering in the recitation of prayers. The crowded saints' room was so small that the congregation, mostly made up of women and older men, had to look on from the center room. The younger folks and children stayed away from the prayers, talking to each other in low voices. Whenever the children got out of control, one of the women would turn and shush them with an accusing finger and a no-nonsense glare.

There was great beauty in the songs preceding the entrance of the encantada, and more enchanting still would be the moment when my father came out of the room of the saints to dance in the center room to the beat of the atabaque drums. He was a slender man, shorter than my mother, and his skin was lighter than ours. That his youth was long gone was obvious from the deep furrows of his face, the ravines of his skin, a daily erosion caused by sun and wind as he planted the crops that won him the right to reside on the planation with his family. To us, Zeca Chapéu Grande already looked like an ancient. He was a guide to the people of Água Negra and its vicinity. They resorted to him for any problem that might arise, whether an argument between workers or an illness that had befallen a neighbor.

The moment arrived. The air was heavy with the scents of sweat and lavender. Stepping out of the saints' room, Zeca, possessed by Saint Barbara, appeared before the crowd in the red-and-white skirt diligently starched by Dona Tonha. My father had also donned the glittering adê, its veil of red beads hiding his face. Saint Barbara was wielding the small wooden sword that Zeca had crafted himself, which sliced the air in agile arcs. "Ê, Saint Barbara, the virgin with blonde hair, her golden sword flashes in the air," sang the crowd in unison, hands clapping to the rhythm of the drums. As the men accelerated the beat, Saint Barbara grew more animated in her steps and sudden turns. Two women dropped to the floor, their eyes half-open, their movements announcing the arrival of more Saint Barbaras. They were led to the saints' room by my mother and Dona Tonha so that they, too, could don the appropriate garments.

During recent Jarê rituals, my cousin Severo had begun posting himself next to the drummers. Having studied the rhythms, he'd duplicate them on the hot leather. Severo had grown tall and strong. His smile was bright, his skin was darkened from toiling beneath the sun, and his muscles strained against the fabric of his shirt, which was a size too small. Belonísia's eyes followed his every move with rapt attention, just as mine did—as she was well aware. Uncle Servó would pull up beside one of the atabaque drums, too, just for a little while, always at the start of the ritual or when an encantado to whom he was particularly devoted, such as Tupinambá, was seen capering among the crowd. Sutério, the farm manager, often participated in the revelry as well, even giving the drums a shot when he took a break from dancing.

The mayor himself put in an appearance that night. Five years had passed since his son was cured of his illness by Zeca Chapéu Grande. Back then, the mayor had sent a car over for my father; it was a red Gordini, a model unknown in those parts. My sister and I had only ever seen the Ford Rural or the random cars that rushed past us on our way to the hospital after the accident. Ever since that Feast of Saint Barbara when my father cured his son, the mayor would come to honor the saint on her day. On that first occasion, my father wouldn't accept payment but asked the mayor, Ernesto, for something else instead: to appoint a teacher from the school district who'd give classes to the plantation children.

My father told us that the mayor looked quite uncomfortable but there was no getting out of it, and the promise was made. Ernesto felt deeply grateful to both my father and the encantada, and he intended to keep his promise. He may also have feared that the spell that cured his son could just as easily be reversed. And so, months later, a teacher arrived in a car belonging to the mayor's office. She'd come three days a week, providing three hours of lessons at Dona Firmina's: Firmina, who lived alone, had offered her small barn for a classroom. Benches long enough to seat seven or eight children were improvised using wooden planks resting on mud-filled canisters. The subjects my sister and I learned from our teacher, Marlene, were reinforced at home by our mother, who could help us with any homework except for math. "Letters I understand, not numbers."

The mayor then made a convenient proposal: since my mother was literate, why couldn't she be the teacher at our school? But my mother, aware of her limitations, refused. She explained that she was no good with numbers, and emphasized that she wanted her children—those she'd given birth to and those she'd helped come into the world—to have access to an education and a better life. The same dream had motivated my father to secure a teacher for us, but that alone wasn't sufficient; he wanted us to have a proper school. My father was illiterate. He'd sign his name by simply pressing his thumb to the paper, a thumb scarred and calloused from toiling in the fields and meeting the wrath of thorns. He'd dip his seamed fingers in dark ink whenever he needed to sign some document. What my father wanted, more than anything, was to have his children learn to read and write. He pursued this dream with tenacity. If you were to follow my father out to the fields or note the seriousness with which he kept his spiritual obligations, you'd think those were the most important things to him. But if you knew the pride folks like us feel in seeing one of our youngsters read a book, you'd understand why education was the inheritance my father had always wished to bequeath to us.

Therefore I wasn't surprised that night when, before any of the other encantados had manifested themselves, Saint Barbara appeared before us, spinning this way and that; suddenly she let out a cry and stopped dead, her sword pointing straight at the mayor. She honored him by singling him out. Treating him as a monarch and yet, somehow, as one of her subjects, she asked him in front of the whole assembly if he would keep the promise he'd made—of which, at the time, I believe we were unaware—the promise to build a proper school for the children of our community. The mayor appeared flustered. He forced a smile before the eyes of forty local families. With something like beneficence, remembering the blessings he'd received but also fearing the retribution of the encantada, the mayor gave in.

12.

Construction of the school began just a few months later. How this happened so quickly we had no idea, nor were we privy to the terms negotiated between the mayor and the

Peixoto family; but the project was authorized. The tenant farmers themselves were to erect the small, three-room structure by working in shifts on Sundays—the one day of the week they could forget about the crops, though they still mustn't forget to feed and give water to the animals. The school would be located at a crossroads; one road led to the Santo Antônio River, the other to the Utinga.

The timing of the project turned out to be providential, for later that year we'd suffer an extended period of drought, a drought so bad that the payment to the workers for building the school, despite being a somewhat modest sum, held back for months, spelled survival for many local families. It was a hard time. The worst drought since 1932, according to my father. Never again would I see enormous rice paddies spreading across the region. Rice needs plenty of water to thrive; it was the first casualty of the drought. Later, the sugarcane would be devastated, along with the bean pods, the umbu trees, the tomatoes, the okra, the squash. We'd stored a reserve of seeds at home and in the barn of the plantation. The drought made us fear we'd get kicked off the land for want of work. Then came the more immediate fear of hunger. Our reserves were running low, the beans were depleted even before the rice, and there was almost no rice left. We still had a substantial amount of manioc flour, something a few of the families produced themselves and would use for barter. We headed out almost daily to the rivers to fish, each time returning with smaller and smaller fish, good just for adding some flavor to the mush we made with the manioc flour. The big fish would only come down from the headwaters when there was a flood, and without even a sprinkling of rain, the smaller and less desirable fish like piaba and cascudo were all there was.

We could season the catch while there was still some umbu fruit around, a kind of plum that, together with salt, made the fish a bit tastier. When even the manioc flour began running out, my father recalled his mother's recipe for a kind of crêpe made from jatoba, a fruit notorious for smelling like unwashed feet. There were jatoba pods in abundance; the leafy, imposing tree could withstand drought conditions. Jatoba was our plan B, to be avoided until we were truly desperate. Well, we ended up eating jatoba for months, until those crêpes made us nauseous.

There was edible cactus as well, though we had to compete with the boss's cattle for it. There was a parcel of land on the plantation set aside for cacti. The only cacti we had permission to eat were the plants we grew in our own gardens. Whoever lacked the foresight to plant their own would have to rely on a neighbor's solidarity to partake of a meal of cactus pad stewed in palm oil. Another possible option was hunting. During the worst of the drought, though, you were more likely to find the carcasses of starved animals than any game. Deer were scarce because they'd been over-hunted, but it was also due to lack of water in the arid stretches. If we searched hard enough, we'd sometimes find them drinking from the shrinking marshes, but their numbers were dwindling rapidly. The paca, whose meat we had a taste for, wouldn't show its face in the woods. Neither would any capybara or agouti. It was possible to catch a bird now and then, a jacu, tinamou, or a bird we called juriti, but they had very little meat, so we'd savor the taste of their bones. Aunt Hermelina once told us about an entire family in Pau-de-Colher that, desperately hungry, had died after eating a large bird called the seriema; it seemed the bird had eaten a rattlesnake, so its flesh was full of the venom.

We'd often manage to catch a lizard, the enormous teiú, easy to find because it would come out to eat the carcasses of animals felled by the drought, the cattle that had nowhere left to graze. If you happened to be walking by a rotting carcass, you just needed to look carefully and you'd catch one of those lizards. If we didn't eat them, they wouldn't hesitate to feast on our own famished bodies.

Children were the ones who suffered most during the drought; they'd stop growing, become terribly frail, and constantly fall sick. I lost count of how many children died from malnutrition, their rigid bodies carried in procession to Viração cemetery. Death would dismount at our neighbors' doors and, despite Zeca Chapéu Grande's every effort to restore their health and strength, many of the sick children succumbed. The candles my father lit for those children refused to stay lit: even in the absence of wind or the slightest gust of air, the flames simply went out. There's no cure, he'd say, but he couldn't accept his own inability to save them. The families would have to find another healer, or put their trust in God.

We continued collecting buriti and palm fruit to take to the public market in town on Mondays. My mother and her comadres, alongside Belonísia, Domingas, and myself, would gather the buriti in the marshes. My father Zeca, Zezé, and the other men would grab the palm fruit that grew in clusters, high above our heads, and we'd turn it into dendê, our palm oil. The buriti trees were tall, too, but the fruit wasn't edible if we picked the bunches from the trees. It was necessary to wait for them to fall to the ground, that's when they were ready to eat. We stored the buriti in large barrels of water to soften their husks. We'd peel each globe with our fingers, very gently, to keep the pulp intact, then carry as much as we could in burlap sacks balanced on our heads, traveling down the road to sell it to the women who made sweets and juices from buriti for their own customers.

On that road, under the unforgiving sun, the buriti pulp would heat up and drip through the burlap, covering us with greasy, orange liquid. Our black skin turned almost copper-colored. We'd arrive in town embarrassed by our stained hair and clothes. We'd place rings of cloth on our heads, beneath our loads, to help us balance the weight, reducing the amount of liquid that would drip down our necks. But there were days when the sun was a bonfire burning us up from head to toe, and our bodies would be drenched in buriti juice. Once, I even slipped from the oily fluid oozing all the way down to my feet. We also took palm oil to market, the dendê produced in our backyards; we'd pour the oil into empty liquor bottles and cap them with used corks. At that time we didn't own a wagon animal, so we relied on the strength of our arms to lug the canvas bags loaded with bottles of oil to the market. We'd arrive with hands swollen and numb.

The drought punished us with hunger, and the ruined harvest left us disconsolate. My father seemed a broken man, and even Jarê lost some of its former brilliance. One day, after we'd packed buriti pulp in those burlap sacks, my mother suddenly fell prey to fever and terrible stomach pains; nothing she ate stayed down. But we needed the money, and so, not for the first time, I'd have to walk to the market with Tonha's daughters. Belonísia stayed behind to look after Domingas, who anyway always dragged her feet and couldn't keep her sack upright on her head.

That particular day I was carrying just one sack on my head on my way to town. I sat down in some shade at the crossroads where they'd started building the school, and waited for Tonha's daughters. The day had barely begun; for breakfast I'd had a jatoba crêpe with some lemongrass tea. There must have been some confusion over what time Tonha's daughters were supposed to meet up with me because I waited and waited, but they never showed. I fell asleep against the fence surrounding the construction site. Someone was calling out, "Bibiana, Bibiana," and I woke up with a start. It was Severo, a sheathed machete dangling from his waist. He was on his way to cut down some palm fruit for his mother to press into oil. Like us, Severo's family would frequently go to the market to sell their oil and buy supplies for the week.

I conveyed to Severo that I was waiting for Tonha's daughters, that we were meant to walk to town together, that my mother had fallen ill and Belonísia was at home caring for her. Severo offered to accompany me, since the market started early and would only go till noon. We really needed the money. I couldn't miss out on this opportunity to sell the buriti I had with me; I'd go with him. He was my cousin, after all, and my family was struggling. I didn't think our parents would give us any grief for going into town together without a chaperone. Severo was very dear to us; my father liked seeing him at the atabaque drums during the Jarê rituals, proud that my cousin took such an interest.

We headed out.

It was a long trek, during which Severo spoke about the things going on in our community. He said the school under construction wasn't sufficient, not for completing our studies, but at least it was something; we lacked so much at Água Negra. I listened as he talked about the drought, the animals dying of starvation, the fish that only seemed to get smaller, the children in our community we'd buried in recent months. I listened as he talked about our family and about Jarê. The only subject we didn't broach was Belonísia; I didn't want either of us to bring up my sister. I didn't want to recall the rift provoked by Severo's kiss. My cousin was already a man, quite muscular; he worked all day, every day. He no longer resembled that shy boy who'd arrived at the plantation. He was of medium height, with a beaming smile, and he seemed uninhibited as he spoke to me, as if this shared intimacy were quite natural. As if there weren't any limitations imposed by Belonísia's jealousy or by our parents' fear that something might happen between us; but we were cousins, after all, raised on the same plantation, and the prohibition on courting members of the same

68

family extended to us as well. Marriage between cousins was frowned upon. It could lead to the birth of a deformed child, a child lacking a limb or cursed with a disturbed mind. Such cases were not uncommon, and everyone in the community had a story to tell about that particular taboo. There were other, vague reasons for forbidding such a marriage, perhaps financial; I never quite understood. In any case, on that day, during the hours we spent together at the market and walking there and back, I didn't worry about the rules. I was focused entirely on Severo. I tried to forget our family connection.

He spoke so eloquently about the land; he expressed such noble sentiments, including a deep respect for my parents, his aunt and uncle, for our entire family. He seemed completely at ease confiding his dreams to me, his plans to pursue his studies; he didn't want to work at the Fazenda Água Negra forever. He wanted to work his own land. He wanted his own farm, and, unlike the owners of Água Negra who didn't know much about land, not even how to till the soil, much less the proper time to plant crops based on the cycles of the moon, or what would grow in the arid stretches or in the floodplain, Severo knew all that and more. He was born from the earth. I found it peculiar, the way he expressed it. I never thought of myself that way, born from the earth. The earth gave birth to plants and rocks, yes. To the food we ate, to the worms. Sometimes, I'd heard it said, the earth even gave birth to diamonds. Severo explained that he'd combine his knowledge of the land with his commitment to painstaking study, to learn new ways of doing things so as to improve his situation. Everything he said was fascinating to me; unlike Severo, I'd never stopped to contemplate why we were there or what could change the course of our lives, what depended on the decisions I made and what depended entirely on circumstance. But as I listened to his words, everything around me seemed illuminated. I wanted to hear more. I'd never heard someone say that a life beyond the plantation was even possible. I was born on that plantation, and, I believed, I'd die there, like almost everybody else.

At the market, we quickly sold the sack of buriti pulp. Money in hand, I stopped by the general store and bought rice, beans, sugar, cornmeal, and coffee. I bought a bottle of Água Inglesa, too, a tonic my father had prescribed to a neighbor who was pregnant and who'd promised to pay us back. I returned home in the middle of the afternoon under the scalding sun, without having had any lunch, but in Severo's company. I've never forgotten that day. Before reaching home, I'd already decided that I would no longer avoid seeing him if he wanted to see me. I began inventing excuses to head out alone and collect buriti, just so I could make my way to the marshes and communicate with him far from the eyes of the others. I wanted to experience life. I wanted to discover what might be awaiting us.

13.

I continued meeting up with Severo on Mondays, almost always at the same spot along the road. My mother's health had improved, so Belonísia was free once more to accompany me. My father would sometimes go to the market himself, taking Zezé along, but usually he preferred to keep working the land in the hope it would produce something. He'd seek out some pocket of cool, humid air, a bit of "luck," as he put it. He'd dig furrows, scatter seeds. The rows of crops had migrated closer to the river, and it wasn't long before areas of exposed riverbed were utilized for planting. Even in the riverbed, however, there were sections that proved worthless due to the heavy concentration of clay. Anything we managed to grow there would go directly to the table. Some okra, some undersized squashes. The manioc wasn't any good, for the root would rot from the excessive moisture. And if we planted manioc in the arid sections during the drought, it didn't develop at all.

With our parents' consent, Severo would accompany us to town. Tonha's daughters would come along, too. We thought of Severo as our protector. Belonísia kept a certain distance; she seemed to understand that Severo's attention was now directed toward me. Sometimes she'd give some excuse not to come, especially when there wasn't enough buriti to fill two whole sacks. She preferred to help our father cut and gather cattails to feed to the animals that had survived. My sister handled a machete much better than me; I admit I envied her skill. She'd wield tools with such strength that it made me feel incompetent. Given her natural abilities, Belonísia became even closer to our father; she accompanied him more and more, together with our brother, and readily expressed her opinion on things, though Zeca would

71

invariably remind her that she was a woman, and therefore banned from certain tasks. But it never demoralized her; my sister seemed always to be waiting for any chance to demonstrate her strength, knowledge, and skill.

Despite her subtle withdrawal, the excitement she felt whenever Severo joined in the Jarê ritual was something she couldn't conceal from me, especially now that we were spending so much time together again. The bond between us had been strengthened by our shared struggles during the drought. I observed the supple movements of her body as Belonísia tried to draw Severo's attention, but while Severo thought highly of my sister, he was focused entirely on me. Perhaps the fact that I was slightly older worked in my favor, or perhaps I benefited from our affinities, which emerged during those long walks to the market: we were both committed to our studies, and we regarded Dona Firmina's schoolhouse with a certain condescension, given our ambitions. We wanted to leave the plantation; it was a fire that had been lit in both of us.

The buriti was bringing in enough money to feed the whole family, and we no longer relied on a diet of jatoba, so no one bothered to inquire about my hours in the woods on the edge of the marsh, collecting the fruit, which became scarce as we neared the end of the season. The scarcer the fruit, the more time was required to gather it. Over those days, I grew close to the riverbanks of the Santo Antônio; I grew close to those fields Severo worked with his parents. Severo and I grew closer, too, whether laughing or disagreeing or even while remaining in silence. Sometimes our hands would touch in an abrupt gesture or while joking around. I could sense his breathing, sometimes calm, sometimes more agitated, depending on his mood. I could hear his heart beating in the silence of the woods, where there was no water, no rustling of leaves, and often no birdsong, for there was nothing for birds to eat there. Eventually, Severo's hand reached for more than my hand: he'd touch my shoulder. I'd push back gently against his chest. And when we grew tired, we'd lie down at any spot beside the river to feel the breeze that didn't blow. But when it did blow, it scattered dry earth over our bodies. I'd wipe the dust from his face with my hands, he'd return the gesture, then one day I let his mouth touch mine, but I could only think about how I felt the time I caught him kissing Belonísia. I walked back home feeling troubled, as though I'd betrayed my sister. I didn't indulge in guilt for long; I quickly got over it, because everything I was going through was too wonderful. The buriti was all gone by then. I went back to the river just for the sake of going back. I'd slip out of the house, and later would have to put up with my mother's nagging questions and reproaches. I couldn't reveal the truth just yet, so I let her think I'd been with some girlfriends who lived farther away.

What was happening to me was so powerful, it was as if my body had been guiding itself. Severo and I became entangled in the same net. The land, blighted by drought, found some relief in the drops of sweat our bodies left behind. The silence of the absent birds, of the animals that had migrated to find water, was broken by our sighs. We'd heard so many stories about dead children. Now nature itself, mysterious and violent, was compelling us to conceive life.

14.

When I started feeling dizzy and nauseous almost every day, I got anxious. I was sixteen years old; I knew of too many young women around the plantation who'd found themselves in the family way. The first thing that made me want to vomit was a jatoba crêpe. I calmly walked out into the yard, and when I was far enough from the house, I threw up what couldn't stay down. I wouldn't be able to look at my mother and father and explain myself. I was even more worried about Belonísia's reaction. If I really was pregnant, I'd have to leave home and live with Severo. My relationship with my sister would come under some strain, to say the least. The bond between us was more than sisterly: something connected us on an even deeper level. About ten years had passed since the accident, and we'd developed our individual personalities, but there was an intimacy, too, that only strengthened with time; there were gestures and expressions only the two of us understood. I suspected that Belonísia still harbored feelings for Severo, even if they'd lessened somewhat. In any case, she wouldn't take the news well. It would cause her pain.

I continued to meet with Severo, lying down with him in the dust, in remote places far from the eyes of others. When we stood back up, he'd pick out the bits of straw tangled in my hair. He knew I was worried about something. He could see how distracted I was, absorbing little of what he said, picking up only the occasional phrase. When I finally communicated my fears to him, and he understood that my period was late, his face seemed to glow. I was a wreck, imagining what my parents would say when they learned the truth, but his face revealed very different emotions from mine: Severo was over the moon. He scrambled up a jackfruit tree, its leaves strangely exuberant in that landscape of withered branches, then yanked a fruit that was hanging off the trunk. He split open the viscous pulp with the machete he always carried with him and smiled. The gooey milk leaking from the husk triggered my nausea, but I loved seeing Severo so enthusiastic, so I ate two wedges, drawing on all the strength I had to make myself swallow—the fruit was mushy, and I started gagging—but at last I held my breath and was able to keep it down.

Severo returned to the topic of leaving home, heading down that road away from the plantation and pursuing our studies, trying our luck; he didn't want to spend the rest of his life in drudgery at Água Negra. "There's no opportunity here," he said. "It's time to get out, come with me." I was dumbfounded. I couldn't think straight. It was all too much, and the most pressing matter was trying to control my body so I wouldn't vomit. The next step would be to reveal the truth to my parents and face my sister. I couldn't stop fretting about how my sister would react. Imagining myself as a mother hadn't given me the same thrill I saw registered on Severo's face; I felt nothing special.

Time passed, and my belly began to show. I don't think anyone really noticed, but I noticed, especially when I went down to the river to bathe. I became more solitary. I felt a sadness, stronger than any excitement. I'd break down in tears over nothing. When he realized this couldn't go on indefinitely, Severo offered to talk to my parents himself; we needed to confess everything. The longer we delayed, the worse it would be for everyone. Severo was young, but he was responsible, even as a child. At the same time, my cousin wasn't afraid of anything; he never shirked his responsibilities. I felt my life intertwining with his, as hardly a day went by without seeing him, even as I continued enduring my mother's complaints and questions about my long walks, about all those hours I was supposedly spending alone.

Belonísia kept her feelings to herself, but she seemed to suspect something. Even if she didn't yet realize I was pregnant, she'd figured out where I'd been going on those walks. She, too, had become more solitary, interacting very little with our siblings. My mother blamed our melancholy on the drought; there was something wicked in the air. My father prescribed ablutions for us; he'd bring back special leaves from the woods and give them to my mother to prepare, hoping they'd dispel the gloom that enveloped us. I felt ashamed, for not only was I hiding the truth from them, I was planning to leave home with Severo in the dark of night. Severo saw no other option, given my paralyzing fear. We'd already planned which roads to take, what day we'd leave and at what time, what we'd take with us and what we would do after we'd left. Initially, I resisted the idea of running away and leaving my family behind. But I liked Severo so much; he had introduced me to the possibility of a life beyond the plantation, his words lit up my horizon. It was hard not to be seduced by his plans, by his enthusiasm. The despondency that had descended over everyone during the prolonged drought contrasted with the breath of life our plans had infused in both of us. If everything turned out as we hoped, one day we'd return, to help our parents and siblings toward a better life. We'd return just to take them with us. Those fields would always be owned by someone else; we were tenant farmers, without any right to the land. Watching Uncle Servó's kids growing up on the plantation, frightening the cowbirds off the rice paddies, it didn't seem fair to me. Watching my father and my mother grow old, working all day, every day, without rest, without any guarantee of comfort in their old age, that didn't seem fair either. But I couldn't match Severo's excitement about leaving home. I felt dejected and confused.

Then something happened to me during one of the Jarê rituals. These ceremonies, more modest now, had been maintained throughout the long drought in hopes of mobilizing the pantheon of encantados to bring rain and fertility to the land. On one of those nights, there appeared before us a mysterious encantada of whom we'd never heard. The names of all the spirits were familiar to us, but of this particular encantada nothing was known. She had never manifested herself in the houses of Jarê in our region. Dona Miúda, a widow who lived alone in an empty field along the road to Viração cemetery and a regular at our Jarê rituals, was the

77

one who received the spirit. When she announced herself as Santa Rita the Fisherwoman, the drums went silent. Then there was quite a commotion. I listened to what folks were wondering aloud: was this a real encantada? Why had she not revealed herself before, since our Jarê community was as old as the plantation itself, going back to the original pioneers of the region?

Dona Miúda was in the ragged clothes she always wore, but now she had donned a veil, old and torn as well. Her feeble voice, almost inaudible, began chanting, "Santa Rita the Fisherwoman, where's my hook? Where's my hook? So I can fish in the sea?" Despite Dona Miúda's advanced age, the encantada was spinning gracefully around the room. Sometimes she'd move as if casting a net over the crowd, other times she'd run across the floor with all the fluid energy of a raging river. Some onlookers grew quite perplexed, indeed; they wanted to solve the mystery behind this apparition. Others just smiled, no doubt incredulous, assuming old Miúda had lost her mind and needed the ministrations of my father.

In the middle of her dance, as the slender thread of the old woman's voice chanted the refrain that sounded improvised, she grabbed me roughly by the arm. I didn't try to free myself, for I was accustomed to the presence of encantados during our Jarê rituals. I was in my father's house, and my father was the healer Zeca Chapéu Grande. I'd grown up among the mad, amid prayers and screams and root tinctures, amid candles and pounding drums. The mere presence of an encantada I didn't recognize wasn't enough to intimidate me, whether it was a true manifestation from the spirit world or just a woman's delirium. Dona Miúda's eyes were cloudy behind her veil; they'd turned gray, almost white. Perhaps it was just her cataracts. But she said something meant only for me, something I couldn't quite explain but understood.

She mentioned a child. Her words didn't follow any clear logic. What she said exactly I can't quite recall, something like "go with child." She said that I'd be riding off somewhere, when we didn't even own a horse, which bewildered me. She said that everything would change. She said something else, too, and the exact phrase that persists in my memory, after the many blows I've suffered, is this: "From your movement shall come both your victory and your defeat."

Her voice was so weak, only I could hear what she was saying, but her message, inscribed in me as if carved into stone, will stay with me for the rest of my days on this earth.

15.

Belonísia found me folding my clothes, placing them in the suitcase that had belonged to our grandmother. I saw the surprise in her eyes, but I wasn't able to communicate anything. Neither could she. She stared at me inquisitively, with a look that was as dry as the air around us, and my shame was such that I didn't even attempt to justify what I was doing. I cried after my sister left the room; I knew I was contributing to her unhappiness. I'd been meeting secretly with our cousin, and maybe Belonísia already suspected I

79

was pregnant, but aside from all that, I was her sister—there were no secrets between us, or at least we'd tried not to keep anything from each other—and yet I'd been in my own world for weeks, oblivious to my family and especially my sister, who seemed ever more distant.

I couldn't bear to think about the look she'd given me. I went out back where I could cry without being detected. I couldn't follow through with my plan to leave Água Negra. I needed to explain to Severo that I wanted to stay on the plantation, that we'd have to face our parents, that in the end everything would turn out fine. We'd build a house near Uncle Servó and Aunt Hermelina's place. That's the way it should be when two young people get together: they make their home on a plot near their parents. They announce their intentions and wait for the plantation manager to give his consent so they can start building. We'd build a house like all the others, using mud from the floodplains and the large, forked branches we'd collect in the woods. We'd cover the structure with the reeds lying in the bed of the drought-stricken Utinga. We'd settle down, and then later, yes, we could plan our departure and pursue Severo's dreams, which had become my dreams as well. I didn't want to spend the rest of my days on the plantation, either, to have the same life as my parents. If anything were to happen to them, we wouldn't have the right to live in their house or inherit their plot of land. We wouldn't have a right to anything, actually. If we left, we'd leave carrying only our few belongings. If for some reason we could no longer work in the fields, we'd be told to leave Água Negra, the land where an entire generation had been born. That larger system of exploitation was pretty clear to me already. But I was still so young; the moment and our circumstances were such that it just wasn't the right time to leave.

I pulled the suitcase back out from under the bed and removed everything I'd packed. I wouldn't follow Severo down an uncertain road, traveling from plantation to plantation until we found something in the city. I decided to meet him that same day and let him know that I was going to come clean to my parents, and that we'd be staying put, as a couple, if he wanted to be with me. If he wanted to leave, he'd have to go his own way, and he should feel completely free to do so. I'd raise the child without him; we wouldn't lack for family. I knew I wouldn't be abandoned by my parents. They could be firm when disciplining their children, but their firmness had a limit. In the end they'd help me, they'd protect me, there'd be no resentment or anger. Even Belonísia would surrender to the baby's smile, and I could ask her to be godmother; it would be a token of reconciliation and forgiveness between us after months of estrangement.

But what to make of the message transmitted by Dona Miúda's encantada, the one supposedly called Santa Rita the Fisherwoman? Hitherto the encantados had had no effect on me; I was so accustomed to their presence that I wouldn't let myself get involved in that world of obligations and prohibitions. My aloofness would keep me beyond the reach of blessings and curses—or so I hoped. And yet I couldn't have been an entirely random recipient of the encantada's message. In any case, she addressed her words specifically to me, when I was fairly certain only Severo and I knew our secret. I remained in that space between doubt and belief. I'd stay up all night puzzling over the meaning of her words, what she meant by my "victory," my "defeat," and what her message might foretell regarding our journey, our child, my life with Severo. My anxiety intensified. I tried to understand why the encantada had seized my arm and not that of Dona Tonha, who'd been standing right next to me, or even that of Crispina, who was also nearby, holding hands with her nephew and her sister Crispiniana. Could Dona Miúda have seen me lying with Severo in the dark of the woods? Her house was nowhere near our usual meeting place, and she seemed too old to go wandering through the woods just to spy on two young lovers.

I found Severo at our usual spot. The jackfruit tree was casting its rare shadow in the blasted landscape of unending drought. I let him know that I'd started separating some of my clothes for the trip, but Belonísia had interrupted me. I gesticulated wildly, expressing how much I'd been agonizing over our decision to leave, trying to make him see that I was too young. My hands were flying between my head and my chest with an urgency that startled him. I wanted him to understand that fleeing home would be a rupture—I crossed my arms then separated them—and an unforgivable betrayal of my parents. A betrayal of everything they'd gone through, everything they'd done for us. And for the same reasons, it wasn't right to abandon Uncle Servó and Aunt Hermelina. It would bring them so much pain—I brought my right hand to my face—and though I was the eldest and

82

often looked after my siblings, I really wouldn't know how to raise a child without my mother nearby.

Severo drew close and took me in his arms. He said it was normal to feel conflicted, but he was already a man and ready to leave the plantation. He didn't want to say anything to his parents because he knew they'd object, but soon, when he'd found a place to live and work, he'd send news and share his whereabouts. I wanted to reassure him that he could go without me, I'd stay behind and wait for our child to be born. I'd remain with my parents and work at Água Negra. After he'd gotten settled, I'd go find him, with Zeca and Salu's blessing. But I lacked the courage. It broke my heart to think about my imminent separation, either from Severo or from my family. We kissed goodnight, upset and uncertain about our future.

The next morning, the farm manager, Sutério, marched into our house and told my father that he needed to finish building the small dam he'd been working on in the stream. And that he needed to organize the men for the slash-and-burn, to clear the land so it would be ready for the rains when they finally came. Having invited himself into the kitchen, Sutério asked where all those sweet potatoes had come from. My father replied that we'd bought them at the street market in town. With what money, Sutério wanted to know. My father explained that we'd sold the rest of the palm oil we'd pressed. Sutério's two enormous hands grabbed the larger share of sweet potatoes and carried them off to the Rural parked outside the door. He also took two bottles of palm oil we'd kept for cooking the tiny fish we

83

sometimes caught in the river. Sutério reminded my father that workers had to contribute a third of the produce they cultivated for themselves in their backyards. But the sweet potatoes hadn't come from our backyard. Not even grass would grow from that parched earth, let alone potatoes. The drought was so bad that not even the floodplains could be cultivated. In the exposed riverbeds, the seeds were rotting in the mud, and nothing flourished but cattails for weaving mats and sacks, or for using as roofing material. I could see the shame on my father's face as he stood there, unable to stop what was happening. Zeca Chapéu Grande was a respected healer, his name renowned throughout the region. But here, within the confines of the plantation, under the rule of the Peixoto family—who barely set foot on those fields except to give orders or pay the manager or remind us that we were forbidden from building brick houses—under their rule and that of Sutério, my father was just another loyal tenant farmer, grateful for the opportunity he'd been given after searching for work and a place to settle down. I saw my mother make a slight movement, her eyes burning with indignation, but she held herself back when she understood that my father was going to just stand there, without protest or complaint. You could say my father was in fact complicit in his own exploitation: as the spiritual leader of the community, it was he who made sure the work continued without disruption, keeping the peace among the tenant farmers. My father was the person Sutério or any of the Peixotos would look to whenever there was trouble, whether it was an animal getting into the crops or a worker building his house with prohibited materials, and they needed someone to step in.

Of course, we wanted my father to take back those sweet potatoes we'd paid for with our own sweat, but he had been humiliated; we didn't want to salt his wounds. How long that night would be for me. I couldn't sleep at all. In fact, for weeks, insomnia had been keeping me company. I was thinking about Severo's judgment on the conditions we suffered on the plantation. We'd end up spending our lives in submission to the landowners, subjected to constant humiliation, such as the theft of our own food. Severo said I had a part to play in how things unfolded; if life was ever going to change for my parents, it would be up to me. He said that, yes, we could buy a piece of land ourselves and one day come back for our parents. It was the only way to achieve a life with any dignity.

I managed to sneak out of the house and find Severo, though we hadn't made plans to meet. I only needed to look at Severo for him to understand that I'd decided to go with him. We thought through everything, down to the last detail: the day, the hour, how far we'd have to walk and where we might hitch a ride out of the Chapada Velha. Early on the morning of departure, Grandma Donana's old suitcase was dusted off and packed so that I could carry the little I owned to the life awaiting me. I rose from bed while everyone was still asleep and prayed to God for the health and well-being of those I was leaving behind. I begged the encantados to help me, to convince my family not to think of me as someone who'd dishonored them, to make them understand that

I'd had good reasons to leave, and I'd prove it to them one day when I returned home with money and we invited our families to join us on land that was our own. I asked God to protect Belonísia; it had been about ten years since the event that changed both of our lives forever. When, in the quiet darkness, I slipped out the back door of our house and started walking down the road to meet Severo, I couldn't stop myself from looking back. I began listing the little I was taking with me, and all that I was leaving behind. I came very close to turning around right then and there and letting Severo go on without me, but the memory of Sutério stealing our modest provisions, and how difficult it then was to conjure a meal for our family, gave me the determination I needed to continue. As I listed the things I was taking on my journey, I remembered what was perhaps the most painful of all: my tongue. My wounded tongue that for years had given voice to the words Belonísia had not uttered, ashamed of the strange noises coming from her throat. It was my tongue that had rescued my sister from the muteness she'd inflicted upon herself, fearing rejection and the cruel teasing of other children. It was my tongue that had so often delivered my sister from the prison of her silence.

II. CROOKED PLOW

1.

I was running through papyrus and cabelos-de-nego and sword-grass near the marshes, opening deep gashes in my dry skin. But there was no blood, no pus. Only sweat soaking my clothes, soaking the strip of cloth wrapped around my breasts. I noticed a boat, an ajoujo, on the river, floating on the surface like a water hyacinth until it was swallowed up in a whirlpool at the confluence and disappeared in water dark as my skin. I was running through the ancient forest of tall trees, looking for the path that would lead me home when the flesh of my arms got caught in the spines of a tucum palm. It was neither day nor night, but the land was burning my feet. A man appeared out of nowhere, well-dressed, his skin pale as the coat of a white horse, his face smiling at me. He blocked my path. I tried to escape, screaming for help, running this way and that, but I was trapped. A wire fence gleamed like silver to either side, and beyond it I saw only spiky tucum palms, mandacaru and other cacti, genip trees and drought-stricken branches. I couldn't get back home. Then I noticed a stone, shining like a jewel. I grabbed it. What looked like a stone from a distance was in fact made of ivory, but I couldn't pull it out from the ground. It seemed to have the weight of the world. Using both hands I was finally able to wrench it free, and with it the polished metal, the pure radiance of Grandma Donana's lost knife, now back in my hands. The knife I'd impulsively pulled from Bibiana's mouth, then from my own, at that tender age when I wanted so badly to feel older, unaware of the blood spilling from my sister's mouth. Unaware of the danger of the blade's edge, which produced such violent light. The light that would sever my tongue completely. Having lost my words, ashamed of what I'd done to myself, I closed myself off to the world as though imprisoned by the wire fence now encircling me. The moment I wrenched my grandmother's knife from the dry earth, blood poured forth. A red river began flowing across the land.

For years, I'd wake from this dream drenched in sweat in the sweltering night. It was always the same dream, with slight variations, always featuring the well-dressed man, the fence, my grandmother's knife, and the blood gushing from the ground. The one positive aspect of my nightmares was that I'd talk nonstop in them, scream out intelligible words, something I hadn't been able to do in years. On the night Bibiana ran away from home, I had the same dream. Maybe that's what led me to start talking to myself this way, in my own head. I woke with a suffocating feeling, then noticed my sister wasn't in our room. I went to get some water, and I didn't find her anywhere in the house. If she'd gone into the backyard to relieve herself, she would have left the back door open. I opened it, and Fusco got up off the ground, limping over to be petted.

I only needed to go back inside and look for Grandma's old, busted-up suitcase to confirm what I'd suspected: Bibiana had left home. Her eyes couldn't hide her intentions from me when I caught her putting her clothes into the worn leather case. She'd been planning to leave without telling anyone, that much was certain. I could've done to her what she'd done to me that time she saw me with Severo under the umbu tree, on one of those nights of Jarê. I could have gone running to alert our mother, so she'd give my sister the same beating I'd received because of a lie my sister told. But that was long ago, and I didn't want to see my sister cry. What would be the point of getting back at her for something that happened in the past? That wound had healed. I didn't want to give her cause to nurse a grudge, the way I'd felt embittered after I couldn't defend myself from accusations that I'd been kissing Severo. All I was doing with my cousin, back then when I was twelve, was admiring the fireflies flashing, far from the lights of our house.

When it dawned on everyone that my sister had run away, which of course was no surprise to me, it caused a terrible commotion, the worst since that day I'd mutilated myself. Seeing my mother so devastated by Bibiana's decision to sneak off in the night like some common hussy, I blamed

91

myself for not having tipped her off; for not having led her to Grandma's suitcase, packed with Bibiana's clothes; for not revealing what I'd discovered days earlier. Later I mulled over my own inaction, telling myself that what I'd done was give my sister the chance to think things through. By sparing her, I'd intimated that I needed her by my side, that she couldn't leave us. Because even if her nausea, her irritation with the heat and the lack of rain, the rage burning in her eyes when Sutério took our provisions while our father just stood by, her urge to do something desperate on account of her belly—even if all of that was prompting her to leave Água Negra, there was still no need. I wanted her to reflect before making a reckless decision. Our parents would be upset at first, but they'd never turn their back on their grandchild. The damage was already done; they wouldn't try to separate her from Severo. My sister had become a woman, and for that reason, perhaps, our mother wouldn't beat her the way she'd beaten me. She wasn't a little girl who could be set straight. I didn't believe Bibiana would follow through with what I'd seen brewing in her eyes.

Eventually, after my sister's departure, there came a period of calm. I'd find my father in the saints' room concentrating, perhaps communicating with the encantados for some news of his daughter. Amid candles, herbs, incense, and chants, he sought to learn the whereabouts of Bibiana and also Severo—a young man he very much liked and had treated like a son, for Severo possessed the character of a leader, a quality my father had never detected in anyone else. My father did his best to comfort my mother, who'd fallen into a depression and couldn't stop weeping. He also tried to offer some comfort to Uncle Servó and Aunt Hermelina; their eldest son's departure—with his underage cousin, no less— had left them bereft. My father forbade us from discussing it with our neighbors or even with each other. Not out of anger, but because he thought it dishonest to talk about people behind their backs. I sensed that my father didn't want us to think ill of Bibiana, even though she'd betrayed our trust. Although my father was a leader in our community, he refused to act like a judge and condemn anyone, for he believed that each of us, no matter the sin, could be redeemed.

Weeks later, we noticed rain clouds finally looming, and from the land rose a freshness that farmers liked to call a bit of "luck." They said you could dig a little into the dry mud and actually feel the moisture arriving, feel that the earth was a bit cooler, a sign the drought was coming to an end. It didn't take long for the first drops of rain to fall, and despite the despondency that had engulfed our home after Bibiana's departure, my mother managed to smile as she put empty buckets out to catch the rain. The plantation resounded with the old songs of the local women bringing their laundry down to the widening river or carrying their hoes to clear their small plots and do some slash-and-burn farming. The men could join the women only after they'd cleared the vast fields for planting the landowners' crops.

Each day the rain fell harder and for longer, bringing out the alluring colors of the sky, the animals, and the people of the region. Francisco Peixoto, the eldest of the heirs, started showing up more frequently. Sutério, who'd lead him around the plantation, seemed to have been taken down a notch; he'd have to wait for Mr. Peixoto to leave in order to feel like the boss again. Sometimes Mr. Peixoto would greet us, sometimes he'd pretend not to see us. On our plantation there was no traditional "big house" where he could unwind; there was only a storehouse, where, if we couldn't get to town, we'd purchase provisions at high prices, much higher than you'd find at the public market. The workers reckoned that there'd never been a big house at Água Negra because the Peixoto family owned other plantations in the region that were larger and more productive, and it was on one of those that the family had their house.

During this period, before the Feast of Saint Joseph, the mayor inaugurated our school. Its construction— including a tile roof, something prohibited on our own houses—had been completed during the summer. The schoolhouse was named after the late Antônio Peixoto, the family patriarch. The man who had reputedly been the actual proprietor of the plantation but had never set foot on it. We all attended the inauguration: the women with their kerchiefs wrapped around their heads; the men wearing their hats, holding their hoes in their hands; the children delighted by the novelty—a small, proper building with three rooms but without a "bathroom," which none of us had at home in any case. The Peixoto family was also represented by the eldest sister, overweight and very pale, a woman we'd never previously seen, who didn't acknowledge us for even a moment. She wiped her eyes with a kerchief while the mayor spoke. When the plaque was unveiled, bearing the name of her late father, she almost fell to the ground, weeping convulsively, and her brothers had to hold her up. Not a word of thanks was addressed to my father who, during the celebration in honor of Saint Barbara, had asked, practically forced, the mayor to keep his promise to build the schoolhouse. But there he was, my father, standing tall in the front row, holding Domingas by the hand, with my mother by his side and a satisfied expression on his face. The slight hardly mattered to him; he was visibly marked by the struggle he'd undergone, borrowing the power of the encantada to open a new prospect so we wouldn't remain illiterate. My father couldn't even sign his own name, but he did all he could to provide a school where we might learn reading and writing and math. I often saw my father arguing with some neighbor who didn't want his child attending school; the neighbor might even agree that his son should study, but his daughter had no need. In disagreeing with his compadre, my father often managed to change the man's mind, such was the respect and prestige in which he was held.

It took some time for them to send us a new teacher, someone to take the place of the woman who'd been visiting us three times a week in Dona Firmina's crowded barn. On my route to the school, every morning I saw the umbu trees with their verdant canopies and the mandacaru flowering beneath the fine rain that stayed with us even after the Feast of Saint Joseph. My thoughts would turn to Bibiana and Severo, and I wondered if the rain had reached them, if they'd found shelter at some plantation or in a distant city. Perhaps the roads they had taken led all the way to the capital.

2.

At school, without Bibiana by my side to help me, my life was a misery. My mother informed the new teacher about my muteness early on, and at first Dona Lourdes paid special attention to me and was helpful when I struggled with an assignment. Thanks to the efforts of Bibiana and my mother, rather than to our previous, rather impatient teacher at Dona Firmina's, I already knew how to read. I thought I'd learned enough. Bibiana felt differently about school because she wanted to become a teacher herself. What I liked was farming, cooking, pressing palm oil and peeling buriti. Math had little appeal for me, much less Dona Lourdes's reading and writing lessons. My mind would wander when she'd go on about the history of Brazil, how we were a mixture of Indians, Blacks, and Whites, how we should rejoice to live in a country so blessed. I didn't memorize a single line of our national anthem; what would be the point? I can't even sing. I noticed that a lot of the other kids weren't really paying attention either; they were thinking about food or the fun on the riverbank they were missing, just to listen to those fanciful, tiresome stories about Brazil's heroic trailblazers, our military leaders, the legacy of the Portuguese colonizers, and other topics that meant little to us.

I grew less and less interested in my studies. It felt like a waste of time being lectured to by that lady with her smooth, slender hands, her perfume overwhelming us like incense in that stifling classroom. I'd gaze at the blackboard, the assortment of beautiful letters; together they'd form difficult words and sentences that just wouldn't stay in my head, and I'd think about my father out there in the floodplain studying the land, throwing himself into some new task, or my mother working in our vegetable garden, feeding the animals, doing some sewing. And the sluggish hours would crawl by ever more slowly before I could finally head back home. I'd sometimes imagine Bibiana, who'd probably be interested in the day's lesson, sitting at the teacher's side, trying to spark my own interest as well. Another reason for my boredom was that I'd been grouped with younger children, some quite motivated to learn, making many mistakes but nevertheless reading aloud while constantly being interrupted by Dona Lourdes to correct their pronunciation. I was able to follow along and even identify errors in their pronunciation, thanks to what I'd learned previously. Domingas and Zezé were attending school as well, but they were on a different schedule, based on their age; perhaps their presence would have helped me stay interested. Daydreaming, I'd wonder if at that very moment my absent sister had a book or a hoe in her hands, if she was pursuing her dream of becoming a teacher. I compared her ambitions to my own and came to believe that these fundamental differences between us brought a certain equilibrium to our relationship.

One day I'd fake a headache, another a stomachache, gradually realizing my desire to get back to work in the fields and in our home. I abandoned my notebook and pencil in a corner of my room, and though my father was put out by my lack of interest in school, I wouldn't be swayed. If a headache was what had kept me from going to class, it would vanish just after class had started, and then I'd join my mother in the kitchen to prepare lunch, or grab a bucket and head to the river, returning with water for the garden. My mother, annoyed at first, didn't take long to accept that I just wasn't cut out for school. I already knew how to read and write adequately; I could write out a shopping list better than she could. I could do simple math as well. My mother kept her disappointment to herself. In any case, she had to agree that my future wouldn't necessarily be improved by school; I wouldn't be able to give classes at Água Negra or in a town nearby. I hadn't seen any ads calling for a mute teacher. Deep down, she knew that so long as I couldn't speak I'd never teach. It was better for me to stay in the fields, the garden, and the kitchen, to limit myself to the marshes and the road to the market, because it was the only way I'd learn to manage on my own.

Working at my father's side was much better than being around Dona Lourdes, with her nauseating perfume and the lies she told about the history of our land. She didn't know anything, really, about why we were working those fields, where our parents came from or what we really did, since her lectures and textbooks only talked about soldiers and professors and doctors and judges. And I didn't need to hear the other kids constantly mocking me because I couldn't speak. Some of them kept wanting me to open my mouth wide so they could see what I didn't have.

With Zeca Chapéu Grande, however, I immersed myself in the woods, walking up and down the trails, learning all about herbs and roots. I learned about clouds, too, how they'd foretell rain, all the secret changes of sky and earth. I learned that everything is in motion—quite different from the lifeless things taught to us in school. My father would turn to me and say, "the wind doesn't blow, the wind is the blowing," and this made sense to me. "If the air doesn't move, there's no wind, and if we don't keep moving, there's no life." He was trying to teach me. Attentive to the movement of animals, insects, and plants, he lit up my horizon, and these lessons that nature had taught to him I began understanding deep in my bones. My father couldn't read or do sums, but he knew the phases of the moon. He knew that under a full moon you could plant almost anything, although manioc, banana, and other fruit liked to be sown under a new moon; under a waning moon, it wasn't time for planting but for clearing the land.

He knew that for a plant to grow strong, you needed to weed around each one every day, reducing the risk of pests. You had to be vigilant, protecting the stalks, making small mounds of soil and watering carefully so they'd flourish. Whenever he encountered some problem in the fields, my father would lie on the ground, his ear attuned to what was deep in the earth, before deciding what tools to use and what to do, where to advance and where to retreat.

Like a doctor listening to a heartbeat.

3.

Several months after the opening of the school, a group of workers arrived at the plantation. Among them was a scrawny woman with straight, black hair by the name of Maria Cabocla. She arrived with her husband and six children. The family was put up in an abandoned house near where Uncle Servó lived. A tall, thin man arrived with them, a man old enough to be my father, looking for work as a cowhand. His body language was restrained, and he spoke very little. He introduced himself as Tobias, and soon he was attending the Jarê rituals at our house, becoming friendly with Zeca Chapéu Grande. Tobias was a man who loved a good story. He and my father would meet in the fields and in the plantation storehouse where the manager would give orders. Sometimes I'd see Tobias on the trails around the fields or the paths leading to the floodplain. He'd nod in my direction and greet me—good morning, young lady— letting me walk ahead of him, but I could feel his eyes burning into my back like embers.

At some point, Tobias must have learned of my disability, but he didn't pester me with questions. He'd pull a sprig of sempre-viva from his hatband and stick it in my hair, making me feel embarrassed and somewhat uncomfortable. I'd never had to deal with the flattery of strangers. In time, I felt like smiling back at him, but, awkward as I was, I'd just look away and keep walking. On the nights of Jarê, I'd see the cowhand talking it up with the neighbors, sometimes with women, like Dona Tonha's girls, and he'd smile and flirt, especially after a few shots of cachaça. At first, it didn't bother me. I enjoyed seeing him in animated conversation with others; something about his eyes transfixed me as I stood watching beside Domingas or my mother. But later I'd start feeling fidgety, a bit jealous, wishing he'd pay some attention to me.

When Tobias eventually earned Sutério's trust, he began leading the herd down the road, for the rains had stopped and the nearby pastures were dried up. Many of the workers would spend hours of time normally spent in the fields in heading out to the parched marshes and cutting cattails to feed the animals. But this wasn't sufficient, so Tobias and the other cowhands would drive the cattle down the main road to pastures along the Utinga River.

He'd sometimes even stand in for Sutério and handle business in town, such as when an order arrived or when provisions came in to be sold later at high prices at the plantation storehouse. Far from Sutério's ears, we referred to the storehouse as the "rip-off." "I can't get to town today, I'll need to head over to the rip-off," that was the name we used among ourselves. Tobias would take the horse and wagon into town and return with the wagon loaded with supplies. On one occasion, he rushed back, seemingly with good news. Whenever I saw someone that happy, my first impulse was to think he'd struck it rich and found a diamond, meaning he'd soon be grabbing his belongings and hitting the road. Tobias dismounted and called out to my father, who'd just returned from the fields. He handed him an envelope. My father couldn't read, so he passed the envelope to my mother. She asked what this was all about, but Tobias just repeated that they'd given him the envelope in town and that it was meant for Zeca. Salu was getting old by then, and in the early evening, by the light of the kerosene lamp, her eyesight wasn't very good. She must have needed glasses, glasses like our teacher had. She passed the letter to Domingas, who examined the envelope, her eyes reflecting the dim light. "Mama, it's from Bibiana."

My father found a chair and sat down, averting his eyes. My mother whispered a prayer, hoping the letter contained good news. Domingas tore open the envelope, which contained yet another envelope, addressed to Severo's father, Uncle Servó. Tobias moved closer to me, his long coat stinking of leather that hadn't been properly cured. His eyes seemed at first to fasten on Domingas, then they turned toward me. My sister began reading aloud, occasionally holding the paper closer to the light. The letter was written in rather faint ink. Bibiana and Severo were doing well, working on a plantation in the region of Itaberaba. Bibiana's due date was fast approaching. They wanted Salu to be the midwife; they'd try to come home for the birth. But if that wasn't possible, they'd come home at the end of the year. Severo was working in the fields, cutting cane, making friends in the labor union. They'd heard that the drought had ended for us; it had rained over there as well. They were trying to save enough money to buy a piece of property. They aspired to farm their own land. Things were fine; they didn't need anything. At the beginning of the new year, Bibiana would pursue her high school equivalency in a program designed for farmworkers, then she could enroll for the certification in teaching. They asked about me and Domingas and Zezé. They missed everyone. They'd send more news soon.

"What's wrong with kids today?" my father asked, not expecting an answer.

Salu wiped a tear away, then carried the kerosene lamp into the kitchen, calling Domingas over to read the letter to her again. I was relieved to know they were well, safe and sound, sleeping under a roof and able to feed themselves through their hard work. But I felt a bit hurt by the attention my mother lavished on the letter, by the commotion Bibiana caused even from so far away. I was upset by the simplicity of her words and the lack of any apparent remorse, as I recalled her voice, the voice my sister had taken away with her. I was just one more name on the same level as Domingas and Zezé. Not a single question asking how I was doing at school, if I had any friends, who was communicating for me, how I was getting along without her.

I could smell Tobias's coat, the mixture of sweat and leather not yet ready to be worn. I thought flies might start landing on him in search of bits of meat. Tobias exchanged a few words with my father, then excused himself, bowing his head toward me before mounting his horse. Watching him disappear down the road, I wanted him to turn around and come back and ask my father if he could take me to live with him. I wanted him to take care of me, as I'd take care of him. I wanted to experience a life like the one Bibiana described in her letter, with her beautiful handwriting, that brought Salu to tears. My father, despite his prickly facade, had been touched, his serious countenance undermined by a glow that said what he couldn't say: he was happy to hear that Bibiana was well, that she hadn't forgotten her family. I wanted Tobias to turn around right then, or the next day or the day after, but not to wait long to make me his woman.

4.

The more babies being born around me, the more my body trembled with an urge to get pregnant, like the humid earth that seems to want to be seeded, and when it hasn't been, nature itself will cultivate the land, bringing forth the scrub and passion flowers of the caatinga and all sorts of leaves that cure the ills of the body as well as the spirit.

Some time after the drought ended, babies began popping up like bracket fungi on the rotting trunks of the floodplain, now transformed into marshland. Almost every week, I'd accompany Salu to help the women in labor. Crispina and Crispiniana were both pregnant again, at the same time, and no one even bothered asking who the father was anymore. We heard that the twins were back at each other's throats. Crispina gave birth to a living baby this time, a great relief to my mother, who worried that Crispina might produce another angel, which would damage my mother's reputation as a midwife. Salu went from house to house to "catch" babies, as we say, borrowing the power that really came from the encantado Velho Nagô, which she always acknowledged, and she'd delight in hearing folks say, "May God reward you." I never heard my mother complain about the number of women giving birth or the hard work of midwifery, such as preparing the medicinal syrup of herbs and ashes to avoid post-natal problems, or burying the placenta in the earth after carefully cutting the umbilical cord. I'll never forget the hiss of the hot spoon cauterizing the newborn's belly button or the smell of dripping fat. I associate the strong smell with that year of hard work, but we received it as a blessing, in contrast to the years of drought when many angels were laid to rest at Viração.

The days rushed by like the wind. Neither Bibiana nor Severo came home at the end of the year as they'd promised. Not even a note to tell us if the baby had been born, if it was a girl or a boy, if they'd named it Severo or José, or Salustiana or Hermelina. Perhaps Maria or Flora, the names my sister and I had given to our corncob dolls when we were small. My mother seemed nervous, on edge every time a merchant dropped by, someone selling blankets or pans, anyone who might show up with a note from Bibiana. At some point, I dreamed that my sister was giving birth and my father, somehow much older, bent by the years, was the one assisting her. In this dream I was singing the old songs the women sang when they washed clothes down by the river, and the child, who should have been born crying, arrived smiling, something I'd never witnessed before.

In December, precisely on the Feast of Saint Barbara, there was a downpour, full of thunder and lighting. Dona Tonha brought over the starched garments she'd put away from the previous year, and it seemed that the older my father got, the more embarrassed he was to don the skirt and adê of the encantada. Not even he, with all his mystical knowledge, foresaw that the rain would wash away a year's hard work in the fields. The drought had just ended, now we'd suffer the ruin of the flood. A number of houses, standing precariously, crumbled under the force of the water and the wind.

"If the water doesn't take our crops, we'll eat," my father said to me as he weeded our plot. But the water took it all. The plots turned into marshland, into lakes, and, instead of the manioc and sweet potato which had rotted beneath so much water, we pulled out cumbá and molé and armored catfish and another kind of catfish we call jundiá, all of them swimming where there had once been arid land. Most families had stored away manioc flour that they'd produced over a period of months. Folks started heading out before daybreak, without the manager's knowledge, disappearing into the forest then arriving in town to sell the fish they'd caught and buy supplies. They'd fish day and night, unless there was a new moon, when the fish seemed to have soft teeth; they just couldn't be caught. To outwit Sutério, the workers would leave their rods and hooks hidden in the woods near the edge of the lake or tied to branches overhead. All summer, along with Domingas and my mother, I'd sink my feet into the muddy banks in order to catch some fish. Zezé and my father kept working in the fields, at higher elevations away from the valleys, taking advantage of the constant rain of those first few months. We'd been cultivating our gardens since the end of the drought, and many other families had done the same, so we were still grateful for the rain and didn't lament the downpour, even when we saw months of work drowned beneath the water. It was hard to watch the cultivated soil flooding, but with the water's return, our strength returned as well, and we were once more ready to toil in the fields.

That year, Tobias came around quite often. I noticed him watching me, encircling me with courteous gestures, but, as time went on, his attention moved elsewhere. He seemed to be just as interested in the other girls around the plantation. Offended, I'd ignore him when I encountered him along trails or on the nights of Jarê. For a time I even believed he was flirting with everyone else just to provoke me. In fact, I couldn't help but follow him with my eyes, tracking him as he grew tipsier during those celebrations. But I'd hold back, because I couldn't get past the fact that I'd been condemned to silence. I couldn't get past my own timidity, which made me gruff and unsociable, and so I isolated myself.

I'd turn away from his glances. But when I noticed him distracted by other girls and other people, or how he applied himself to his work, I'd study him from afar and feel my interest grow. My body was like a filly refusing to be controlled, sweating, giving off strange odors and trembling, moving this way and that, heart pounding. I was reminded of how I felt when Severo, still a boy, first arrived at Água Negra. But my desire back then didn't have the same strength; it was something pleasant, like fragile wings beating within. Now my desire was a ripened fruit inviting birds to peck at me, like those cowbirds we'd scare away from the rice paddies when we were children.

One morning, as he sat at the table where Salu was straining coffee, filling the room with its aroma, my father turned to me. He told me that Tobias had approached him, respectfully, with the proposal of taking me to live with him. He told me that Tobias disliked being alone in that old house by the Santo Antônio River. That Tobias was very fond of me and held me in high esteem. For an instant I pictured my father warning him about my defect, telling him that I had a disability, that I was strong-willed, wild like a jaguar, but that I had a good heart. I pictured my father making him promise to take good care of me, to see to it that I wouldn't know suffering. I pictured a conversation that may or may not have taken place, because nothing was said to me about it. My father told me I didn't need to decide right away, I could think about it, he'd only give his consent if I felt I was ready, because he would never grant his daughter's hand to just any man. He'd come to know Tobias well over the course of that year and considered him a hard worker, worthy of respect.

I don't know why, but, at that moment, the image of Grandma Donana came to mind. She appeared to me in all of her fierceness and wearing that big hat she had, with the ivory-handled knife and the stories that had been told to me, her three marriages and the mystery surrounding her daughter, Aunt Carmelita, of whom no one had any news. I thought about the answer Donana would have given were she the one being courted. On a brown piece of paper tucked under my mattress, I'd write the word that would define the rest of my life: yes, or no.

5.

Perched behind Tobias on his horse, clutching a bundle of clothes, I left my parents' house. I recalled that Bibiana had pulled Donana's old leather suitcase from under the bed when she left. If she hadn't taken it, I probably would have. I felt my chest tighten. The amble of the horse was invading that part of me beneath my hips like an echo. We moved slowly. Tobias was silent, when I would've preferred for him to say something cheering. With one hand I held on to his waist, and with the other, my bundle.

"So this is your house now, young lady." I looked around. I noticed a long shadow extending from the crown of a jatoba about twenty meters from the house. A bright green that drew my attention. Tobias dismounted, then guided his horse to a trough full of fresh grass he'd probably gathered that same morning before fetching me. I felt paralyzed, already longing to return home. "Go in." I was stunned by the chaos of his smelly three-roomed hovel, strewn with dirty clothes and all sorts of trash, never mind the poor condition of the structure itself, the dilapidated walls and the gaps above through which light poured in. The house badly needed repair, maybe a whole new roof. After just a few days, I would feel terrible regret for having written "yes" on that brown piece of paper I'd handed to my mother. I understood that my life from that day forward would be very hard.

He walked over to an old wardrobe and opened the door, which promptly came off its hinges; he tossed it among the nameless objects spread about the house. He told me to put my things in the empty compartment. I was overwhelmed with dread, but I did everything I could to hide my sadness. Despite my fears and doubts, I had no desire to hurt the man's feelings. My revulsion was quite natural; after all, I'd never left home before. Here, in Tobias's decrepit house, everything was strange to me, but I'd soon transform this hovel into something I could be proud of. One thing I'd been taught at home and at Dona Firmina's school: there's nothing in the world that doesn't benefit from a woman's touch.

Tobias seemed quite pleased. He took the bundle from my hand and threw it on the bed. He grabbed me by the arm and started walking excitedly through each room, showing me this and that, junk everywhere I looked, ruined things that could never be fixed. He was keen to lead me out back where there was a jirau; I saw some firewood and the mud oven, partially collapsed. It was all so disheartening, but I wanted to show him that I was paying attention as he led me to the piece of land behind his house. I took note of the araçá tree, its ripe fruit strewn on the ground and pecked by birds. Tobias explained that the birds left not one fruit on that tree, and since he didn't really care one way or the other, well, what could you do? A piglet was tied to the trunk of another tree, and I noticed a small plot of edible cacti.

He led me back to the ancient outdoor oven, pointing out two pans, black with ashes from the firewood. He repeated everything twice, as if he were teaching a child who'd just arrived from the city and knew nothing about country life. In the kitchen I found some grease-stained bundles atop a counter of rotting wood, where heaps of uncooked rice and beans had been scattered as if to seed the spaces between the opened packages and Tobias's leftovers, all of it beneath a heavy cloud of flies. He said I could go ahead and make us something to eat, and if I lacked anything, I'd find it growing out back behind the house. What could I say, looking at that pigsty? I thanked God I was mute.

Having brought the tour to its conclusion, Tobias went back outside, put on his leather hat and unhitched his horse. He told me he was heading back to work; he'd be expecting a meal when he got home. He rode off into the distance, and I found myself alone. I had no idea how far I'd have to walk to reach my closest neighbor, or what I'd do if I were in danger, if a chicken-snake or rattlesnake got into the house. I sat down in an old wicker chair; it promptly collapsed and I fell on my backside. I remained on the floor for a while, listening to the buzzing of the flies.

I figured that being left alone in the house wasn't the worst thing in the world, for I had no idea what I would've done had Tobias wanted to take me straight to his bed that morning. I'd worry about that later; better to confront one fear at a time. If I could stand it, I needed to start tidying up this dump that would be my home. I decided to begin in the kitchen, sifting through and separating the grains that had been scattered everywhere. I discovered the reason for the cloud of flies: fresh fish, two cumbá that Tobias must have caught that morning before the sun came up. I covered the fish with a cloth before the insects could devour them. I sorted the beans and was about to put them to soak, but there was no water to be seen, not even a jug for storing it. So, the first thing I had to do was locate the river. I grabbed a large canister, smelling of rust, and brought it with me. I walked through the woods and climbed down a hillside to reach the valley of the Santo Antônio. The river was overflowing its banks at the time, so it wouldn't take long to find it. I searched my memory for the configuration of houses where the locals lived; most of the houses had been built along the river, within easy reach of fresh water. I came to the bank of the black current, the water rushing along without obstruction and carrying fish and broken branches to the confluence where it fed into another river. I dunked the canister into the shallows, then, after filling it, I had trouble carrying it all the way back home. But I'm used to this kind of work, I told myself, and soon my feet will come to know this stretch of land so well, I won't even need my eyes.

I put the canister on the ground, beside the jirau, and left the beans soaking in pails I was finally able to locate. I went through the heaps of rubbish and separated out anything that could still be of use. I took the fish to the jirau where, fortunately, I'd found a knife. I gutted the fish, salted them—Tobias kept salt on the table at least—and left them to marinate in the seasoning I'd made with fresh herbs and lime from the backyard. In the meantime, I put the firewood in the almost-useless old oven. But how would I start the fire? I couldn't find matches or kerosene. I looked around the jirau, on the table, through the rubbish. Nothing. I didn't waste more time looking. I'd already started putting the house in order, and I didn't want to stop. I was going to transform that house into a home. As I began sweeping the cobwebs from the corners of every room, I wondered if I should try to find a neighbor and ask for some kerosene or even embers to get the oven started. I thought Tobias must have some friend or acquaintance nearby. He'd been living there for some time, and the workers usually treated one another like extended family, sometimes getting into lively disputes, too, just as real families inevitably did.

I decided to head out and find something with which to light the oven. By then the sun was at its peak, and a warm breeze touched my skin, dripping with sweat. I took a piece of firewood with me. Whoever I met as I wandered would understand that I needed a flame.

6

The sun was setting, the heat less intense, when Tobias finally returned. I felt weak from hunger, but I'd fooled my stomach with some of the pecked-at araçá scattered on the ground. Earlier, I came across Maria Cabocla's house, where I found the flame I needed. She didn't seem surprised to see me; we recognized each other from the Jarê rituals. When she saw me, Maria explained she didn't need any firewood. Then she perceived that I wasn't responding, that I was just standing there, waiting for something. She asked if I was the one in need of firewood. Eventually she grasped that what I needed was a light, and gave me an ember from her oven, glowing at the tip.

Tobias smiled the moment he stepped into the house. At first, I was worried he'd complain that I'd been messing with his things when I'd tried to straighten the house, even though I hadn't managed to do everything I'd wanted during those hours alone. But the difference was immediately clear to him. He noticed the swept corners and the made bed; the rip in the mattress, a mattress stuffed with corn husks, was now mended with the thread and needle I'd brought with me. He noticed the clean table and the absence of flies, and he noticed, too, the smoke rising from the oven outside. He didn't thank me. He was a man, after all, why should he be grateful? That's what went through my mind. But his eyes betrayed a deep satisfaction, for he'd come out way ahead in this deal, bringing a woman to live with him in that dump of a house. I filled his plate, then stood beside him, waiting for him to eat. I wanted to see the delight on his face when he tasted my seasoning. He ate greedily, using his bare hands, pouring large amounts of manioc flour over the food, until he cleared his plate. I tossed the fish bones into the woods. I didn't wait for him to ask but went ahead and dished up more beans and fish. He cleared his plate with the same enthusiasm as before. I left him alone so he could wash in the water I brought from the river when I'd finished with my attempt to clean up the house. Exhausted, I finally stepped into the shallows of the Santo Antônio to bathe.

Night had fallen, and I lit the lamp using some kerosene I'd discovered buried in the rubbish. I sat in the lamplight and began stitching a bed sheet, torn and threadbare, one I'd washed that morning. I was in an agony of tension, just trying to concentrate on my needle. Tobias closed in on me; he'd been drinking the cachaça I'd left on the table. He began talking about his day, the livestock, Sutério, all the work he'd been doing around the plantation. I put my sewing down and turned to look at him so that he wouldn't think I was snubbing him, sewing at that hour. So that he wouldn't suspect I was scared of what was about to happen between us on that bed, the bed I'd been mending and beating with the handle of a broom to remove the dust. But all it took was for our eyes to meet, and I quickly looked away, focusing on my needle as it pushed through the fabric. My heart was pounding, and I told myself: one fear at a time.

He laid me down on the bed and began kissing my neck, then lifted my dress. What happened next didn't justify my fears. It was like cooking or sweeping the floor, just another chore, albeit an unfamiliar one. I was a woman living with a man now, so I understood this was something I'd have to do. As he entered and exited my body with a back-and-forth motion that brought farm animals to mind, I felt something uncomfortable deep in my womb; it was the same feeling that had invaded me on leaving home that morning, when I felt the trotting of his horse. I turned my head toward the window. Through the gaps in the walls, I tried to find the moon, which had appeared earlier in the evening. Then I felt something being released from his body inside of me. He got up and went to wash himself with the rest of the water. I pulled my dress back down and turned to lie on my back, looking up through the thatched ceiling for threads of moonlight, for a lost star to show up like an old friend and tell me I wasn't alone in that room.

The next day, just after Tobias had left for the fields, my mother appeared at the door with my sister, Domingas. She'd packed a lunch for us: jerky, some honey, eggs, and shelled green beans. She wanted to see how I was doing; they'd made an early start to avoid the midday heat. I was relieved to see them. Salu had an apprehensive look in her eyes. If my mother weren't so embarrassed by such questions, she would have asked if I'd become a woman the previous night, if he'd treated me with respect. My mother and sister were shocked by the amount of rubbish I'd removed from the house. I grew agitated as I communicated with them, my hands slicing the air. Domingas tried to keep up with my signing, then burst out laughing when I listed my chores as the new lady of the house. We spent some happy hours together that morning. I felt a tightening in my chest as I watched them head back home.

Tobias would always return in the early evening, and the first thing he'd do was take a swig of cachaça from the bottle on the table. Then he'd either have a bath or sit right down for his dinner. I'd stop whatever I was doing to serve him. At first, he seemed to really appreciate my cooking; he told me as much. Later he started complaining that I put too much salt, or too little, or that the fish wasn't cooked properly: he'd indicate pieces that were supposedly still raw, or pieces that crumbled apart, claiming I'd overcooked it. I'd become very upset and berate myself, feeling stupid for having been so careless. But that would be the extent of his complaints; his tone didn't alter, and he didn't yell. He'd talk as though he'd been looking out across the fields and noticed some problem that needed to be addressed.

As time went on, however, Tobias seemed more dissatisfied with me. He grumbled whenever he couldn't find some item he was searching for. He'd tell me to leave his stuff alone, because something might appear out of place but it was exactly where it should be, where he wanted it to be. I'd agree, nodding my head, but I'd avoid looking him in the eye. In those moments, a yearning grew in me, a yearning to leave, to go back home; but what would the neighbors say? We kept attending the Jarê rituals at my father's house, and everyone knew that I was no longer "Zeca's Belonísia" because I was living with Tobias. I became "Tobias's Belonísia." I tried not to indulge my sorrow, especially on those nights when he'd lift my dress and enter me. Then he'd fall asleep, snoring. He never complained about his woman in bed, so I silenced my feelings, as though everything were fine.

I'd jump out of bed when he started to stir, before sunrise. I only needed to wake up for more complaints to come my way: the coffee was watery, he'd say, like angel's piss, or it was too bitter, like sludge. He'd look around for his hoe or sickle, things I never touched. If he couldn't recall where

117

he'd put some particular item, he'd snap: "Where is it, woman?" and I'd get all flustered and stop whatever I'd been doing to help him look. If I found it, he'd act like he found it, without a word of thanks. It got so bad, I tried to anticipate everything before he could complain. I started preemptively putting things in his hands: his belt, his shoes, his hat, his leather coat, his machete, just to avoid hearing him call out "woman." It made me feel like a bought object, and in my head I'd scream, why the hell won't he call me by my name? When we went over to my father's house, every two weeks, or during my mother's visits with Domingas, on those occasions he'd call me by my name, but I'd pretend not to hear, I wouldn't even nod in agreement. I could sense that my mother was studying my facial expressions, the way I'd turn and look away, hiding what I was feeling, revealing nothing. What bothered me most was that I wasn't really like that. I'd been impossible to tame. I even stopped going to school, against my father's wishes. The local boys never got close to me, because they found me ugly or because they couldn't talk to me without Bibiana's help; or perhaps because I was always challenging them, never bowing to the authority they believed they enjoyed. That's how I used to be. But living with that man, between the crumbling walls of his hovel, I felt like an outsider, unsure of myself. I just couldn't react, even calmly, even without the violent outbursts of my gestures.

7.

One day, just after Tobias had ridden out with Sutério, Maria Cabocla burst in without knocking, scaring me half to death. I thought maybe some man was breaking into my home now that I was alone. Her clothes were torn and she was crying, her body shaking. She was carrying her youngest boy, also in tears. I couldn't understand much of what she was saying, except for one phrase she kept repeating: "He's gonna kill me." Her eyes were wide with terror, her wispy hair stuck to her sweaty face, and mucus ran thickly from her nose.

She sat down. I shut the door, hoping she'd calm down and trying to muffle the sobbing that seemed to reverberate across the whole region. I brought her some water, then took the boy in my arms, but nothing seemed to ease their anguish. Only after some time had passed could Maria Cabocla finally explain that she was fleeing from her husband, he'd gone crazy, he'd lost his mind, and her other children were hiding in the woods. I got chills just thinking he might come into my house looking for Maria Cabocla, maybe even slap me around as well for having broken a cardinal rule: don't stick your nose into someone else's marriage. I was trying to calm myself. Tobias was a brave man, respected in our community. He knew Aparecido, they got along; they weren't compadres, but as neighbors they were on friendly terms. Aparecido wouldn't dare step into our house without having been invited. I went out back and gathered some lemongrass, then I put the water to boil. When I brought the tea over to Maria Cabocla, she wouldn't even look at me but kept on sobbing like a child. I lifted the cup to her lips. It was the right temperature; she needed to drink something. I became distraught, for I noticed then the black eye, a cut just above her eyelid.

I made a poultice with what was available in the garden, remembering the ingredients and method passed down to me from my parents and my grandmother, without me even being aware that I'd learned so much. I applied the mixture to her wound. I gathered her hair up and tied it back with a strip of old cloth that was lying around. Only then did I see more clearly Maria Cabocla's face, the coppery skin of an Indian woman. Whenever I sought her out for a fire-lighter, or to accompany her down to the river to wash our clothes, she'd tell me stories about her past, about her long journey, but I had never studied her features as I was doing at that moment. I always listened most attentively to her tales about the various plantations she'd passed through and about her grandmother, who'd been abducted from her tribe by White folks, or at least that was the story. Maria was skinny; she always looked hungry. Her slight body was dotted with purple marks; it was easier to see them in the light. A beautiful and battered woman, my mother would say. We are women of the fields, already battered by the sun and by drought. By arduous work and hardship, by the children we bear when we're too young, one after the other, withering our breasts, thickening our ankles. Looking down at Maria as she sat, distressed, in the chair, I could see her small breasts rising and falling as she breathed. My heart swelled with pity, and though I wanted to share with her the modest meal I'd prepared, I didn't offer her any, worried how Tobias might react.

Just as suddenly as she'd entered, Maria Cabocla left through the front door, murmuring thanks. Her boy, no longer sobbing, was asleep, clinging to her. She said she was going to look for her other kids, her husband must have left the house by then, his anger would have abated. I could almost read her mind; she was thinking how silly she'd been to flee her own home, to get so scared. A woman's place is beside her husband. A woman shouldn't go from house to house yapping about things that were private, making her life a subject of gossip.

From the door, I watched her nimbly stride along the trail. I asked the encantados to protect her and her children.

Tobias arrived home later, dripping sweat, his eyes blood-shot. I could tell from a distance he'd been drinking. He hitched his horse with some difficulty, then stumbled into the house. I put the pans on the stove to get them going, and before he even sat down he asked what was taking so long, he was hungry, he'd been working all day. I grew uneasy; feeling uneasy had, in fact, become routine for me during the short time we'd been living together. I often thought about how stupid I'd been to leave home, but, that day, he wouldn't allow me even a moment's peace with my distracted thoughts. He began bellowing insults about every-one: our neighbors, Sutério, the Peixoto family. I was afraid someone might have told him along the way home that I'd received Aparecido's wife, Maria Cabocla. I put his plate on the table, he dug his dirty hands into the food and brought it to his mouth. He mumbled something I couldn't quite make out; he seemed to have burned his fingers. I stood beside him as he ate. Tobias lifted the food to his mouth again, then snapped at me that it needed salt. He was drooling.

I'd never seen him so completely smashed. At parties he often drank quite a bit, sure, but he could hold his liquor. His lips would get flushed and his eyes would squint behind drooping eyelids, but he wouldn't slur his speech like he was doing at that moment. I tried to understand what he was saying, but without warning, he threw his plate at me. I stared at the food now scattered all over the floor. The floor I'd swept with such zeal. Anger welled up inside of me. Who did that filthy cowboy think he was? In the beginning, I'd swallowed my pride and accepted his insults; they were more measured. Now he'd gone too far. Soon this macho would start slapping me around the way Maria Cabocla's husband did to her. But something had changed in me. I wasn't going to be afraid of a man. I was the granddaughter of Donana and the daughter of Salu, women who made men bite their tongues in their presence.

Tobias had tipped his chair back against the wall. I looked down at the mess; he must have been expecting me to clean it up at once. Instead, I stepped over the enamel plate, avoiding the pigeon peas and pieces of chicken strewn on the floor. I wiped my hands on my dress, walked out into the yard and started digging in the garden where I'd been growing tomatoes and onions. I waited to see if he was feeling brave enough to come after me, if he'd raise his hand to strike me. From inside the house, he began hurling curses. Telling me I was an idiot, that I couldn't even talk with my crippled tongue. I absorbed each insult and began violently hacking at the soil with the hoe, breaking up large clods of earth. If he dared try to hit me, I'd do the same to his flesh: I'd tear it from his skull with just one blow. Before any man had the chance to strike me, I'd cut his hand off, or his head. He'd be wise not to take my anger lightly.

Tobias continued spitting insults, but my heart was calm. Working the land can have a very soothing effect. My mind was far away, oblivious to the man who was losing all composure in that shack he called a house. Dusk fell before I knew it, and after all my hard work the garden was looking beautiful. I went back in to clean up the kitchen. The food that had been thrown disrespectfully to the floor I put aside for Fusco. I'd go to my mother's house next morning, no matter what he said. I felt a longing in my chest for the patch of land I knew like the back of my hand. I would no longer make food for that man. I had my pride. I wasn't submissive, I wouldn't forgive. If the food wasn't to his liking, he could cook for himself. But how would I communicate all this to him? There was no point in writing a letter, he couldn't read it. Tobias only knew how to sign his name, as was the case with most of the workers. To express my displeasure with his fits of temper, I'd simply stop making food for him. I walked over to the bedroom. I could hear him snoring. He hadn't bathed in the river, he'd gone to bed filthy from the fields. Patience, patience, I thought to myself, one mustn't disturb a sleeping beast. He's capable of turning against me.

The next day, Tobias left the house earlier than usual. I stayed in bed. I heard the door close behind him, then his horse trotting off into the distance. I got up and started my day. I watered the garden. I cooked the breadfruit. I delighted in the smells of my cooking. I wondered about Maria Cabocla, present in my thoughts and prayers before I'd fallen asleep. I prayed that she and her children were well, that she and her husband were getting along. So that God might tame that husband of hers, I'd encourage Maria to talk to my father; many had been cured of drunkenness by his elixirs and prayers. There was an encantado for every problem, there was an encantado to remove that vice from her husband. Maria seemed older than Bibiana and myself. She wasn't quite as old as my mother, but she'd told me that her eldest child was aged eleven. If Maria and I stood side by side, folks would mistake her for my mother because of how worn-down she looked.

I shut the door and started walking. I was going home. I felt something good take hold of me; I experienced shivers of pleasure, as though I were about to receive some long-awaited gift. Along the way, I renewed my acquaintance with the places I knew so well, the trails, the houses, the river, the buriti trees. If things didn't work out with Tobias, I could always make my way along the Utinga River. I could go home or make a new home.

I caught sight of my family's house in the distance and almost smiled to myself. I hoped my mother wouldn't be standing by the door; I wanted to give her a surprise. We'd laugh, and I'd sit at the table like I used to. I'd listen to her talk for the both of us, asking questions and responding to herself as though they were my answers, until I disagreed with something, interrupting her with a gesture. All those feelings would flow back again, positive and enduring. I arrived at the door and stomped my feet to announce myself. I heard voices: Dona Tonha must be visiting, I thought. I stepped into the house and saw the silhouette of a woman sitting with a baby on her lap. Bibiana had come home.

8.

It was many years ago, but I remember that day well, the day of the accident that made my mother and father fly into a panic, rushing off to find Sutério so we could drive to the hospital in the Ford Rural I'd always dreamt of riding in, just not amid all that bawling and blood. On the way to the hospital, I couldn't stop thinking about Grandma Donana's desperation when she saw the blood pouring from our mouths, her alarm when she noticed that her suitcase had been moved from its usual spot, not even thinking, perhaps, of the knife covered with a cloth that had been removed, the knife with the ivory handle. Only when our mother, alerted by Dona Tonha, hurried over and became frantic at the sight of us, asking over and over again what we'd done, shaking Bibiana and me with a violence we'd never seen in her, only then did my sister, screaming and spitting blood, say that we'd found the knife in Grandma's suitcase. I didn't see how Grandma reacted when it dawned on her she'd been keeping an object whose danger we, as children, couldn't have anticipated. To us, the knife was a curiosity, an object to feel in our hands and then—we must have been bewitched—in our mouths. The blade's radiance was a warning, but it took possession of our eyes, making us forget the rest of the world and all we'd learned about sharp objects—"be careful with knives"—ultimately luring us to the event that would destroy our innocence forever.

On that morning, tired of playing with our corncob dolls, I turned to Bibiana and suggested we head over to the jirau and fetch some embers, maybe catch a lizard in the woods and do the wicked things we'd seen the neighborhood children do to animals. She said no. "How about we take a peek inside Grandma's suitcase?" "She's right there, roasting potatoes." "Just wait," she said. Grandma Donana often drifted into daydreams. She lived in the past, and soon she'd be lost in thought again, wandering through the woods beyond the orchard and the old chicken coop. We sat in the doorway, catching a glimpse of Grandma's shadow disappearing out back. Most likely Bibiana had no clue what was in that suitcase, but I thought myself cleverer than my sister, though I was younger. I'd already watched Grandma pack and unpack it many times, despite the heavy layer of grime the winds of September and October had deposited on its surface, as though a long time had passed since Grandma last delved into her belongings. I'd spied her, one morning, removing the knife with the ivory handle. I saw her polish the silvery metal with a dirty cloth as she talked to herself about Carmelita, her daughter who'd disappeared. We could seize that knife, use it to cut back the brush outside the house, or dig in the dirt, or butcher the animals we hunted in our imaginations. We could grab that knife and use it to sharpen our busted pencils.

The knife shone like nothing else on earth. We saw ourselves more clearly in the blade than in the shard of mirror Grandma kept in the same suitcase. In the quiet of the room, away from the jabber of birds outside, I whispered to my sister: "I wonder what it tastes like." "It must taste like a spoon," Bibiana said. "Let me see," I replied excitedly, jumping up and down on the peccary hide that covered the bumpy dirt floor. "No, me first." Bibiana imposed her authority as the older sister, an authority she enjoyed exerting. But what if Grandma Donana suddenly appeared and found Bibiana with the knife in her mouth? All her posturing would collapse and she'd reap a good beating. I leaned back against Grandma's bed and gave it a shove so Grandma might hear the noise from afar and hurry back. She'd catch us, and the fun would be over; after all, it had been my idea to grab the knife. The alarm I sounded didn't work, so I thought of crying out, but my sister would be quick to put the blame on me. I decided to take the knife from her. "Like a spoon, huh?"

I yanked the blade from her mouth. I had to struggle for a moment against the strength of her hand. I thought she'd fight back more than she did, the way she'd fight whenever I took something that was hers, the way I fought whenever she took what belonged to me. I paid no mind to her widening eyes. I placed the knife in my own mouth, spellbound by its radiance. And my daydreaming grandmother grew ever more distant. The object I held was heavy as a stone. I sensed that the knife's spell would turn against me, and I'd be the one to get caught; Bibiana would deny everything. So I rapidly withdrew the knife. That's when I noticed Bibiana was bleeding, and it felt like something had ruptured in my mouth, too. But my nervous excitement, my quickened breathing from the fear of getting caught, kept me from feeling the pain I'd feel soon afterward. I was holding a piece of my tongue in my hand, thinking my father and grandmother could use their magic to put it back. My father, the healer Zeca Chapéu Grande, could do anything. On the nights of Jarê, he'd transform into any of the encantados. He'd speak differently, he'd sing and whirl with wonderful agility around the room, endowed with the powers of the spirits of the forest, the waters, the mountains, the air. My father could cure people of insanity and drunkenness, and he could put that piece of tongue back in my mouth. As I hastily thought of some way out of my misfortune and before Bibiana could return the suitcase to its place, Grandma Donana surprised us. I saw her hand strike the side of my sister's head, just as I had wished minutes earlier. With the same force, her hand struck my own head, but I was starting to swoon; I'd lost so much blood.

I remember hearing the doctors say I'd have difficulty speaking and eating. I'd need to go to the city regularly for speech therapy. But it just wasn't possible, we were stuck at Água Negra, we lived in the middle of nowhere, we couldn't travel that far and that often. And there was no one at the clinic in the nearby town who could help me.

So I fell silent.

Time went by, and eventually I decided to try to speak. I walked alone down the same path Donana liked to take. I still remember the word I chose for myself: plow. I enjoyed watching my father drive his old ox-drawn plow, tearing up the soil so that later he could toss rice into the red and brown clods of turned earth. I liked hearing the word "plow" enunciated; it's a strong, resonant word. "I'm going to work with the plow today." "I'm going to plow the land." "A new plow would be nice, this one's old and beat-up." But the sound that came from my mouth was an aberration, chaotic, as if the severed chunk of my tongue had been replaced by a hard-boiled egg. My voice was a crooked plow, deformed, penetrating the soil only to leave it infertile, ravaged, destroyed. I tried other times, alone, to say that word aloud, and later other words as well, attempting to restore speech to my body, to become the Belonísia I used to be, but in the end I gave up. When the edema went away, I still couldn't reproduce a word that even I would recognize. I had no intention of making sounds that provoked my own grief and disgust, and I didn't want to be teased by the children at Firmina's school or by Tonha's daughters.

For many years, only when I was alone, and even then, rarely, I'd attempt to speak. It was a kind of torture I'd impose upon myself, consciously, as if Donana's knife were running through me, shredding the strength I'd been cultivating. As if the plow, old and bent, were running through my insides, tearing me apart. All the courage I'd tried to instill in myself would drain away, the courage needed to live in that hostile

129

land of perennial sun and occasional rain, that abusive land where people were dying constantly, denied all succor, where we lived like cattle, working and getting nothing in return, not even rest, and our sole rights were to reside on that land for as long as the owners were willing, and, if we never left Água Negra, to be buried in the grave awaiting us at Viração.

But I persisted. On the paths I walked alone, I'd recite the most hideous words to myself, words no one would wish to hear, and over time I did it more frequently. I wasn't shy of saying things that would've made others run away, frightened off by my tongue's virulence. I'd repeat those words in a strange, distorted voice, full of anger about so many things, an anger that only grew with time. And now, suffering my husband's abuse, the words became viler still, words cried out by my ancestors, by my mother and grandmother and the great-grandmothers I never knew, words that came to me to be uttered in my horror of a voice, and thus those words acquired the sad and enduring contours that would keep me alive.

9.

By my count, barely two years had gone by, but how my sister had aged! Her hips had widened, her skin had lost its youthful glow. The only thing she retained from adolescence was her acne, its yellow dots protruding visibly from her face. Otherwise, she looked ten years older. Time, it seemed, had been rough with her, and now she was the mother of a baby boy. I could see her breasts through her clothing, swollen and drooping from nursing Inácio, but this was nothing to women like us. From childhood onward we were being prepared to produce future workers for our bosses, for their plantations or those nearby. What surprised me was just how fast my sister had changed from a girl into a woman.

She was happy to see me, glad that I seemed well, but her face betrayed some apprehension, for she'd returned after having abandoned us and eloped with Severo—the sort of reckless decision many young women make. Indeed, we knew too many stories like hers. Bibiana's movements, familiar from observing the animals around me, reflected her maternal instinct. She got up, sluggishly, and moved the child to Salu's lap before embracing me. I badly wanted to give her a strong, meaningful hug, for I'd been taken by surprise by this blessing, to see my sister's face and see her child. But the pain bloomed in me again, though less intensely, given everything I was feeling all at once; nevertheless, it was a pain I couldn't stifle. For that reason our greeting was rather restrained, lacking the vigor our relationship had once known.

The reason for my arrival that morning suddenly seemed less important. I certainly hadn't been expecting to see Bibiana. I sat by her side and listened to her talk to Domingas and my mother, sharing details about her life far from Água Negra. I tried to move past my astonishment and join in the conversation with the same gestures that had once been understood and translated by Bibiana. How I tried, truly, to

131

recapture the bond that used to make us almost one! But she couldn't interpret my gestures as easily as before. She got them wrong, once, twice, then many times, until we both grew tired of trying. Domingas understood me better. Bibiana had lost much of her ability to transmit my feelings, that incessant capacity of mine to communicate, lying dormant ever since her departure.

Bibiana told us that she'd finished her high school equivalency. The following year, she'd pursue her teaching certification at the public university. She'd been babysitting some of the local girls whose mothers worked outside the home. She earned very little doing this, but it was all she could take on with a baby on her lap. She told us that Severo was working in the fields and that he'd been active in the farm workers' union, a real learning experience. He'd faced a lot of intimidation and adversity, but he kept on fighting to improve the lives of his fellow workers. He was admired and respected, even by the old-timers.

Severo walked in through the back door, accompanied by my father and Zezé. He took off his hat to greet me, calling me "cousin Belonísia." I was so happy to see him. He'd changed, too, looking more like an adult; he'd left his adolescence well behind. He seemed to have kept only that familiar restlessness of his. As soon as he walked in, I knew that all the resentment they'd caused with their childish decision to leave would, at least superficially, remain in the past. I'd believed, for a time, that there might be a rift between our families, but forgiveness blossomed with the blessing of their return. Just the same, it was impossible for me to completely draw a veil over the nonsense Bibiana had invented about Severo and me when we were younger. Severo had always held me in his spell, but it wasn't passion I'd felt, it was admiration for my older cousin, for the energy and vitality emanating from his gestures, his stories, and especially his actions. Severo was naturally seductive; he was like some woodland creature always surprising us with his astuteness. It wasn't so much the array of his physical gifts; it was something about the way he moved in the world. I admired Severo's strength, wisdom, and leadership, qualities I desired for myself. To me, he was like an older brother, for what I most admired about Severo was an ability he shared with my father: the ability to guide people along the most tortuous paths.

The impression I'd always had about certain things would be reinforced by Severo's words to us. He began speaking bitterly about our condition on the plantation, and I could sense my father growing uncomfortable. Zeca had taught us it was a mark of ingratitude to speak ill of those who'd taken us in, who'd given us a place where we could live and work. He refrained, however, from arguing with Severo, perhaps due to the occasion and to his own desire to rise above lingering resentments. But it was a sign of things to come should Severo and Bibiana ever return to the plantation. When my cousin described our work and our subservience, his assertions were forceful and decisive. I'd remember what I could of his words, hoping to decipher the new concepts he was introducing and applying to our situation so they might have more meaning for us.

133

I looked closely at the baby boy, back in Bibiana's arms. She noticed, and that's when she told me the boy's name. I found the name quite beautiful, and I smiled to express how much I liked it. I tried to take the child in my arms, but he drew back, burying his head in his mother's shoulder. He was my nephew, my blood, who'd grow up to seed the land at Água Negra or elsewhere, that is, if illness didn't take him from us, one of those illnesses that take our children too quickly. It was hard to tell if the child's eyes resembled those of his father or his mother. I reached out to caress him. My mother kept repeating with unbridled joy, "I'm your grandma!" My hand felt the heat of Inácio's small body and recognized it, the child's skin so alive and warm, the color of wild honey, filling me with strength and love for him.

Bibiana said she'd bring the boy to the Senhor dos Passos Church to be baptized. "You'll be his godmother," she said to me. Her decision meant that I'd have a very important role in the boy's life, even if my sister and I were far apart and despite any lingering tensions or estrangements. It was her way of reinforcing the bond between us.

I visited Bibiana and Severo almost every day, either at my parents' house or at Uncle Servó and Aunt Hermelina's place. I couldn't get enough of the stories they brought back with them. I wanted to listen to Severo's analysis of our situation at Água Negra. His words echoed my own anger, as if he were speaking for that deformed voice of mine that tormented me and sometimes tore me apart. His words evoked the suffering that united so many of us across great distances. Together, perhaps, we could break free of the fate others had allotted us. Not even Tobias's ill humor and fits of rage could keep me from visiting Bibiana and Severo regularly until the day of their departure, when they promised they'd soon return.

I knew they'd come back, carried home by the strong winds that bring rain and change. I prayed they wouldn't delay.

10.

In the months that followed, Tobias would lose his temper more and more often, to the point where my mother brought me a message from my father: he was worried and wanted me to come home. He said that our family wouldn't see any shame in it. That it was his responsibility to look after his daughter, to make sure nothing bad happened to her.

Tobias griped about the most insignificant things, and usually it was my fault. He'd drink enormous amounts of cachaça, then aim his bloodshot eyes at me and fire off insults: he'd rub in that I was mute, and unlike my sister I couldn't get pregnant. Plus I was an awful cook, I wasted too much time tilling the fields, and he didn't want me hanging around Maria Cabocla. Maria, incidentally, told me it certainly wasn't my fault I hadn't gotten pregnant. Tobias used to sleep around with this one and that one, she said, and it never led to any babies. "He's shootin' blanks."

I often considered returning home. But something told me that I could bend that man's will. I wasn't about to slink off with my tail between my legs. If there's one thing I'd learned by then, it's that you never accept someone else's protection. If I didn't take care of myself, no one else would. The concern that Bibiana had shown for me in the past was part of a larger desire, one she'd always nurtured, to save everyone; maybe she'd been influenced by our father's beliefs. The truth is that I was the one who'd protect her when she got scared of the silliest things, like when we needed to go deep into the woods or wade into rivers and marshes and she'd make me go in front, so that if we came across a snake or some wild animal, I could frighten it off. "You're the brave one," she'd say.

On those festive Jarê nights, Tobias still seemed to fear my father. He'd drink and raise his voice and draw attention to himself, but he wasn't the only one getting carried away, so no one paid much attention to his antics. Nights like those were an opportunity for folks to loosen up after day on day of relentless hard work. But because, back home, I had to put up with him yelling at me constantly on account of the drink, I couldn't stand to look at him or listen to him or even accompany him when it was time to leave. I preferred the company of others, helping my mother with her tasks, spending time with Domingas or Dona Tonha's daughters.

I blamed myself for having accepted Tobias's invitation to live with him. He wasn't ever as horrible as Maria Cabocla's husband or so many husbands who'd turned their wives into punching bags. Only once had Tobias threatened to hit me. It was the time he'd ordered me to look for a pair of pants I'd mended for him days earlier. He yelled in that rude way of his, and I, offended by his tone, didn't budge from my chair, where I'd been stitching up a tablecloth. Tobias raised his hand as if about to land a blow, and he kept it hovering in the air while I paused my sewing to fasten my fierce eyes on him, daring him to follow through, interested to see if his bravery could match my will. There was a nasty beast deep inside of me, eager to claw its way out. Perhaps Tobias caught a glimpse of my fury. He lowered his hand and didn't say a word. Embarrassed, he left the house and went in search of more booze. I assumed he would stagger home eventually and collapse, filthy, into bed.

I wondered if it would have been better to have died the day I left my parents' house. To have fallen off that horse, to have broken my neck. Because no good ever came of my lamenting. I knew I'd always bear the shame of having been so naive, falling for Tobias's flattering sweet talk, no different from that of so many other cunning men who'd carry young women away from their parents' houses to turn them into slaves. Making their lives hell, hitting them till their blood, or their very lives, poured out, leaving a trail of hatred on their bodies. Complaining about the food, the mess, the poorly behaved children, the weather, the house falling apart. Introducing us to the hell that so often is a woman's life.

My mother's happy marriage, or my sister's—these seemed the exceptions. They suffered hardship, for no woman was free of hardship, but they were respected, they had a voice in their homes. I'd never heard my father insult my mother. While they weren't particularly warm or affectionate, neither were they cold to each other. Each partner considered the other's feelings, making compromises when necessary. I came to understand, rather quickly, that with Tobias things would be very different. Things could, indeed, get even worse; look at how Aparecido mistreated Maria Cabocla.

With no explanation, Tobias began spending more and more time away from home. He stopped going to my father's for the Jarê rituals and started attending them somewhere else, miles away. When it wasn't Jarê that took him away, it would be a saint's day, a birthday, or a christening. He'd come home drunk, clothes smeared with all sorts of stains, from dirt to lipstick. He'd often sleep elsewhere. At first I worried that his explosive temper and threats and habit of swearing vengeance might get him into trouble. I worried, too, that Sutério might get wind of Tobias's behavior and expel him from the plantation. Were that to happen, I'd already decided I wouldn't leave Água Negra. I'd return to the house where I was born.

I often felt a chill run through my body; every time Tobias disappeared, I prayed for no one but myself. I prayed for the strength I needed to endure my life. I kept on working out back, taking care of our crops and the many responsibilities he'd abandoned. I never rode his horse; that was one thing I never learned to do.

One morning, after a sleepless night with no word of Tobias's whereabouts, I saw one of the cowhands, Genivaldo, approach my door, hat in hand. He didn't say anything, but I saw doom in his expression. He was like one of those birds, harbingers of death, and I felt goosebumps up and down my body. He asked me to accompany him to the spot where he'd found the fallen man, the man who'd taken me from my parents' house.

11.

I knelt on the ground and closed Tobias's eyes, then stood up and walked to the side of the road where his horse was cropping grass, head lowered, ears twitching to shoo away the flies. I caressed its belly as if that horse were the most important being in the world. I gave it a couple of light slaps on the rump, indicating it was time to move on. I held the reins and started walking with the others who were carrying Tobias's body back to our house.

Maria Cabocla once told me that Tobias had upset a woman by the name of Valmira, a healer who lived in town. Tobias was drunk, as usual, and a bunch of Valmira's followers decided to expel him from her house. The kerfuffle had something to do with Dona Miúda's encantada, Santa Rita the Fisherwoman, who'd appeared at my father's Jarê. Now manifesting herself at Valmira's house, the encantada became the butt of Tobias's invective. He publicly doubted her authenticity and demanded she demonstrate her powers; he went so far as to claim that Valmira herself was a fraud, that none of it was real. Several times the healer intervened, asking him to quit talking nonsense, but he wouldn't stop or apologize. The encantada who'd mounted the body of Dona Miúda then focused her attention on Tobias and uttered a single sentence, which no one but Tobias could hear. "But he continued disrespecting the encantada," Maria Cabocla concluded, "so don't be surprised if some misfortune befalls your home."

"Just like your grandmother, just like your grandmother," my mother repeated, seizing me by the shoulders as I was wrapping a black kerchief around my head. My mother recalled the occasions, for there were more than one, when Grandma Donana found herself a widow, the several times she had to bury a husband. At Tobias's wake, my eyes wouldn't weep, the result, perhaps, of some enduring drought. Something in me had dried up ever since I agreed to our union, ever since I stepped into that trash-filled house and allowed Tobias to lift up my dress, ever since I absorbed those insults without retorting in the way I would have preferred. I stood by his coffin, not too close, but near the doorway, welcoming the many neighbors who were arriving to pay their respects. I felt unconcerned, empty of affliction, as I watched the mourners come and go. Domingas and my mother attended to them. Unable to fake any expression of sorrow, several times I felt obligated to send a mourner out of my presence. They were expecting me to play the inconsolable widow. They wanted my grief to be conspicuous: I should exhibit due respect for the man I'd been living with. More than once I had to restrain myself so as not to let slip a smile or gesture that would be deemed disrespectful by those present, particularly my father and mother. They'd better not expect me to start wailing and tearing my hair, I said to myself, observing the exaggerated sorrow and lamentations of neighbors and compadres.

During the vigil, standing aloof from the corpse, I looked just once at Tobias's face. There was a small wound on the forehead, which, even after being cleaned, continued to leak a transparent liquid the color of faded blood. But I wouldn't reach out my hand to him, not even to adjust the lace adorning the casket. I wanted this moment in my life to end as quickly as possible. I tried to hurry things along by urging my sister to usher the mourners out the door, but it was no use. I had to suffer the endless eulogies. Then the comadres began reciting the rosary, praying for Tobias's soul. I prayed for his soul too, but that's as far as I went. They needn't have waited for my tears. At last I watched as his body was carried away from the house he'd built, where he hoarded every little thing he found as though it were treasure. I watched as he was lowered into the ground, feeling a serenity that had never been available to me in that hovel where we'd lived for little more than a year.

My mother said I should close up that house and come back home, where we could enjoy each other's company. I didn't want that. What I wanted now was to be left by myself. I wanted to live in the silence I'd found far from everyone else. I understood why Salu was worried; I would be alone, without a man, and she thought I'd be vulnerable to all kinds of danger. No one would've believed that I was the one who protected Tobias; he'd often fall into bed dead drunk, and was absolutely useless when it came to watching out for our safety. I allowed my sister Domingas to keep me company for the first few days. My sister quickly understood I was fine, busy with the day-to-day chores I'd handled since moving into that house near the banks of the Santo Antônio. She asked if I was afraid to live alone. I shook my head repeatedly to indicate no. I'd find a dog to keep me company, like old Fusco, who was dead by then. Tobias had left a rifle behind, under the bed. There was no way I was going to let that parcel of land fall into someone else's hands after I'd worked so hard to turn the backyard into a productive garden. I'd grown attached to my plants, to everything that flourished as a result of my hard work and that of Tobias. But the house is falling apart, Domingas argued. She was right, but I'd seen walls built many times, and I knew what was needed to turn that place into a proper home. First, I'd gather the rubbish Tobias hadn't wanted to part with and carry all of it to the dump. That house, shaded by the jatoba, would soon be transformed. As for marriage, never again. I had no interest in finding someone else. I'd take good care of the house and the surrounding land; maybe this was all I'd ever have.

On the path I'd chosen for myself, I'd come to know the suffering that united the workers of Água Negra and nearby plantations. Alone, I'd experience all the hardships I'd seen my parents undergo over the course of their lives. I didn't have children to feed; nevertheless, I insisted on working with more strength and determination than many of the men around me. Suffering would come from whatever didn't turn out well, but this made me feel alive and connected to all the workers who faced the same adversity. I never complained of bad luck, for luck stood by me, with all its power. I shelled corn, filled bags and bags of manioc flour, labored every day in the field that in time would grow green. If the sun was too harsh, killing what I'd planted, leaving a trail of withered and burnt crops, or if the rivers flooded, the waters swallowing up what I didn't have time to harvest, I simply applied myself where I had to. When there was no farming to be done, I stuck to gathering buriti and palm fruit, and headed out with Maria Cabocla and the other women to the street market in town. Sometimes a truck driver would see us walking along, covered in the juice of the fruit balanced atop our heads, and he'd let us hop in the back of his truck.

One day, while climbing the buriti tree, I gashed my foot on its spiny trunk. I felt like a hunted animal, brought down in the marshes. I was only able to walk back because Maria Cabocla had sent her two small boys to find Zezé and Domingas to help me. They tried to persuade me to come back home with them. Even Zeca Chapéu Grande came, with all his authority as father and healer, to sway me from my stubborn insistence on living alone. I appealed to his faith, which was, for the most part, the same as mine, by pointing up at the sky and then at the small shrine I kept in my living room—a statue of Saint Sebastian riddled with arrows; a picture frame, missing one of its sides, that held a darkened image of Saints Cosmas and Damian; a small picture of Nossa Senhora Aparecida; one of Saint Barbara; a newer one of Our Lady of Perpetual Succor, given to me by comadre Nini; and an empty Coca-Cola bottle holding a bunch of sempre-vivas from the plantation. I was trying to explain to my father that we are never alone. God and the encantados remained by our side.

My foot never fully healed because the thorn, like a dagger, had sunk all the way in, and the pain kept coming back, along with swelling and redness. I traveled to town a few times with Domingas, my mother, and Dona Tonha for the doctors to have a look and prescribe something, but nothing they did worked. My father made a root tincture and asked me to be patient, and in fact the pain diminished considerably. But after an arduous day the inflammation would return, and the pain became more acute. It never undermined my determination, however, to transform my surroundings through hard work, though I knew that, since I didn't have children to feed, Sutério would claim a generous percentage of the food I produced. That's why I often used to head out before sunrise, carrying part of my harvest to my parents' house to be divided among the family. Maria Cabocla would drop by with her children just to check in on me, and I'd always insist she take back with her some manioc, black-eyed peas, squashes, and potatoes.

When I got my strength back after my injury, I began building my new home. There's really no way to renovate a house that's made of mud; the only thing to do is to start from scratch in a different spot. That's how we did it on the plantation: we'd put a new one up nearby and let the old one fall to pieces. Zezé helped me cut branches for the walls and carry back mud from the river. It was thrilling to see a house rise from the ground, from the same mud where, if we'd sown the seeds, our food grew. I had seen that ritual of construction and ruin so many times, and still I marveled when walls were raised to provide us with shelter.

On the day I finished transferring my belongings from the old house to the new one, Maria Cabocla came running in and crouched in a corner of the room, a nasty cut on her lip. She didn't need to explain. Aparecido was getting worse. He said that if she was still there when he got back home, he'd kill her in front of her children. It was revolting, and it brought back painful memories of Tobias, although I do believe one shouldn't think ill of the dead; they should rest in peace. I had to drag Maria back to her house. She'd arrived at my door with just three of her children, the others she'd left behind. They shouldn't have been left in the care of a drunkard. I couldn't stand to see Maria utterly forsaken. She didn't want to go home, I saw the fear in her eyes, but she gave in. I grabbed some clothes from my closet and threw them in a bag with a few other things. I wanted to ask one of the local men to accompany us, but before I could even communicate my thought, Maria warned that if another man got involved, things would get much worse, there might be bloodshed, because Aparecido was insanely jealous. I desisted and decided to go with her by myself.

The door to my house was somewhat misaligned, so I had to pull it hard to slam it shut. My bag fell to the ground, and Maria bent over to help gather my things. She paused, enchanted, to examine the ivory handle of the silver blade that was still, after so many years, pure radiance. Maria's eyes reminded me of Bibiana's the day we put the blade in our mouths. She gave it back, then handed over my bag, not daring to ask why I was bringing a knife.

12.

As misfortune would have it, my foot began throbbing along the way. When I paused to adjust my sandal, I saw my foot had swollen up. I arrived at Maria Cabocla's house limping. The first thing that caught my eye was two empty bottles of cachaça lying in a corner. Then I noticed the dirty clothes, the leftovers on the table and houseflies everywhere, loyal companions living off our crumbs, awaiting the hour, perhaps, when our flesh, too, might nourish them. In fact, they didn't have to wait for us to die completely: it was enough to find an open wound to host their larvae. We knew all about flies. There were times of year when, no matter if we were falling asleep or waking, we'd hear them buzzing. Were they to suddenly disappear or fall silent, we'd know at once that something wasn't right.

The walls of Maria's house were eroding; I could see through the holes straight through to the other side. I helped gather the children for their bath, then I tackled the dirty dishes and cups and the empty bottles scattered everywhere. It was a cool afternoon with cloudy skies, and as evening approached, Maria's face grew tense; she knew a storm was coming. Several times she assured me everything was fine and implored me to leave, but I refused. I started straightening up the place, putting things back where they belonged, fixing what was broken. I don't know how I was able to go about it without the slightest twinge of fear. Maybe it had something to do with Tobias's death, the solitude in which I'd immersed myself. Maybe it was the memory of my grandmother, Donana; from the stories I'd overheard, I knew she was a woman not to be messed with. Or maybe it was all the adversity I'd faced by that point, although I wasn't yet twenty. Or the desire I felt to defend this woman, Maria, for I was familiar with a man's abuse. Tobias had never struck me, but I couldn't forget his insults or the outrage that had taken root in me. I wanted to believe that Maria Cabocla just lacked guts. If she could show her husband that she didn't fear him and that she could hurt him just as badly, he'd think twice before raising his hand against her.

Night fell slowly, and I prepared coffee and sweet potato for the children. The cool evening air came in through the doorways and windows we'd left open, despite the mosquitos we were smashing between our hands. Maria lit the only lamp she had, and the fresh breeze mixed with the smell of burning kerosene. Maria had told me a while back that she wasn't yet thirty, though she looked a lot older. Her wispy hair, reaching down to her shoulders, had started turning gray. The oily skin of her face always seemed to shine, and now it shone more brightly against the shadows cast by the lamplight. I looked at the children surrounding their mother. Sometimes they'd gather around me, trying to get me to join in their little games. They'd play house or pretend to be in school, or they'd pretend to be working in the fields or hunting, and I watched them with longing, recollecting my own childhood by the banks of the Utinga, playing with my corncob dolls and frightening off cowbirds from the rice paddies. Some of the children resembled their mother, others their father, but all of them shared the same marks of neglect: swollen bellies, scrawny limbs, and most of all that sad, fearful look in their eyes from the daily violence they endured in their own home.

After the children went to bed I sat with Maria in the main room, the doors now shut, and listened to her talk about her life before Água Negra. "I was born already a prisoner. I was born on a plantation, like you," she said, searching through a small box that held pieces of fabric, along with needle and thread, as well as rosettes of various colors. "But my father wandered like a gypsy, looking for work, trying to make a better life for his kids," she continued, not looking at me. "Anyway, before I got here, I lived on six different plantations. That's why I can't read or write." She pulled out three rounded pieces of fabric, each the size of her palm, and placed them on her lap, looking for the needle and thread to transform the pieces into flower buds. "If it was up to me, I wouldn't be living on a plantation, no way. They put a bridle and reins on you, like you're some sort of animal." She brought the needle close to her eyes to run the thread through. "But Aparecido, he's got the earth in his blood, and during that last drought, he asked the boss here for permission to live on his land."

She spoke as though she were reciting the rosary, each memory a strange and ancient prayer, speaking the way some folks do, the ones who've made the same pilgrimage to Água Negra or to plantations nearby. "When I arrived here, I thought this place was called Fazenda Boa Sorte, can you believe it? A plantation called Good Luck?" She was laughing almost without meaning to. "He went on and

148

on about a place called Good Luck, how there was fertile land there, nice houses for all the workers, but somehow we ended up here, and there's nothing here that's any different from the other places we knew, certainly not any good luck. You know, I was just fourteen when I became Aparecido's woman." She got out of her chair and grabbed an empty cup. "You want more coffee?" She was looking at me, hoping my body language would indicate that we could confide in each other. "He didn't drink back then, no. He was a good man. The drinking ruined him." She placed the cup of coffee on the small table beside me. "I already asked Aparecido to go see your father for one of his root tinctures, but he refused."

Maybe she'd been working on those rosettes of fabric to alleviate her anxiety, but she seemed unable to focus and put the small box off to the side. She stared at me. Even in the dim light of the kerosene lamp, I could make out Maria's knobby hands trembling, reaching toward my head.

"But what about you, a widow all of a sudden . . . It seems so sad, so lonesome. Still, you're probably better off than me." As she spoke, she undid the kerchief I'd wrapped around my head and I felt a hot wave move across my chest. She ran her hand slowly through my kinky hair, letting her fingers get tangled in it, and this gesture was deeply soothing, unlike anything I'd ever felt from someone's touch. Rarely had I laid my head on Donana's or my mother's lap so that they could do what Maria was doing to me. The pores of her skin gave off a scent I recognized, like fresh water. "Your hair is so black, Belonísia. I never see you without a kerchief on your head." I didn't look at her, just let her fingers go deep in me.

Then she stopped. She went into the next room to get something. When she returned, she began combing out my hair and braiding cornrows. I closed my eyes for just a moment so I could concentrate on feeling her fingertips weaving strands of my hair as she spoke to me, though sometimes she fell silent, and I could hear the sound of her breathing; she was almost panting, while I began breathing more calmly, as though about to fall asleep. When she finished, I was almost dozing off, but against my head I could feel the warmth of her body. She didn't have a mirror, so I lifted my hands to my hair, and, without meaning to, I touched her rough skin. My whole body blushed, and the cornrows beneath my fingers seemed to form paths encircling my head.

After that night, I'd often close my eyes and try to feel Maria Cabocla again. "You must be tired, go lie down in my bed. I'll stay up, I can't sleep." She said this as she put the comb away. I folded my kerchief and tucked it into my bag, where the knife was, then remembered I'd brought her some potatoes from my garden. I refused the offer of her bed at first, then I yielded. "Don't worry," she said. "Lie down here, on the side I sleep on. My boy Tião tosses and turns." She moved the legs of her little boy and those of the two girls, all of them asleep in her bed. "And if that man shows up, I'll wake you."

I could smell the scent of fresh water in her bed sheet, and for some time I couldn't fall sleep, trying to calm what was happening inside my body, still throbbing from her caress. When I finally dropped off, I dreamed of Tobias. He was watching from a distance as I tried to escape from him. I was climbing a slope, my legs already giving out, when I came up against a shining fence. I tried to get around it, but all I saw was more fence. Retreating, I saw that the trees were on fire. The woods turned to ash, though nothing happened to me. But there was no way out. The ivory handle of Donana's knife appeared again as I tried to somehow get back to the river. Bibiana and Severo were standing before me, but they couldn't see me. I was calling out their names, my voice loud and clear, but they couldn't hear me. When I pulled the knife out of the earth the ground opened, and the hole swallowed them before they even realized it.

I woke up startled and panting. I got out of bed, it was almost daybreak, and found Maria Cabocla sitting by the front door, asleep. She'd been keeping a lookout for her husband so he wouldn't surprise me while I slept in his bed. I made it home before the sun came up; I had to feed the animals. I was still worried about Maria, but I knew that if something were to happen, she or one of her children would find a way to reach me and ask for help.

13.

Not even a week had gone by when one of Maria's boys came to fetch me while I was out back, weeding. The boy said his father had gone crazy and was beating up his mother again. I made a sign for him to wait. I went back into the house to grab my things, figuring I'd better throw some manioc and bananas in a bag, too, and asked the boy to help out by carrying it over to his house. I didn't change my pants, filthy from the field, or my long-sleeved shirt that, I recalled, had once belonged to Tobias. I approached Maria Cabocla's house like someone who just happened to be passing by, but even from a distance, I could hear her sobs echoing down the trail as I hurried nearer. The door was open, but I knocked on it anyway, announcing myself. Aparecido turned to look at me. The cowardice of other men had made him confident, men who'd hear a woman's desperate cries and do nothing about it. I walked right in as though it were my house, set the food on the kitchen table and started assembling the crying children. I wiped their faces with a cloth I found by the stove.

The man barked at me to leave, to mind my own business. I hadn't yet paid any attention to Maria, who was still sobbing loudly in her room. When she looked at me, she'd notice I was still wearing the braids, she'd see in my eyes what had arisen from that intimate gesture of hers. I stayed right where I was, daring him to drag me out, because I wasn't about to just walk away. I heard him say that he respected my father, that he was his compadre, but he wasn't going to be disrespected in his own house. Maria came out of her room and headed straight for Aparecido, but a vicious slap from the back of his hand knocked her to the floor. His hands had been thickened by toil, by a hard life. My eyes widened with rage as I looked at Maria lying on the ground, but she didn't back down and kept insisting that I wasn't going anywhere. As Aparecido rushed forward to remove me by force, my heart began pounding, but I felt something in me go cold like the early morning breeze, and I stood my ground, like my ancestors did. Nevertheless, Aparecido grabbed me by the wrist, intent on dragging me outside. My other hand brought out the blade I'd been hiding behind my back and held it under his jaw. I looked into his bulging, bloodshot eyes. I was holding the knife in my right hand, the blade's handle cool in my palm like a stone lifted from the river. Maria seemed stunned by what she was witnessing but didn't hesitate to tell Aparecido to get out of the house. She ran to their room and gathered some of his things, then came back yelling that she'd had it with his abuse, that he should leave at once, that she and the kids would manage without him. The knife was pressed firmly to his neck. I could almost see the moment when the blade would slice it open.

His eyes, previously red with fury, softened like the eyes of a child frightened by some apparition in the woods. Aparecido was sniveling, begging forgiveness, saying he wasn't the type of man to do these things; the liquor had ruined his life. Maria Cabocla took advantage of this moment of weakness to send him off, once and for all. She pointed to the wounds all over her body, the ones that had healed, the ones that hadn't, and those that were quite fresh. Her anger revealed, too, the wounds in her soul—of which she did not speak. Wounds slow to heal, those which, when they come to mind, we wave away so we can move on. She told Aparecido never to come back. Two of the younger children started crying when Maria threw her husband's clothes out the door, pleading with her, "Mommy, no, don't make Daddy go away." Maria was deaf to their cries, shouting at him to go stay with the whores he liked so much. He shouted back, through tears, that the house was his; he was the one who'd asked the boss for permission to live there. But Maria wouldn't relent, and I stood with her.

After Aparecido had staggered away, we straightened the house and fed the children. I wanted to take care of Maria, clean her wounds, make her something to eat. She thanked me but said everything was fine. I started home, nervous that Aparecido was out there somewhere. I was worried for Maria, too, with all those kids to feed and care for. What would happen to her? What if they kicked her off the plantation? What might her husband say to the farm manager, Sutério? I struggled to go to sleep as these questions hammered in my head. I couldn't stop thinking about Maria getting hurt, without anyone to protect her. I wanted to please her in some way, to be the one to comb her hair this time, to braid it, if its oily gloss allowed.

The harvest was good, so I brought her manioc and potatoes; it gave me an excuse to drop by each week and check on her. There was too much food just for me, really, and around here one hand washes the other. After all, my people and Maria's people, like so many others, had arrived from distant places, but gradually we became kin; we were children of the same midwife, or we were connected through godparents, neighbors, husbands, and wives; through in-laws and cousins and even through our enemies. Many of us had married within this community and had become true relatives, relatives by blood and affection. Others were like adopted family. And so our hearts commanded us to share what we had with one another, and that's how we survived the most arduous difficulties.

Weeks later, I heard that Aparecido had returned. The news made me sad, but I thought to myself, "As the father of Maria's children, he should get a second chance." Maybe the man could change. Who knows, the affection he felt for Maria might grow stronger than his anger. Or maybe, deep down, she'd come to realize that things could actually be worse—to be alone with all those kids, unable to farm the land on her own and to feed so many mouths? Maybe that's why, after I'd confronted Aparecido, courage coursing through my veins, Maria withdrew from me somewhat, ashamed of having called on me for help in the first place. As time passed, she seemed to change, sinking into depression, growing ever more solitary. She'd say hello whenever we bumped into each other, but she no longer lingered to chat, to talk about her problems, her husband's beatings, her struggle to put food on the table. I had no wish to hurt her more or offend her in some way, so I stopped going over with the produce I'd grown through my hard work.

A great many folks would step into the loneliness of my little ranch and compliment me on what I'd made of that bit of land, more impressive than anything the menfolk in the region had cultivated. They were amazed to discover I'd done it all on my own. They'd look me up and down incredulously. I half expected them to challenge me to arm-wrestle one of the local guys. They wondered if the strength required to till the soil, to work the land, came from these

arms of mine, or if the strength really belonged to the encantados. Sutério would swing by each week like clockwork,
and he took what he could. But I wouldn't let him take the
best, as my father would do out of gratitude. I separated the
largest vegetables for myself and for my parents. I never let
my crops wither on the stalk out of spite, for that would be
disrespectful to the earth. But if I could give extra to the
animals, I'd do so, just to deny Sutério the chance to claim
my sweat, my pain, my calloused hands and wounded feet,
as though all these belonged to him.

14.

Years later, Bibiana and Severo moved back to Água Negra
with their four children. They'd visited regularly to celebrate
the holiday season at the end of the year or the Feast of Saint
Sebastian. On one of those visits, I baptized two of their
children, as I'd promised: Inácio, the eldest, who'd grown
almost as tall as me, and Maria, their third child. My sister
Domingas baptized their second, Flora, and Domingas and
my brother Zezé became her godparents. Dona Tonha's
girl, Santa, was the one who baptized Ana, the youngest of
the four; Ana, named after our grandmother, was already
three years old. My mother traveled to assist Bibiana when
she was about to give birth to Flora; later, she accompanied
Bibiana to the hospital for the births of the third and fourth
child. The year of Bibiana and Severo's return to Água
Negra was also the year the very first television set arrived

at the plantation. Damião, an old-timer, had been given the television as a gift from one of his children who was working in the city. It was a black-and-white set. It had a gray box with two antennas that needed to be wrapped with balls of steel wool because they barely got any reception.

At first, what we watched was mostly noisy snow on the screen. But later the first satellite dish was installed, "a big plate turned to the stars," as Damião explained to my father on one of the Jarê nights. I still recall the expressions of surprise and laughter from folks in the community when they watched TV for the first time. We'd known about it from our visits to town and such, but no one in our community had a TV set in their home. However, this set arrived before electricity did, so in Damião's house they made it work by hooking it up to an old car battery, which as a result regularly needed to be jumped. That's to say, we'd watch a telenovela for two weeks straight, then we'd spend another two weeks not watching anything, until someone from Damião's family lugged the battery into town to get it recharged. The TV set turned out to be something that brought the community together at night. Whenever the battery gave out, you'd hear folks moaning about it in the fields, at the market, in every corner of Água Negra until someone came back with the battery recharged and ready to go. Even Sutério would occasionally show up and shuffle over, "just for a look-see." Folks would crowd around the set and start discussing the show, others would demand silence. Latecomers could only watch by clustering around Damião's window, poking their heads in because there wasn't any more room inside the house, not even if you were willing to sit on the floor. Bibiana said she'd buy a TV for our parents as soon as we had electricity.

Before my sister returned home, we'd suffered several cycles of flood and drought. The landscape was changing, for the enormous fields the men cultivated were shrinking year on year. The Peixoto family had already lost all interest in farming. Recently, one of the brothers, the one in charge and from whom Sutério took orders, had passed away. He was quite old, and his children seemed completely uninterested in taking over the operation. The periods of drought had been brutal. Rice was no longer a viable crop, and the Peixotos claimed they didn't have the money for fertilizer and seed. Not much flourished around Água Negra, but we had our individual plots near the marshes, and we had our telenovelas on Damião's TV as well as our Jarê rituals. My father was getting old, bent over by the years, his hair turning gray, but he was still out there working in the fields, Sunday to Sunday. He never spoke of stopping, even though many of the first arrivals at Água Negra were starting to retire. They'd been instructed by Sutério to go ahead and request the rural pension, though Sutério admitted that even he lacked the proper Work and Social Security Card. That pension mattered a great deal to folks; it improved a worker's precarious condition. An official copy of the Peixotos' rural real estate tax, a required document, had been passed around so that the old-timers might finally have what they'd never had before, devoting so many years of hard work just for this moment when they'd finally receive their meager pensions from the bank in town. It was as if, having worked for so long without pay, they finally understood, too late, that they'd always had a right to a monthly wage. Even after retirement, they continued working their plots, growing their own food, and often putting up their stalls at the public market. But at least they were free of the back-breaking labor that had wrecked the bodies of so many, that had meant enduring servitude for their ancestors, for their grandparents and great-grandparents, a subjugation they wished to put behind them.

Despite some progress, many of the prohibitions imposed by the landowners were still in effect. What little money folks received from their pensions couldn't be spent on upgrading their houses, which were made of mud; we were still forbidden from using brick as building material. So people embarked on more modest, interior improvements: foam mattresses rather than sacks stuffed with corn husks; a real bedframe; tables and chairs; medicine, better clothes and food; now and then, the pans and quilts the wandering gypsies would peddle door to door.

Bibiana had obtained her teaching certificate. She spoke differently, beautifully, and I could see the pride in my father's face as he watched her teaching her children. He wanted Bibiana to teach at the Água Negra school; he was planning to discuss it with the mayor at one of the upcoming Jarê rituals. Bibiana and Severo built a house close to our parents', as was usually the case when a couple married and intended to remain on the plantation. I continued living in my home near the Santo Antônio River, spending weekends with the family. I liked being around the children, and I liked hearing Severo talk about politics. I was learning so many things. My cousin continued traveling far from the plantation for his union meetings and his activist causes. Though I enjoyed his company, I kept a certain distance; I sensed my sister was suspicious of her husband, even of me. Maybe I got that impression from seeing her hackles rise whenever some woman got too close to Severo, drawn to his eloquence and the wisdom that seemed to emanate from him, lured by his rhetorical gifts and by that smile I recognized from long ago when Severo was a boy and I too had been enchanted, wanting so much to emulate him.

Whenever Severo went away to join the people who were teaching him new ideas, ideas about job insecurity and the hardships of simple farmers, I'd sleep in Bibiana's house to keep my sister company. Inácio, my godson, was growing up so fast; already he seemed to have a man's body, and he enjoyed working with me out back. He'd take the hoe from me, or from his mother, and start tilling or clearing the ground while we kept an eye on him. Like his parents, he was passionate about books. As for Maria, my goddaughter, she was a mischievous girl, constantly fooling us. She'd climb the branches of an umbu or cashew tree, then suddenly vanish into the woods. On one occasion, she fell and broke her arm, and immediately I recalled the day, long ago, when the Ford Rural took us to the hospital, a day that came back to me like a vivid dream. My mother looked over at her granddaughter and said, "I wonder who this one took after! I'll never forget what you girls put me through, having to rush to the hospital." Her words upset Bibiana, but I laughed quietly, thinking to myself how a life could be repeated like an old story. My father, concerned for my sister, comforted her, telling our mother not to make Bibiana feel bad, for Saints Cosmas and Damian were her protectors, and he was to blame for neglecting them. That's why we two had had such difficult childhoods; my father hadn't given Saints Cosmas and Damian the attention they deserved, and when he did honor them, he did so with displeasure. He never enjoyed being possessed by those two saints, saints who acted just like children, clambering up trees and jumping out of windows. Our house didn't have a proper tile roof, but if it had, my father, possessed, would've climbed up there like an unruly boy.

The year of Bibiana's return also marked the last time my parents traveled together for the religious celebration held in Bom Jesus da Lapa, our mother's hometown. Years before, my parents had promised that, should Bibiana and Severo come back home, they'd make the pilgrimage, entirely on foot, as a sign of gratitude. We only learned about this promise as August drew near and our parents announced they'd be joining the pilgrims on the journey. The pilgrimage that year was also meant to show thankfulness for the rain, never mind that less and less rain was falling. The need to give thanks had motivated many devotees around Água Negra, especially the old folks, to make the journey. It would take seventeen days, there and back, and for that reason we grew concerned for our parents' well-being. Bibiana was especially worried; she felt responsible for her parents' burden and feared something bad might happen to them, then she'd carry that guilt with her for the rest of her life. But our mother and father made it back safe and sound, burnt by the sun and exhausted, yet spiritually reinvigorated, as always after a pilgrimage to Bom Jesus; thankful for having been able to complete that journey, for having the legs and the stamina to walk for so long. They returned full of divine grace and brought back portraits of the saints, as well as rosaries and ex-votos. They returned older in the flesh, granted, with aches and pains that would persist for weeks or years, perhaps for the rest of their lives, but their eyes shone as though lit by candles, and that was enough to tell us that they did what must be done.

After that pilgrimage, however, my father would never be the same. His strength faltered. Maybe the journey had been too arduous for a man his age. My mother returned bone-weary, yes, but Zeca Chapéu Grande was in much worse shape. Suffering under that sun beating down on the asphalt, trudging amid prayers and spells and reliving the trek that had brought him to Água Negra so long ago, overwhelmed, perhaps, by the emotion of seeing the Bom Jesus, then seeing his children and grandchildren gathered around him—all this had prepared my father's body to leave us.

15.

In the last year of his life, which happened to be a leap year, my father went against the edicts of Jarê, contradicting his own teachings regarding certain prohibitions related to leap years. In those first few months, with the help of his son in-law and his son, my father laid the foundations of our new house, put up the large, forked branches and built the center room. We suspected what was going on, but we didn't talk about it so as not to attract bad luck. My father planted two jackfruit trees in a spot about half a league from the house, three cashew trees near the doorway, some banana trees in the backyard, and a mango tree along the short path to the old house. My father used to say that during a leap year it was forbidden to plant trees with deep roots and culti-vate perennial crops, such as coffee. Nor were you allowed to build the center room of a house. However, if you'd done all the real work the year before, such as laying the founda-tion, then you could finalize things during the leap year: hang the doors, thatch the roof, and paint the walls with whitewash. That year, however, my father didn't mention the prohibition or the fatal risks involved, in that to violate such laws was to court misfortune. But no one dared ques-tion him when my father planted those seedlings and asked for help raising the walls of the new house.

My mother did try to broach the subject with him, wonder-ing if we shouldn't wait until next year to start building. He said it made no sense to wait. He even suggested that what he'd said before was mere superstition and we shouldn't get hung up on such details, we should live our lives. The previous winter had brought a lot of rain and strong winds, damaging the house where our parents were living by themselves, now that their children had left. The mud had begun to erode, exposing the wood lattice that supported the front wall. It was like a decomposing body, allowing everyone to see its bones, to see a house's intimate spaces, for the holes and cracks were now gaping. To look into the interior of a house was to see all we possessed, secrets that should never be revealed, secrets fundamental to who we were. My father wouldn't be drawn into explaining why he was in such a hurry to build, but we could intuit the reason: his body was falling apart, like the walls of his house. It was a matter of months, perhaps. He was by then quite old. We sensed that the hour of his final rest was approaching.

Meanwhile we'd watch his tired body go up and down that road, from one door to the other; throwing himself into his task; heading off as dawn was breaking, carrying his hoe and straw bag down to the floodplain. We found it reassuring that my father never lost his desire to work. Indeed, he was always at it, from Sunday to Sunday, hauling sacks full of corn, dragging back his mesh bag heavy with manioc. He brought home fish on days when he took his rod to the black waters of the river. He ate with his usual appetite, and he continued with his work as a healer, lighting the candles, gathering herbs, and preparing medicine for our neighbors. He didn't forget Saint Sebastian on his feast day, even if the encantados who'd been beside him his whole life no longer took possession of him. Even if the clapping hands, the old songs and the rhythms of the drums could no longer conjure nimble dances from my father's body, or even get him off his chair. The filhos de santo and filhas de santo who followed my father were as numerous as reeds in the floodplain; they'd encourage him to get up, to move to the music, but it was useless. Santa Rita the Fisherwoman would manifest herself, riding Dona Miúda, casting her nets in the air. But my father just sat smoking his pipe, his eyes vacant, staring off somewhere far from the dancing in that room. During the Jarê rituals, while they were outside his house or, later, as they began walking home, the guests would comment on the feebleness of Zeca Chapéu Grande.

The time came, just after the Feast of Saint Joseph, when I noticed that even the energy my father once mustered for work had drained away. He'd wake up and light a cigarette, but he wouldn't head to the fields. He'd rise as early as usual, but then he'd stand in the doorway and gaze out across the distance at those fields that had meant so much to him. He'd gaze at the land he'd seeded with his own hands. He'd step down from the threshold, moving gingerly, and wander over to the plants in the backyard, where he'd relax for a bit. He'd touch the fresh dew on the leaves before the sun had risen to its full, terrible strength, a strength that blessed us but also punished us. He'd study those drops of water, then smear them between his fingers and walk back to the house, tossing his cigarette butt in the dirt.

My mother would be standing in the kitchen, waiting for him, ready with hot coffee and some sweet potato. He'd sit at the table but not touch the food, letting the coffee get cold, then he'd make his way back to the center room and sit by the doorway, nodding off while my mother talked to me about the weather. She would try to conceal her worry, but upon walking away I'd overhear her asking my father if he was feeling unwell. He wouldn't respond. He'd just indicate no by raising his left hand, a thick hand with knobby fingers.

I closed up my house by the banks of the Santo Antônio. Every now and then I went back to harvest the crops that were ready, before heading over to work my father's plot with a lump in my throat that sometimes threatened to suffocate me. Bibiana's house was next door to my parents'. She'd walk to the school to teach her classes and return during the lunch hour, uneasy, to check on our father. My mother looked after the grandchildren, cooked meals, watered the garden, and regularly sent away any visitors and anyone seeking help with maladies of the body or the spirit. We had a hard time making them understand that my father was too tired, that he was in no condition to attend to anyone. We asked them to wait until my father felt stronger. He often took daytime naps, but he'd still wake up early each morning, open the door, and then just stare at the path leading to the floodplain.

My brother alternated between working in his plot one day and in our father's plot the next, by my side. He tried to spark our father's interest with news that the pepper plant had flowered, or that the squash vines were struggling. But nothing could reach him; our father seemed disconnected from the world. With each passing day he moved about less and less, until eventually he didn't even get out of bed. His loss of weight and his apathy kept my mother looking constantly worried. My father made just one request: he didn't want to be taken to the hospital. Domingas tried to convince him otherwise, so did my brother, so did Bibiana and Severo. Now that the silence had been broken, suddenly everyone began expressing an opinion regarding what measures to take. There was an ambulance available to transport my father to the hospital, but we didn't want to contradict his wishes. I expressed my own feelings as best I could, but my gestures weren't understood, a source of enduring frustration for me.

The doctor arrived in an ambulance and, after examining him, decreed that he needed to go to the hospital right away. His lungs weren't working properly, there was fluid in them, and he was dehydrated and malnourished. My father kept his eyes shut during the doctor's visit, but we knew he was awake and lucid. He wouldn't say yes or no to any of the questions put to him. Bibiana spoke separately to the doctor, asking for just a little more time, and later we'd call for the ambulance. "But the ambulance could be on its way somewhere else by then. The right thing to do is to take your father to the hospital now. We already drove all the way out here; there's no point wasting time and gasoline." We watched the ambulance drive away, without my father.

At once we started trying to persuade him to change his mind, saying we weren't able to care for him properly in his worsening condition. "The doctor said you need oxygen." My father didn't open his eyes, but his lips, lips that had so often announced whether or not a life could be saved, firmly reminded us: "I'm still alive, and I'm the healer, not he."

His condition got so bad that he was forced to sit up so as not to choke on the fluids bubbling in his chest. Sometimes it was Domingas who'd hold him up so he wouldn't lean back; sometimes my mother would do it, but she tired quickly, though she never complained. Bibiana headed out each day to teach, but during her free time she'd put in a shift, and I'd help as well. Once, I fell asleep while on duty, and woke to find Zezé lifting my father up from my lap, where he'd been suffocating. I hadn't noticed that my father had slid from my arms and was resting his head on my lap, a dangerous position for him. When I realized my own carelessness, having almost let my father die, I got so angry at myself that my mutilated mouth let out the first cries anyone in my family had heard in many, many years. The only thing that could console me as I wept was my mother's embrace. Everyone seemed astounded by my body's involuntary cry. To them it was a miracle, showing everything could change, and my father could even be well again; after all, it was the first time in almost thirty years that they'd heard a sound from my mouth. The astonished look in Bibiana's eyes was the exact look she gave me on the day I was silenced.

Holy Week arrived, and my father seemed to have found his second wind. He accepted some stew without resistance. He was still dehydrated, but we respected his wish not to be taken to the hospital. That Friday, we had more of the beef stew that my father had enjoyed the previous day. My mother said it was more nutritious than fish, even if we weren't supposed to have meat on Good Friday. She sat down beside him, using an empty vegetable crate for a chair, and when she brought the first spoonful to his mouth, he gulped it eagerly. He seemed to be concentrating all his strength on chewing. It was, for us, a sign that Zeca Chapéu Grande wasn't going anywhere.

On Easter Sunday, my mother told us she'd felt a strong gust of wind, cold and damp, blow through her room in the early hours before sunrise. She roused herself, out of sorts, thinking she'd left the window open during the night, but the window was closed. She lit the kerosene lamp to see if my father needed anything. My father's eyes were open and his expression was serene in the dim light, in that play of shadows around the bony contours of his face. My mother cried out to us, her voice tearing through the song of the insects. Zeca was gone.

16.

I grew up hearing stories about José Alcino, my father, the man known as Zeca Chapéu Grande. Some of those stories came from him, from his own desire to share his past with his children, his filhos, and with his children of the spirit, his filhos de santo. But most of the stories involving my father actually came from my mother, for she'd heard stories about this man before she even met him, before he asked her to live with him. It was from my mother that I heard the most stirring tales, and those hardest to believe. I first heard them as a young child, and didn't remember much. As I grew older, I'd listen more attentively whenever my siblings asked our parents about the past, and they'd respond while we'd sit and listen to whatever they needed to get off their chests. Such stories often emerged while we were being reprimanded for complaining about our chores.

"You kids haven't gone through half of what your father went through," my mother would say, shelling beans to be sold at the market. "This happened long ago, long before we got to Água Negra . . ." My father, she went on, was born almost thirty years after enslaved Blacks had been declared free, when in reality they were still captives of the descendants of their grandparents' masters. My grandmother, Donana, gave birth to José Alcino, named after his father, in the middle of the sugarcane at the Fazenda Caxangá. He was born right there in the marsh because they wouldn't let Donana take the day off. My father came into the world surrounded by women who, like my grandmother, were racing to cut cane under the watchful eye of the foreman. Donana recalled that my father came out with his eyes wide open, and he didn't cry for those first few minutes. She barely had the strength to lift him to her breast to nurse. Only after he'd been sated did he finally cry out, announcing his arrival, a cry that could be heard for miles around.

My father was the first of eleven children my grandmother had with different men. My grandmother was nicknamed Donana "Chapéu Grande," or "Big Hat," because she'd always wear the same straw hat that had belonged to her first companion. He died just before my father was born, and it took a long time for Donana to accept what fate had decided for her. Despite her small stature, she could be seen cutting cane from far away because of that hat, which she'd wear for the rest of her life. It protected her eyes from the harsh sun, but it also fueled a suspicion folks already had about my grandmother—that she was a witch. We never learned the name she inherited from her mother's or father's side; we only knew that "Donana" was what she called herself. My mother thought her real name must have been Ana. We couldn't find a single document about her after she died, and since she was buried at the Viração cemetery on the plantation, no one said anything about her papers.

Donana told us almost nothing about her own life. She'd make vague allusions to her daughter Carmelita or to her fear of jaguars, but she wouldn't elaborate. Salu was the one who'd tell us stories from her time in Caxangá, but she waited until after her mother-in-law had passed to share some of them with us. She only knew those stories from what she'd heard in her youth after she'd left Bom Jesus da Lapa with her parents and they'd made their way to the plantation where she met Donana Chapéu Grande and her son, both of whom were already legendary in those parts.

My mother related that when Donana was just a girl, she lived with the family of the plantation foreman. He was her guardian while she worked in his home as a live-in maid. During that time, just before her first menstruation, she began experiencing dreadful pains. She had a fever and felt exhausted during the day, but when night came, she couldn't sleep. She threw up almost everything she ate. The

171

lady of the house said that some evil spirit must be involved, that Donana wouldn't last long. Days before the blood began running down her legs, Donana started to see objects shaking violently, the dry woods ablaze everywhere she walked, even the clothes on the line consumed like straw. The family, terrified, took the girl to a healer who was well known in that region, and left her with him. There, Donana would watch as doors and windows suddenly slammed shut when there wasn't even a breeze. She'd been given a straw mat to sleep on; when she looked at it, it caught fire. The healer said he couldn't help her.

Donana's guardians traveled for miles around, from one healer to the next. "They knocked on sixteen doors, sixteen houses of Jarê," Salu said, gathering dead leaves from her small vegetable garden behind the house. "They sought the most famous healers in all of the Chapada Velha." At some point, the girl began receiving the encantados, and it was the spirit of Velho Nagô who'd most often possess her. Donana's guardians were told that the problem came from the realm beyond, and it had been resolved. The encantados would wait for Donana to reach adulthood so that she herself could become a healer; she'd direct the powers of the spirits to benefit those needing help. It was in that final house of Jarê, the one belonging to the healer João do Lajedo, that Donana learned to work with herbs and roots to make tinctures and medicines for the illnesses that befell folks of all types: from big-shot coronéis to farmhands, from rich city girls to women laboring with their husbands in the fields.

When destiny brought her a man named José Alcino, the young Donana had no doubt that she'd find protection under his wide-brimmed hat, a hat that had sheltered him from the sun throughout his long journey. José Alcino had left the Recôncavo, on the coast of Bahia, for the Chapada region in the interior, tempted by the discovery of diamonds and the promise of sudden wealth. As soon as he arrived, he found that diamond prospecting had transformed the region into a battlefield where coronéis ran their own militias and got rich off the backs of desperate men who risked everything—their bodies, even their sanity—to find those gems. José Alcino decided that mining wasn't for him. When he reached the plantation called Caxangá, he set down his rucksack, which held only two changes of clothes and a few other possessions. He'd do what he had learned to do from his parents, the work that had always sustained him. José Alcino asked for a hoe, then demonstrated his ability to work the land. He was given permission to reside on the same plantation where Donana was still living as a captive. She never tried to run away from her guardians; she kept on working in exchange for food. José Alcino built his mud house, covered it with reeds, and soon made friends with the foreman who had raised Donana. After some time had passed, José Alcino said he needed the company of a woman; he wanted a family, he couldn't live alone anymore. He'd noticed the young lady who kept staring at his hat. Though he wouldn't look her in the eye, he brought her back to his house.

Just as Donana was about to give birth to my father, José Alcino fell badly from his horse while escorting a shipment of sugarcane. My grandmother's strange powers became once more the subject of gossip, in the big house as well as along the paths the workers followed to their plots under the scorching sun. My mother continued with her story, saying that Donana walked very slowly, helped along by her neighbors, to the spot where the accident had occurred. She didn't cry when she saw him lying lifeless on the ground, just as I hadn't shed any tears for Tobias. Perhaps for very different reasons. But it was strange how, after everything that had happened, history was repeating itself. Donana picked up his hat, which had rolled a short distance off, then climbed into the ox cart that would transport his body. He was the man who'd given her a home and companionship. She cradled his head on her lap.

Later, when my grandmother became a widow for a second time, she received a message from João do Lajedo, the healer, who by then had reached an advanced age: it was time for Donana to fulfill the obligations God had assigned to her. She must attend to the encantados who accompanied her. She must open her house to people seeking help and cure them of those maladies of the body and the spirit. Her power was a gift, and it must be used to alleviate suffering. Should she continue to turn her back on this gift, bad luck would follow her for the rest of her days. She'd already seen ample proof of this sentence.

But Donana wouldn't listen. She wanted to live her life. She'd continue making root tinctures for folks and acting as a midwife, but that was enough. There was no way she was going to turn her home into a house of Jarê, organizing celebrations for the feast days, offering room and board to the sick. She wasn't made for that life of deprivation and unending obligations. Donana sent her reply to João do Lajedo through his messenger: "There's no point begging. I'm not doing it, and that's that."

Not long afterward, at least as I understood it, her son Zeca, almost a grown man by then, began suffering awful headaches. He couldn't put in a full day's work beside his mother and siblings. He'd return home early from the fields, and sometimes he couldn't even manage to wash himself in the river, to scrub his hair and skin clean of the dirt that flew in every direction when he turned the soil with his plow or hoe. He'd just curl up on the floor, unable to eat or sleep. He spent days like that, in agony. It got to the point where Zeca began howling like some beast of prey. His screams would echo across the fields, and his gaze would pierce through you. Donana knew that her refusal had brought madness to her eldest child. The local children would gather outside her window and taunt Zeca, chanting, "You're crazy! You're crazy!" Donana, in her large hat, would chase after them with a broom.

She tried every way she knew to help her son come back from his madness. She made him root tinctures, she consulted João do Lajedo and other healers, but they all said the same thing, that there wasn't much to be done; this was the price for turning her back on her purpose on earth. Donana didn't feel capable of so great a sacrifice. And so she prayed, and lit candles, day and night, many of them going out before the wax had fully melted—the sign that her prayers were falling on deaf ears. She started locking her son inside the house whenever she headed out to the fields. She'd leave Zeca in his room without a blanket or a glass of water or a candle or food or anything that might somehow be turned against him. He spent whole days like that, alone in the dark of a windowless room.

Until one day Donana came home, and Zeca wasn't there.

17.

If I knew that this procession of memories, these thoughts passing through my mind while my hair turns gray, might be valuable to someone, I would have dedicated myself to the craft of writing. I'd have bought notebooks with the money I made at the market, filling them with the words that won't leave my head. Had the curiosity that led me to the knife with the ivory handle been directed elsewhere, I'd have discovered the person I might have been. For my mouth has so many stories to tell, stories that could've inspired our community, our children, to cast off their servitude to the owners of the fields and of the city houses where my people work.

After Bibiana and Severo came back to us, I began reading every book I'd seen in their hands. I developed a hunger for books. I'd even bring books with me to the fields, for those moments of rest in the shade. Today, the stories I encountered on those pages and heard from the mouths of my people keep unrolling in my mind like a fishing net.

176

When I sit quietly to mend an article of clothing, when I raise my hoe and swing it back down, opening gaps in the soil and tearing at roots, all the while the thread of my thought keeps weaving a fabric. In these moments, I, who once felt so much rage toward men, never wanting to lie with one again or remarry, entertain the idea only because I wish I had children, so I could sit with them and pass these stories down. Maybe I'd hand them a pile of old notebooks, blotched and moth-eaten, so they'd read those pages and learn what we're really made of.

We buried my father after a full day's vigil, allowing those who had once sought out Zeca Chapéu Grande to pay their respects to the healer. My father had placed his hand on the heads of so many who now knelt in reverence and prayed for his soul. Each of them had had some experience with madness or drunkenness, or needed to break a curse or to ward off the evil eye, and their eulogies formed a flood of emotion that broke over the entire community. On that warm morning, my mother, my sisters, and I took turns bringing out lemongrass tea from the kitchen to calm the weeping of the mourners. The old, dilapidated house where my father had lent his body to the encantados so that they could dance, and heal, and impose respect and forbearance and order, now received the folks whom the healer had always welcomed during his life. I could hear conversations, each person telling a story about Zeca to explain why he'd be missed around Água Negra. Some of the women went into the kitchen to see if comadre Salu needed any help. They had brought bags of ground coffee and bags of sugar, as well as thermoses from their homes, and started serving coffee to the mourners in the center room. As the day wore on, people began arriving from farther away. They arrived in their cars, on horseback, and on oxcarts, but the vast majority came on foot, carrying small umbrellas to shade them from the sun. "I believe this heat's addled my mind," Dona Miúda announced as she stepped inside. "May God bless you, comadre, and bring you comfort."

Amid the hushed voices and more lively conversations, I heard the buzzing, like a constant companion, of flies. I was the one who shooed them from my father's casket. When I recall that day, the hum of insects together with people's voices always comes to mind. It was the same hum I'd heard at Tobias's wake. Our neighbors and relatives began withdrawing into their own silence. They doffed their hats before my father's casket and bowed, down to their waists, and now and then they whispered words I couldn't hear.

As if some good news were awaiting me, I went up to the casket and began covering my father's body with small flowers, a white blanket borrowed from the earth. I looked at my father's hands: aged and thickened by hard work, they looked like they'd been covered in several pairs of gloves, gloves of skin and callus. His hands seemed disproportionately large compared to his arms, which were like dry sticks. Maria Cabocla hugged me, holding me up, but she was unable to find the words to console me. After the vigil, after serving many cups of coffee, having covered our heads in mourning, we headed in procession to Viração, the plantation cemetery, where Donana and Tobias were buried.

And those babies who hadn't survived. And the misery and memories of so many families. It's where we buried those who had died of illness or overwork. Those who had died from witchery. Those who had died just because it was, as they say, part of God's plan. My father's grave was ready. Beside it, a mound of earth. After we'd said our prayers, the earth would be tossed over his casket.

18.

Donana feared someone would show up unannounced at the door to tell her that her son had been found dead. Zeca had disappeared without a trace, and many days had gone by since my grandmother came home to find her front door busted.

As it was impossible for her to concentrate on farm work, she stopped going to the fields for a while. She sent her children out in all directions in search of their brother, while my grandmother went deep into the woods with her machete, opening paths, calling out for Zeca or for José Alcino, using his full name and sometimes holding her breath, in case the silence yielded some clue as to his whereabouts. They'd return home at night and gather in the light of the lamp and the candles to report that they'd seen footsteps by the riverbank. Or that a woman out on the edge of the plantation claimed she'd seen Zeca, but she wasn't sure because she couldn't see very well, but, if her eyes hadn't deceived her, it was Zeca, wandering around like a lunatic. Or that some folks spoke of a jaguar prowling in the woods where the boy might be hiding. Or that someone had been stealing eggs and fruit from their backyards, that clothes had disappeared from the line.

Time seemed to grind to a halt as the news trickled in. The sun took slower steps across the sky; the nights seemed endless. Then one of Donana's boys came running home to report that a cowhand, miles away at the Fazenda Piedade, had observed a young man, a Black man, naked as the day he was born, spending his days beneath a jatoba tree on the boundary with another plantation whose name he couldn't recall. My grandmother left Carmelita in charge of the little ones, told the foreman she needed to find out if that youth was her son, and struck out with some of the older kids. She took with her manioc flour, rapadura candy, and some crêpes for when the kids got hungry. She had no idea how far they'd have to walk.

They followed the road until arriving at Piedade. The cowhand said it had been several days since he last saw the young man. "Something's not right there, ma'am. He sleeps beside a jaguar under the jatoba, and the jaguar does not harm him." He said the beast seemed to be under a spell: it would circle him, guarding him, as if he were the jaguar's cub. The man didn't say another word but remained quiet, huddled in a corner of the room. It was the same jaguar Donana would see, years later, when she looked into Fusco's eyes.

Donana set up camp near the jatoba tree. She had a bit of flour with her, having come across a shed earlier where, luckily, someone was grinding and roasting manioc and didn't mind sharing. She gathered the fallen jatoba fruit and used the seeds to make those humble crêpes that had killed the hunger of her ancestors and would kill the hunger of her descendants. She slept poorly in the primitive shack she'd improvised to shelter her children from the night. She was afraid of the stories she'd heard about the jaguar.

She remained vigilant, and very early one morning she heard a rustling of leaves, a sign that her son might be lurking nearby. Donana got up from her mat and woke the eldest of the sleeping children. She let her ears guide her through the forest trails. She came across a marsh where fireflies were flashing excitedly over a glistening pond. An animal of some kind was there, on four legs, lowering its head to the muddy ground, lapping water. But as night gave way to morning, my grandmother could see that the beast was her son who'd been lost for months. She called out to him, "José Alcino," and "Zeca," but he vanished into the dense scrub, scrambling away on all fours through the cacti and dry branches. Donana knew how to move stealthily, without alerting her bosses or neighbors, and could wield her machete more powerfully than many a man. She followed Zeca deeper into the forest and at last she found him, cornered, staring at her with widened eyes, baring his teeth. Donana said a prayer, asking permission of the encantados of the forest, then lassoed her son as though she were roping a calf. His naked, filthy body was covered in cuts and sores. He reeked like a peccary. Ignoring his screams, she covered him with a blanket and bound his hands together, then told her other

181

children it was time to go home. She left behind her make-shift shack and the remnants of her jatoba crêpes.

João do Lajedo's house was along the way to Caxangá. "My boy's been carrying my burden for me," Donana said to the old man when he opened the door. "I was disobedient, I wouldn't listen. I defied the saints, and they punished me for it." João's neighbors had started gathering round because Zeca was howling and whining like a dog, struggling to break free and run. "Cure my boy, compadre. Cure my boy. And if he must be the one to bear my load and become a healer, so be it." She turned away and led her other children home.

19.

It would be some time before anyone else was buried at Viração, the cemetery at Água Negra. Not because no one died during that time, but because the plantation was sold shortly after my father's passing. The heirs had grown old, and their children and grandchildren wanted Água Negra off their hands. The elder Peixotos knew us well, but their descendants had no idea who we were, though they were sure we'd be a headache for them when it came time to sell. They sold Água Negra to a couple with two children; they sold the entire property, including our mud houses, including our very bodies as furniture. Accustomed to the Peixoto family's longstanding ownership of the plantation, we were taken by surprise and had no idea what might happen to us. The more naive among us believed that everything would stay the same. The pessimists feared for our future, imagining we'd be evicted. We knew that the land had had tenant farmers on it since at least the arrival of Damião, the pioneer of our community, who showed up during the drought of 1932. The Peixoto family had inherited their lands from the colonial sesmaria holders. Not even God can explain how things turned out the way they did, but, in any case, Severo said, we should keep an eye out for anyone suspicious lurking around our houses, on our way to the school or the fields, and later we'll get together and try to reconstruct our families' histories from the days before we even arrived at Água Negra. I paid close attention to what Severo was saying. He explained that, a long time ago, a White colonizer came to this region and ruled it as his kingdom. Then another White man appeared on the scene, a man with an important last name, and the two of them decided to divide everything up between themselves. The Indians were pushed aside, or killed, or forced to work for these owners of the land. Later, Blacks would be brought in from far away to take over the work that the Indians had been doing. Our people couldn't find their way back home; we got stuck here. When the plantations stopped being productive because the owners had grown old and their offspring couldn't care less about agriculture—being educated types who only knew how to get rich in the city—they came looking for us while fencing off the plantations, and so we started calling ourselves Indians. Because we knew there was a law, even if it was regularly violated, that forbade Indians to be expelled from their lands. But it's also true that Blacks had mixed with the Indians who'd been drifting around the region, unable to return to their villages.

Folks say that, way back, people began pouring in after hearing that diamonds had been discovered in these parts. What's more, some say that the first person to find diamonds here was one of our forebears, but the precious stones he found in the Serrano River were promptly stolen from him. They accused him of having killed a traveler from Minas Gerais. If he wanted to live, he'd have to tell them where he'd found the stones. Others say that he'd only been transporting the diamonds to be marketed else-where, and they'd actually been discovered by the slaves of a certain Prado. Still others argue that the first diamond was discovered by someone from Minas. What is certain is that the news attracted more workers and more slaves to the interior of Bahia, along with foreign consulates and mining companies, all eager to extract diamonds from these mountains. It's well known, too, that blood was spilled, a lot of blood, and that many men surrendered to the call of the stone, to madness, to the stones' enchantment. Many lost their reason searching for that radiance. Many perished under the spell of those gems, many more were murdered outright. For years, the coronéis waged war against each other. Enslaved men were brought in from the outskirts of the capital to dig for diamonds, and more came from the sugar mills that were no longer so lucrative, as well as from the gold mines of Minas Gerais. Folks even affirm that one child born to a miner was, in reality, the grandson of a king of the Oyó people in Africa, the last to keep his kingdom united, until he fell into disgrace.

Severo reminded us how, for generations, our lives had been shaped by the hunt for diamonds. As children, we learned to play games in which the objective was to identify gems that resembled the coveted stone. We heard stories, told and retold, of the legendary coronéis who ruled this region and battled one another for dominion of the mountains rich in diamonds. Ordinary folks used to be terrified of traveling, for fear of ambush. Every day was a life-and-death struggle in the Chapada Velha, and we were still living in the shadow of that violence. In the past, if a landowner happened to fall out with some coronel, then anyone working at that plantation was in mortal danger. That's how it used to be; but fear travels across time. It has always been part of our story.

The fear of being kidnapped from your home. The fear of not surviving the journey over sea and land. The fear of being whipped, of hard labor under the scalding sun, the fear of the powerful spirits of those people. The fear of leaving your house, the fear of displeasing those people, the fear of simply being. The fear that they don't like you, they don't like what you do, they don't like your smell, your hair, the color of your skin. The fear that they don't like your children, your songs, your sense of brotherhood. Wherever we found ourselves, we'd find a relative, we were never alone. If we weren't family, we made family. Our salvation lay in our ability to adapt, to create that sense of brotherhood, even when targeted by those who preferred us to remain weak.

And for that reason, they spread fear. Whenever Severo spoke in this vein, I'd grab hold of every word I could and keep them in my memory.

He'd speak, and the people of our community would reinforce what he said, sharing their own life experiences of how, at a certain point, diamonds no longer attracted so many incomers to this region; what was left was the land itself, known for its abundance of fresh water and for the floodplain that gives us everything. Água Negra was a piece of land between two rivers that almost enclosed it, forming something like an island in the heart of the Chapada Velha. Workers would make their way here in search of a place to live when drought struck. They were brought by the farm manager, or by workers who'd already settled in and were calling their brothers and compadres to join them. Others arrived singly, carrying out the trek on foot, to make a life here with the permission of the landowners. For many years, Água Negra was blessed with water and plentiful crops in the otherwise dry sertão of northeastern Brazil.

One day, the new owner, who'd built a fancy house for his family at the edge of the marshes, sent his new manager to talk to us, for Sutério had retired. He explained that we could no longer bury our dead at the Viração cemetery. That it was a crime against the forest, against nature. That the graves were too close to the riverbed. That there was a cemetery in town, and there the mayor's office had agreed to transport the dead in the future.

The younger folks didn't care much one way or the other. However, for our elders, this new prohibition was an insult.

They protested that Viração cemetery was over two hundred years old. The womenfolk announced that, when they died, the only place they'd be buried would be Viração. No more damn-fool talk of prohibitions. It was their destiny to be buried in that ground, beside their family members and compadres. The same ground as compadre Zeca, in a plot of dry earth with a meter-high wall on one side and caatinga scrub on the other. "Viração, and nowhere else," that's what a lot of folks started saying after the new ban had been announced.

Fortunately, no one passed away that first year, but everyone seemed tense about what was to come. Indeed, the message delivered to us said much more about our lives than it did about our deaths. If we couldn't bury our dead at Viração, it meant that very soon we wouldn't be allowed to remain on the land at all.

20.

Many months passed before Zeca was considered cured of his madness. Donana visited João do Lajedo's house every day to help with the root tinctures, prayers, and ablutions. In time, Zeca would return to his previous life, though it was clear something inside him had changed forever. His eyes no longer brimmed with innocence. A weight bore down upon his slender shoulders. Zeca remained alert and attentive whenever the healer performed his rituals; he committed to studying the rites and precepts, and he assisted at the

Jarê rituals, summoning the encantados in song. He could easily identify the various entities that would appear, and he'd switch the rhythms when appropriate. He'd modify the tempo of the atabaque drums when he needed to stir up, or calm down, a spirit in the room. He became familiar with the order in which the encantados manifested themselves. When the occasional surprise came along, he didn't panic.

Zeca eventually went back to work alongside his mother, but he still slept in the healer's house. He went back to the sugarcane fields. He'd set out with his mother and two of his brothers before the sun came up, but he never forgot about his prayers, or the candle he needed to light, or his obligation to return to João do Lajedo's house at nightfall.

When Zeca was ready, when he could distinguish between the various maladies that arrived at the door, when he understood the nature of childbirth, of the life cycles of animals and crops, he left João do Lajedo's house, only returning to participate in the ceremonies. He went back to live at Caxangá, where he continued learning from his mother how to identify and gather wild herbs, how to prepare ointments and tonics for a wide range of afflictions.

But the time came for him to make his own way in the world. He wanted to travel to other regions and search for work. The fields of the Fazenda Caxangá were suffering the effects of another drought. The mandacaru cactus hadn't flowered when it was supposed to, and the caatinga branches were completely bare. People had to fetch water from farther and farther away, and even the marshes were drying out. The plantation owners began arming their men to guard the water they'd stored for themselves. The rivers were shrinking, and the fish, abundant during the rainy season, had vanished. That hostile landscape, short of water but spilling over with violence, was the environment in which my father spent his first years as a grown man. During that period, he often came across travelers passing through in search of water and opportunity.

I'm not sure when he first heard of Água Negra—between one hand-rolled smoke and the next, between gathering herbs and saying prayers to ward off the evil eye, between the houses and the horses kicking up the dry earth of Caxangá. Word went around about a plantation where rivers of dark water flowed. About its plentiful fish, its rice paddies, its abundance of palm fruit and buriti, and its great pond where the Utinga and Santo Antônio Rivers converged. Word was that the landowners were happy to take in more people, as long as they had no objection to hard work. Folks who didn't mind sweating from sunrise to sunset, from Sunday to Sunday. They wanted folks who'd cultivate their own vegetable gardens, who'd make the vast fields productive and thought nothing of shredding their hands during harvest.

In return, they were free to build modest houses of mud and cattails, structures that would crumble over time from rain and sun. A worker's house should never be thought of as an asset, a possession that might attract the greed of heirs. The house must be easy to demolish when required. They'd put you to work—according to those travelers passing through Caxangá—they'd put you to work, but the land you farmed would never belong to you. It belonged to the Peixoto family, their claim officially recognized since the Land Law of 1850, so it was beyond dispute. The folks who'd turn up there in search of work were foreigners to the region; they'd be allowed to reside on the land, sow crops, and make a home. They could fence in their gardens and even plant in the floodplain in their free time. They could feed themselves from what the land provided, but only if they were obedient and loyal.

After probing the travelers for information, folks with news from relatives who'd already left, Zeca decided it was time to depart. He informed Donana, whose tired eyes filled with tears. "Please don't cry, Mama." She took the crucifix from around her neck and put it over her son's head. "Mama, don't worry. Velho Nagô will be with me." He assured her that if he started early, he'd arrive at Água Negra the very next day. Zeca put on the clothes his mother and sisters had sewn for him. "May the encantados and spirit guides protect you," Donana said to her son. "I call on them: Sete-Serra, Iansã, Mineiro, Marinheiro, Nadador, Saints Cosmas and Damian, Mãe d'Água, Tupinambá, Tomba-Morro, Oxóssi, Pombo Roxo, and Nanã."

Zeca set off before the sun rose. The birds were fluttering wildly, a commotion of wings, alighting then soaring up again, a good omen. In the straw bag she'd woven for her son in her spare time, Donana put some jerky, a container of manioc flour, and a small bottle of honey for the journey. Maybe, before leaving, Zeca kissed his mother's face or Carmelita's forehead, maybe he embraced his brothers. "God bless you, Mama. I'll be sure to send news, good news.

I'll come back for you, so you can live close to me." Donana wiped her eyes. "God be with you, my son."

He took the bag with the food and the few items of clothing he possessed. Some paper to roll tobacco, a comb with missing teeth. A rusty blade for shaving. He walked for a day and a night and arrived at Água Negra, where he would spend the rest of his life.

21.

One day, my brother Zezé asked our father what it meant to be a tenant farmer. Why didn't we own the land ourselves, when so many of us had been born there, when we'd always been the ones who worked those fields? How could the Peixoto family own the land when they didn't even live there? Why didn't we just make the land ours, if we sowed the seeds for our daily bread, if it was the land that sustained us?

That day is branded on my memory. It'll never be erased, never leave me, no matter how long I live. There weren't any clouds in the sky that day, and the way the sun was beating down, everything around me glared white. My father took off his hat, the heat drenching him with sweat that trickled down his temples and dripped from his chin. On his threadbare shirt, I could see large, damp stains around his armpits. His pants were covered in dirt, as were his arms and his hoe and the wide-brimmed hat he held in his hands. I was feeding corn and leftovers to the chickens.

"Being a tenant farmer means you got nowhere else to go. It's your only chance to find work, to survive." He squinted, looking into the ditch at his feet. "So, you go ask someone who's hiring, 'Will you let me stay, sir?'" Then my father looked straight into my brother's eyes. "Work more, think less. Don't set your eyes on things that don't belong to you." He stuck his hoe into the ground and rested his elbow on the handle. "A deed to the land isn't going to give you more corn, more beans. That's not what puts food on our table." He took out some tobacco and rolling paper. "See all this land around you? A man's eyes can get too big. He wants more. Are your hands strong enough to work all that land? Do the work that's in front of you. From this land a forest grows, and the scrub, and the buriti, and the palm fruit, but without our hard work, it's nothing. Worthless. Now, maybe it's worth something to those folks over there who don't do any of the work. Who don't dig with their hands, who don't know how to sow or reap. But for folks like us, it's work that gives land its value. Without our hard work, the land is nothing."

My brother went back to his chores without pursuing the conversation. My father hadn't mentioned Severo's name, but he knew his son-in-law had been going around talking to people about the union, about workers' rights and the law. He was holding those conversations out there in the fields. My father knew that Sutério must have heard about it, too. Zezé, out of respect, didn't bring the subject up again in front of our father, but he kept ruminating on the matter, disregarding our father's instruction. When Zeca wasn't nearby, he'd return to those issues and offer his own opinions. From the older folks, he heard the same arguments Zeca had made. But the younger folks thought he was right to ask those questions, for their parents and grandparents had died with nothing. The only bit of land to which they had a right, that no one could take away, was the grave awaiting them at Viração cemetery. To retire was just another humiliation, asking the owners for a copy of the rural land tax or any document establishing that a worker had some connection to the plantation. The owners would drag their feet when the time came, after having exploited the workers for so long, even denying them a wage. When folks finally decided to retire, when the day came to head over to the government office to apply for their benefits, they lacked the necessary documents.

The way the system operated, it was the workers who were indebted to the owners of the land, for having been granted the opportunity to work; except for that debt, they had nothing to bequeath to their children and grandchildren. The only thing they could possibly leave them was the house itself, almost always in a state of ruin. But the old-timers at Água Negra didn't get upset about such things; their priority, in fact, was to keep the peace between workers and landowners. Perhaps they felt some deep gratitude for having been taken in, gratitude that subsequent generations wouldn't understand, having been born and raised on the plantation. The younger folks started to think of themselves as having a right to the land, more of a right, in fact, than their elders, whose names had been recorded on a document

193

somewhere, paperwork the managers always rigged to the disadvantage of the worker.

My brother wouldn't let it drop, though he avoided talking about it in front of our father. He'd accompany Severo when, between tasks, his brother-in-law went around the plantation, engaging with his fellow workers. "We can't keep living like this. We have a right to our own land. We're the descendants of those original escaped slave communities, the quilombos. We're quilombolas." This dream of freedom kept growing inside of us, affecting everything we did. As the years passed, the dream would create conflicts between parents and children. Some of the younger folks had already decided to leave the plantation. They hankered for a life in the city. Such relocations were nothing new—workers would sometimes leave on the backs of animals for other places, for the city or a nearby town—but now the departures were becoming frequent. Life in the city, full of people coming and going, busy with trade, was very tempting. But the work we'd been doing for generations was what we knew, and it weighed heavily on anyone's decision to leave. Zezé wanted to tell our father that being a tenant farmer just wasn't enough for our generation, and it had nothing to do with ingratitude. Domingas and I listened as Zezé made his point: "The landowners, they're the ungrateful ones. And now we hear rumors that they want to sell this plantation without a thought for what it'll mean for us." We'd formed a circle beneath the jackfruit tree by the side of the road. Severo weighed in on what Zezé had said: "We want to be in charge of our own work, to make decisions about what to plant and harvest, and I'm not talking about our little gardens. We want to take care of the land where we were born, the land nurtured by our sweat."

But this dream of freedom would poison our homes.

22.

He walked for a day and a night. Before the sun came up he'd reached a group of houses sitting atop a plateau, and all around there was good land. A herd of cattle went by, followed by some cowhands on horseback. He'd always remember that day when he first arrived, the cattle kicking up a cloud of dust. He walked close behind, the dust blowing in his face, while one of the cowhands, at some distance from the rest, kept his eye on him. He kept walking, slowly, holding on to his mother's crucifix. From the position of the sun, he figured it was about six in the morning. He said a prayer to greet the new day.

His feet ached. During the night, he hadn't wanted to stop and rest. He was afraid in those unfamiliar woods. He walked in the company of his encantados, but there was danger all around. Perhaps his own guides had instilled this fear, a strange gift bathed in moonlight, precisely so he'd remain vigilant? Perhaps this fear would help him reach his destination safely? The encantados opened paths for him. He sensed them driving the dangers away. Dangers such as snakes, peccaries, jaguars. The coronéis with their armed thugs. Even the danger of greed, the greed for land and gemstones. God was his true guide, looking out for him and directing the encantados.

Velho Nagô, following behind him, drew closer as he approached the end of his journey. Velho Nagô, bent over his walking stick, wearing a white hat, his pipe in his hand. Back in Caxangá, ever since being cured from the disturbance of his mind, he already felt Velho Nagô's presence. He could feel the old African's touch and his wisdom covering him like a mantle. But Velho Nagô wasn't the only encantado protecting him. Mineiro was walking just ahead. Elegantly dressed all in white. Mineiro had arrived in those parts with the migrants from Minas Gerais; he stayed around because he'd developed an affinity for those diamond prospectors. He never refuses a sip of white wine. He never refuses a white cigarette. He's the encantado who warns us when someone will be touched by madness.

Oxóssi is the hunter, the one who knows his way around the woods. The one who always steered him away from danger, from venomous snakes. The one who'd charm the hunted prey, so he wouldn't go hungry in that new land. The beef jerky his mother had provided would sustain him for now, but Oxóssi would never let him down. Oxóssi traveled between earth and sky, he was there in the commotion of birds, and he was present in the medicinal herbs and roots the young man had gathered into his straw bag.

Mãe d'Água guided him along the rivers; she made sure he never went thirsty. She was there when he left the cattle trail and made his way down from the plateau, finding the path that, he'd heard, led to the plantation. She kept showing up between green leaves and tree trunks, among cactus thorns and twisted branches. She'd hurry this way and that, appear and disappear, her feet merging into the clear, dark river, the river that was his path, the promise of a new life. The current seemed to bless his own feet. Ventania was there, too, spiraling up as a whirlwind, blowing dirt in his eyes. The encantado seemed to be traveling along the same path as Mãe d'Água to let Zeca know there would be both soil and water for sowing and reaping, for himself and for those to come. Ventania ran ahead of everyone, and when Zeca reached the houses on the plateau Ventania rose up, blinding the cowhands and their cattle, forcing him to cover his own eyes, lifting dry leaves off the ground and into the air, whipping his body to keep him alert at the end of his journey.

On that day Zeca recalled certain things that had happened to him, things folks had described but he hadn't previously been able to remember. He recalled spending many nights sleeping next to a jaguar. A jaguar that hardly seemed to notice him. He'd eaten the fruit that fell from a tree; he'd torn into small birds and fish with his teeth as they pulsated with life, the blood dripping from his mouth. The memory of the fields came back to him as well, the hard work he did for the landowners. The story of his widowed mother, too, came back to him; how she'd given birth to him in those fields of cane. Her refusal to serve as a healer. He remembered his sister Carmelita, still so young, her hands mending shirts and braiding the fibers of buriti palms. And his younger siblings helping with the chores, watering the garden.

197

He reflected on everything. And he said to himself, if there's good land at Água Negra, if they give me permission to build a house, to farm the land, if I could have a garden with access to water, if there's a river nearby and fish to put on the table, then I'll bring the whole family here. I'll find a good, hard-working man for Carmelita. And if I meet a nice girl, I'll invite her to live with me, have children with me. And if it pleases the encantados, I'll organize the festive rituals so they can manifest themselves. And when folks come to me for help, I'll say healing prayers and make root tinctures for them.

And so he walked for a day and a night in the company of the encantados, bringing memories and stories with him. Bringing wild honey and beef jerky. Filthy from the dust clinging to his sweaty body, completely exhausted as he walked up to one of the men on horseback.

"This here Água Negra?"

"That's right. Who sent you?"

"No one sent me. I'm looking for work. I'm young, and I'm strong. I'm good with a hoe. I know powerful prayers and the medicine for jiggers."

"Then you've come to the right place. Some make their way here, some don't stay long, but we always need folks who'll work hard. Take this note with you, give it to a Black guy by the name of Damião. He lives down that road you see there. What's your name?"

"José Alcino da Silva, but you can call me Zeca Chapéu Grande."

The man took out a pencil and a wrinkled sheet of brown paper, and wrote down some words Zeca couldn't understand. But what the man said rang in his ears: "Find Damião. He'll tell you what to do." My father folded the paper and tucked it away as though it were an official document. He headed down the path to find Damião.

23

"Your father's hand is still on your head, comadre. You need to take his hand away. Go to the house of another healer." That's what Tonha's daughters told me. Crispina and Crispiniana said the same thing. And Maria Cabocla, stopping by the old house where I'd been living with my mother since my father had fallen sick, repeated the message. I took no notice. Their advice was based on beliefs my own father had spread across the region, but none of it meant anything to me now. Take his hand away? My father was gone; he took his hands with him. Even if I believed them, I still wouldn't take his hand away. Zeca Chapéu Grande was my father, my guide on this earth, responsible for the person I am. His followers, his filhos de santo, had been visiting other Jarê houses in the region, to remove his hand from their own heads. They feared they'd be condemned to follow him into the next life. I was incapable of fearing anything, not the threats Tobias directed at me, not the sight of Aparecido charging toward me. I didn't fear the living; I wouldn't fear the dead. I could hear the womenfolk weeping outside the door, telling me I was going to die. On more than one occasion, Salu had to send them away. "Leave my Belonísia alone. If she doesn't want to, she won't do it. I appreciate your concern, but please, go mind your own business." After a while they forgot about me. I thought to myself, "Careful, ladies, you might go before I do." How I'd laugh if that came to pass.

It was a long time before my sorrowful mother was able to drag herself out to the fields to work. She started drinking cachaça, even before noon. It was strange to see her behaving this way, for my mother never drank, not even at a party or celebration. I started hiding the bottles, but she'd go to the market and find a way to sneak them back into the house with the provisions. She'd tip her head back and take long swigs, then fall asleep in her chair, snoring. She'd let the food burn if she was cooking. She lost interest in relating to her grandchildren. When she was sober, she'd pick up some item that had belonged to my father and say, "Look what he left behind." Or, "He never got the chance to finish this." She'd lose herself in such nostalgia when anyone came seeking help, accustomed as they were to knocking on Zeca's door whenever there was a problem. She'd explain that she couldn't do anything, she wasn't a healer. "I'm not going to stick my nose into something I don't understand," she said to Domingas once, fanning the flames in the oven. "I wasn't born with the gift."

The new house my father had gotten started was left unfinished and remained that way for months, without anyone taking over. No one believed they had the authority. My mother put her foot down one day as she glanced over at the unfinished house, already smothered by weeds:

"I'm going to demolish that thing. I'm not leaving this old place." "But your house is falling apart," Bibiana replied, "so maybe we should finish the construction, and you could move sooner rather than later." My mother had lost all desire to move, and she wouldn't be swayed. "No one is to do a thing. Let time have its way with it."

When the sun began lingering on the horizon, signaling that another dry season would soon be upon us, Salu found herself burning with fever, unable to get out of bed. Dona Tonha stopped by, and the two talked quietly in her room. The next day, my mother told me that she had to travel to Cachoeira: she'd been cursed with the vice of drinking because, after my father died, she refused to take over his obligations regarding the encantados. Dona Tonha would accompany her on her journey. She understood it was time to remove her husband's hand from her head. She set off to find a healer, and I stayed behind alone. I went back to work in the fields because I wanted everything to go back to how it used to be. I reckoned that farming was the only way to remember my father without feeling so much pain. I followed my brother down the trails to the fields, and sure enough, plowing the land, planting and harvesting, mending fences, all that hard work began healing me of the pain of my father's absence, just as it had healed me of my sadness after I moved in with Tobias. The same way it had healed me when I became a widow and lived by myself by the Santo Antônio: work is what kept me alive. I saw things revive in my hands, and I wondered about the direction our lives would take without my father's guidance, without the powers of the encantados who'd lived among us for so long.

Salu finally came back from Cachoeira and announced that she'd finish building the new house. That she was done with drinking. Her decision was a relief to us. It didn't take long to complete what my father had left half-made. We cleared the land around it. We got ready for the move. The same pai de santo who had taken care of my mother in Cachoeira came to Água Negra to oversee this operation. In our old house, there had lived a powerful man, my father, who directed energies between the world of the living and that of the dead; who handled positive feelings and negative ones, healed the land, healed people, called forth the spirits of nature. And so everything he had done, all that spiritual activity, was still hovering in that space, and it needed to be transferred somewhere. The old house would have to be dismantled. The doors, windows, and thatching were removed. The pai de santo began batting the walls with a bundle of herbs and chanting prayers we'd never heard during those nights of Jarê.

"If there's some power still left behind in this house, would you want it to go to you, Salustiana? Will you follow your husband's calling?" the old man asked. "No," she replied without hesitation, her eyes fixed on what the sacred healer was doing. "Then may I direct the power to myself?" he asked, standing beside my mother and holding the herbs high in the air. "You may," she replied.

The old man left the walls as they were. He didn't touch a single stick. Time took care of bringing down our former home. No longer providing us with shelter, the house seemed to collapse with an urgency it borrowed from the surrounding woods. With every heavy rain, a wall would crumble, until at last the wind finished the job. Those walls of earth, made from the mud of Água Negra, became earth once again. Grasses and tiny flowers flourished in the humidity of the dew and of the rain that fell when it was the will of the saints. I was attentive to what was happening. I knew that none of it would come back. I watched as though under a spell as time advanced like a horse, wild and indomitable.

24.

Indomitable, Severo traveled every road, lifting his voice, giving speeches, challenging the new landowner and the manager he'd put in charge. Himself transformed as the rest of us also got swept up in the movement, Severo wound up reinventing Água Negra. It became a different place. When Zeca Chapéu Grande was alive, Severo would defer to him, holding back rather than confronting those who'd given us shelter. Questioning their authority would be a form of ingratitude. Severo understood he couldn't argue with my father, who was both his uncle and his father-in-law; it would've shown a lack of respect for everything my father represented to our community. Zeca Chapéu Grande had kept us all united, he'd been our leader for many years, and, never allowing the owners to mistreat us, he often intervened where necessary without directly confronting Sutério, preventing injustices worse than those that already existed. Thanks to my father's beliefs, a system of order had been established, one that had helped us to make it that far.

His death left a void in our community, and the sale of the plantation was an unexpected shock. The news that reached our ears was that Água Negra had been sold cheaply; our presence on the land had reduced its value. The new owner was determined to get rid of us, but he was aware that after residing there for so long, we enjoyed certain protections under the legal system. So, at first he acted as a peacemaker, reassuring us that nothing would change. He wanted us to know he was a very sympathetic person. If someone needed a doctor, he'd offer a ride to the city, then announce to the four winds how generous he was to his workers. He opened a proper store, stocking it with provisions, and decided to raise pigs on the plantation. Anyone prepared to work hard, he claimed, would have the right to a real salary. But then he'd pay us for our work with goods from the store, and somehow we'd leave with an unpaid balance and find ourselves in debt.

The playing field would never be level. Severo raised his voice against such measures, which we all found unjust. He swiftly became an enemy of the landowner. Severo would deliver speeches about our rights, reminding us that our ancestors had migrated to Água Negra because, following abolition, being a tenant farmer was the only option available to most Black folks. That we had worked for the previous landowners entirely for free, without even being allowed to build a proper house. That we were only allowed to build mud huts whose walls needed to be rebuilt after every rain. That if we didn't unite as workers, very soon we'd be homeless. Every time Severo and his siblings took action against some oppressive rule, the landowner responded with greater tyranny. He tried to divide us, alleging that "a bunch of good-for-nothings" were trying to take over his land, the land he'd bought with his hard-earned money. For some of us, Severo was the answer to the abandonment we'd felt after my father's death. But others didn't take kindly to Severo's activism; they openly opposed my cousin, contradicting him at every turn and joining the landowner's side, undermining our collective strength. They'd lead their animals out of their pens in the dead of night to wreck our plots in the floodplain. They'd knock over our fences, and months of cultivation became mere pasture in the mouths of cattle. Once, late at night, we were awoken by a fire raging in the chicken coop. The eggs started exploding like fireworks at one of our June festivals. We put out the blaze with water from the trough and by throwing dry earth on the embers. Other coops had been set on fire as well, making it obvious to everyone that this arson had been committed by the landowner and some of our neighbors, as retaliation. I wasn't going to leave my mother and sisters to fend for themselves. I decided I'd never return to my house by the Santo Antônio River; my place was with my family on the banks of the Utinga.

Severo started collecting signatures to establish a labor union. He said that unless we got organized, we'd end up being kicked off the land. The idea of leaving Água Negra was, for many of us, unimaginable. I overheard Dona Tonha talking to my mother, explaining that she could never move to the city: "What am I going to do, pace the sidewalk? You can't till it. In the city, you need money for everything. You want an onion, you pay for it. Want some seasoning, you pay for it." Bibiana was active in the movement alongside her husband. In the midst of all the mobilizing, I was content to watch the children so that my sister could write letters, teach, and travel around on the back of Severo's motorcycle. They'd attend union meetings. They'd come back and organize more meetings, clandestine ones, held in this house or that. Our own house hosted plenty of meetings. I'd been worried that my mother might react the same way as my father, who dismissed this activism as mere ingratitude. But no, she seemed enthusiastic about it, inspired to tell more stories of the past. She was a living book. She'd tell stories about her grandparents and great-grandparents, about the Caxangá plantation, where she'd lived for a time, and about Bom Jesus, where she was from. She'd speak confidently, aware of the importance of the history she knew. And it became clear to folks that if we didn't start making some real noise, we'd be packed off with nowhere to go.

A police car began paying visits. The officers would routinely get out of the car to question us, marching into houses, upsetting the residents. It frightened us. One house would warn another if the officers came by, if someone was late returning home, if someone was away somewhere. We were all in it together; we understood that this was the only way to protect ourselves.

Bibiana and Severo were heading out again, this time to the notary to register our union, which would represent the farm laborers and fishermen of Água Negra. They were taking the list of signatures with them. Previously, one overcast morning, the sky almost white, the heat stifling, Salu recalled that she was still in possession of Sutério's note, a note he'd given my father maybe seventy years before. Everyone agreed it would be wise to make a copy and attach it to our paperwork. Zeca had kept the note, written on a stained piece of paper, in a brown envelope along with some other documents. The paper was so old, it was almost disintegrating. I still remember the time my father asked Bibiana to read it out, so everyone would understand our situation. Bibiana drew the note out very carefully and began reading aloud. When she finished, I insisted on confirming the veracity of what was written there: "Mr. José Alcino asked if he could live here I gave him a spot by the Utinga told him he has to work in the fields he can build a house with mud, no brick."

Bibiana had already climbed on the back of Severo's motorcycle when she remembered the note. She handed her helmet to Severo and came into Salu's house to get it. Maria and Flora were washing dishes out back, while I was trying to get a fire started in the oven, my clothes damp with sweat from the effort of fanning the flames.

I heard a series of popping sounds, just as I did that time the chicken coop was torched. The eggs had exploded, and all the hens had burned to death. I felt a pain in my chest that night, seeing our animals killed for no other reason than sheer wickedness. We never rebuilt that coop, so there were no eggs to explode, to make the popping sounds that once again made me weak with worry. I ran to the front of the house. Bibiana and I got there at the same moment.

Severo was lying on the ground. The dry earth at his feet had cracked open, and in that rift there flowed a river of blood.

III. RIVER OF BLOOD

1.

My horse has died, so I cannot go forth mounted as I
should, the way an encantada should present herself to
human beings, the way she should reveal herself in this
world. I've been wandering aimlessly ever since, here and
there, searching for a body to take me in. My horse was
a woman named Miúda, but when I possessed her flesh,
she became Santa Rita the Fisherwoman. For a period,
Miúda, who lived alone, was my chosen mount. Days and
years mean nothing to me. Miúda lived for a century; I'm
much older. I've found refuge in many bodies, long before
Miúda's, ever since humans began penetrating the forests
and rivers, mountains and lakes, ever since human greed
began digging those deep holes, with people clawing at
the earth like armadillos, looking for the shining stones.
Diamonds cast a terrible spell, for everything beautiful

carries within it a curse. I've seen men make blood pacts, cutting their flesh with sharpened knives, staining their hands, their faces, their houses, their tools, their sifters and pans. I've seen men go mad, never sleeping, hunting day and night along the Serrano River, over the mountains, down the mines, burrowing in the dark to catch the stone's sparkle. Yes, the diamond casts a spell. In pitch darkness you can see it flash—it would blind an owl—as it travels from one place to another like a spirit, flying from a mountain, crossing the sky, coming down a slope or a stream, taking the form of light, drawing all eyes to it, even from afar. Men went mad for it, waiting for sunrise to dig craters where they'd seen something flash, only to find nothing there. They grew crazed, not eating, not bathing. They perished deep in their holes or while trying to steal the finds of others. They died of hunger, surrendering the energy of their bodies and minds to the hunt for diamonds. And they led their families down that same road of insanity. Many lost their minds quite suddenly, without sign or warning. They made offerings to the encantados in the houses of Jarê, encantados such as Mineiro and Sete-Serra. They sacrificed animals, spilling blood to help them find that radiance. They weren't out to hoard the stones or admire their light; they wanted to fill their baskets to purchase a house, or their own freedom. Every now and then, it's true, someone would get lucky and get the chance to buy his freedom, become his own boss. Some acquired slaves of their own and said goodbye to servitude, to the searching that had lacerated their hands and their souls. But what most of them found was a chimera; what most of them found was madness, dread, disquiet, hurt, violence. So many were broken beneath their own illusions, defeated, buckling under a heap of gravel.

My people were always moving from one place to another in search of work. In search of land, of somewhere to live. A place where they could plant and harvest. A hovel to call home. Abolition came, and the landowners could no longer own slaves, but they still needed them, so they began referring to their slaves as "workers" and "tenants." They couldn't ignore the law completely; it might cause trouble. The owners drummed into their workers just how kind they were for providing shelter to those Blacks adrift in search of a place to live. How kind they were, no longer reaching for the whip. How kind they were, allowing their workers to plant their own rice and beans, okra and squashes. Some sweet potato for breakfast. "But you gotta pay for this patch of land where you plant your sustenance, you gotta pay for the food you eat. An empty sack won't stand up. You'll work in my fields, and during your free time, you can look after what's yours. Ah, but no building with brick, and no tiled roofs. A worker can't have a house like the owner's house. If you don't like it, go ahead and move on, but think twice about it; it'll be hard finding anything else."

I hid among these people whom the landowners called workers and tenants. The same who carried me on their backs when they were slaves in the mines or in the sugarcane fields, when they were slaves of Nosso Senhor Bom Jesus, owned by the Catholic Church. I'd find shelter in one body

213

and then another, back when there was abundant water in these parts. But diamonds never brought us good luck or fortune. They brought only illusion, for after the dredging machines were installed, the rivers started filling up with sediment. They became dirty and shallow. Without plentiful water for fishing, there was no point in making offerings to Santa Rita the Fisherwoman. Ah, and then electricity arrived, and those who could afford it bought a refrigerator. The small fish that remain in the river won't satisfy anyone's hunger. They embarrass even the fishermen.

So no one bothered to learn my songs. They seemed positively shocked, once when I revealed myself. They looked at me as though I were a ghost intruding on the ceremony; some even mocked me. Miúda toiled in the fields like the others, but her passion was fishing, waking up at dawn and wending her way to the river. She'd bring her children along, but after they left home, Miúda fished alone. She used to sleep on the riverbank, without fear of jaguars or snakes. I was her encantada, riding her body without ever frightening her. I protected my horse. My horse who danced, casting her net in the house of Zeca Chapéu Grande, the healer. She didn't wear shoes, for her feet were my roots connecting me to the earth. Her arms were my fins, propelling me through the water. I've ridden my horse for so many years, I've lost count. But now, without a body to possess, I wander the land.

2.

The morning was cloudy, the sky a field of cotton, thick and warm. I floated over the land, across the cornfield and over the river, but my reflection didn't appear on the surface of the water. The air was heavy and it was difficult to move, until, all strength spent, I became completely still. But only for an instant, for the feeling of heaviness quickly dissipated in a powerful gust rising from the earth, tearing through the stifling, oppressive atmosphere. A cry sliced space like a sharpened sword. Everything was stained red. I followed the river of blood back to its source.

The river was flowing from Severo, the man who'd been mobilizing the workers of Água Negra. His body lay on the ground, pierced by eight bullets. The cry had come from Bibiana, who I found cradling her husband's head on her lap. The river was made of blood and tears, copious and slow, like a current of advancing mud, calling on the people to come together or flee the plantation. In moments of heightened emotion, I lose myself, I overflow, unable to hold myself together. If I could still mount a horse . . . but no one remembers Santa Rita the Fisherwoman. No healer calls to me, no house of Jarê. Slowly the people unlearn what they once understood; so much has changed.

I felt profound sorrow at the sight of those two on the ground, forsaken. Even if I've grown numb in the face of cruelty, I can't help but grieve to see men spilling blood to destroy dreams. I've witnessed masters hanging their slaves as punishment. Cutting off their hands for having stolen a diamond. I once came to the aid of a woman who had set herself on fire rather than remain enslaved. I've seen women tear their children from their wombs, to free them from being born into slavery, and many of those women would also die as a result. I've seen women go mad after being separated from their children who'd been sold off. I remember the cruelty of a master who'd sleep with Black women, then beat them to death and walk away, as if purging himself of the wickedness that had made him surrender to lust. I saw a master use the body of a slave as a plug for his leaking boat. The boat made it safely to its destination, with the enslaved man drowned inside. In times of drought, I've seen men and women barter their plots for a bag of beans, a hunk of beef, because they couldn't stand the hunger any longer. Severo was killed because he went into battle for his community, for their land. He fought to liberate his people. He wanted their rights to be recognized, the rights of families who'd lived for so long on that land, where children and grand-children had been born whose umbilical cords were buried in the earth of their backyards. The land where they'd built their homes and erected their fences.

I became a fine rain falling on those folks in the middle of nowhere who were fighting to save Severo's life. I entered his mouth to wash out the blood. I broke against the shoulders and heads and backs of all those gathered around the two of them, husband and wife. I saw a strange wagon come racing down the road. It took Severo to the city, but they were too late to save him. Through Água Negra, a river of blood was running.

Belonísia unwrapped the kerchief from her head and embraced the children who were crying, calling for their parents. In their desperation to save Severo's life, the adults had let the children get too close, and they saw what had been done to their father. It was Tonha who moved quickly to shield the girls and take them back inside. Salustiana began lighting candles, praying to the saints and encantados for Severo's life. After that, there was only silence. No rain was heard, no wind. Salustiana hugged her grandson Inácio tightly, asking him not to lose faith. Everything had gone awry. Severo's parents and siblings soon learned what had happened. I saw Hermelina pass out and hit the ground like a decapitated hen. Not even my breath could stir her.

When Bibiana came home in her bloodstained clothes, her mother knew that something inside her had been irremediably torn. She made her daughter take off those clothes marked by violence, and wear something appropriate for the wake. She didn't try to make her eat. She saw how her daughter's eyes stared past any person or thing in front of her. Belonísia longed to embrace her sister but felt herself fading into the distance, like her voice. She couldn't make sense of what had happened, so she focused on caring for her sister's children, trying to lessen the pain, a dim light spilling from their eyes.

They mourned Severo in the house he had helped to build. Bibiana remained at his side, not budging even for a minute, like the ipê tree that does not yield to the blows of the machete. The mourners gave their eulogies, listing Severo's virtues, praising him for bringing a fighting spirit

217

and political consciousness to the workers of the plantation. Some swore vengeance. Severo had made enemies, too, the people who disagreed with his activism, but even they came to pay their respects.

It had been some time since anyone was buried in Viração cemetery. The entrance had been locked by Salomão, the new owner who'd succeeded the Peixoto family. Someone thought to ask Bibiana where she wanted Severo's body to be buried. She wanted her husband buried beside Zeca Chapéu Grande, in Viração. Severo's brothers, with the help of Zezé, carried the body down the path that led to the cemetery. Belonísia followed behind with Severo's children. Hermelina joined the procession, walking with the support of her husband Servó and their daughters.

The simple gate had been fastened shut with a padlock and chain. The procession came to a halt so folks could decide what to do next. Bibiana, who'd said nothing for most of the day, asked them to open the gate, in a voice so quiet that most of them couldn't quite hear her. They obeyed what they thought they'd heard. The hands of the mourners started shaking the old gate violently, with the same force their ancestors had needed to cast off the chains of bondage. The gate clattered to the ground like a busted shackle.

3.

A year after the death of Zeca Chapéu Grande, the new owners of Água Negra came by. The man was tall and burly.

218

He'd visited the plantation a few times while negotiating with the heirs of the Peixoto estate. His skin was the color of sand, a rusty shade, like the banks of the Santo Antônio. He'd often point to his skin color when arguing with Severo and the other workers, to indicate that he wasn't prejudiced, that he himself had Black ancestry and was proud of it. A woman accompanied him on those earlier visits, and later she'd reside with him on the plantation. She was White and petite, not quite thirty by the looks of her. They had two children who only came to the plantation much later, and for very brief stays; they attended school in the city. The couple would wander around Água Negra, the man's eyes widening as he examined his property more thoroughly, the woman faking an interest. She seemed perpetually bewildered, entering rooms hesitantly, repeating the same expressions of surprise, and barely concealing a smile at the ignorance of common folk whenever she put a question to the workers and heard their responses.

Salomão, on the other hand, was interested in just about everything on the plantation. He was eager to listen to the workers and then argue with them, convinced he understood more about this or that: he'd seen it all before, somewhere no one had heard of. The new owners lunched at Firmina's place during a visit to survey the property and choose the site for their future house. Firmina prepared a small feast for the occasion, killing a chicken and serving it with squash, okra, diced cactus, and rice. Água Negra had been her home for more than forty years, but in Salomão's presence she felt like a mere tenant; and though Salomão was new to the plantation, she sensed she was expected to go out of her way to please him, since she was on his property. Salomão ate heartily, but his wife wouldn't touch the food, thanking Firmina but explaining she was on a special diet. It was clear the woman was repelled by everything. By their dilapidated houses, by the clothes they wore, by the lack of clean, running water. Once, when she had an upset stomach, she was horrified to discover there wasn't a single bathroom in any of the houses, not even in the school. Her face began changing color, from sunburnt to completely pale, and though she refused at first, she ended up relieving herself in the woods. She was given some paper to wipe herself, and afterward tried to hand the soiled scrap back to one of the ladies. "No, ma'am, you can just leave it in the woods," explained the women watching from a distance, outraged yet unable to restrain their laughter. She emerged from the woods thoroughly vexed, wondering how she'd ever adapt to life in this place.

For Salomão, however, the plantation was the apple of his eye. He had ambitions to become a big coffee producer, not knowing if it was even possible to cultivate beans in this region. Later he tried to raise pigs. Ecstatic about how this plantation, unlike much of the Chapada, was so rich in fresh water and unspoiled forest, he eventually decided that Água Negra should become an ecological sanctuary. Not one of his schemes took any account of the people who actually lived on that land. They were simply workers who could be relocated. In fact, they were squatters, and should go live somewhere else.

Salomão hired men to bring in construction materials and build his new house. When it was finished, the house offered a bizarre spectacle to folks who'd been living at Água Negra for a long time. The buriti and palm trees that were so abundant in the swampy part of the plantation were all chopped down. Having had the area drained, there Salomão built his house, a house of wood and glass. To Severo that house was an affront, because, way back—long before Zeca Chapéu Grande had passed—he had organized a petition asking permission to upgrade the workers' mud huts, which were cesspools of disease and in danger of collapsing. They needed to be built with more durable materials. Some of the workers agreed with him, others didn't. Some argued that the land belongs to the owner, so he gets to make those decisions. That's the way it's always been; no reason to start changing things now. Others, however, were aware that they had certain rights. Eventually Severo and some of his fellow workers reported back that their request had been denied. Many workers, in fact, were critical of the prohibition, but it was necessary to bite one's tongue or face eviction. These days, however, folks talk openly about the rights of Blacks, the rights of the descendants of slaves forced to wander from place to place. They also discuss the law, and the possibility of securing land, for they no longer live at the mercy of the landowners like their forebears did.

I'm an old spirit, an ancient encantada, and I've been with these people ever since they came here from Minas Gerais, from the Recôncavo, from Africa. Maybe they've forgotten all about Santa Rita the Fisherwoman, but my memory won't let me forget how I suffered with them when they fled from land disputes and armed conflicts and the ravages of drought. I've traversed centuries; it's like walking over the surface of a rough river. The battles were always unjust. I've watched these people endure the annihilation of their dreams.

Two weeks before Severo was murdered, Salomão and his wife, Estela, left the plantation. They were taking a trip, apparently. After Severo's body was buried, what folks wanted was to burn that house of wood and glass to the ground, to see it consumed by flames, reduced to dust and ashes. They wanted to destroy the things that had been denied them.

4.

One man spoke up and said that there was still a chance those responsible for Severo's murder would be brought to justice. Painful as it was to lose a leader, they must honor his memory by pursuing their shared goals, still waiting for them on the horizon. He added that it would be irresponsible to get carried away by violence, to put their dreams at risk, to hasten their own defeat. Then someone else chimed in, agreeing that cooler heads must prevail, despite what had just happened. Yet another voice likewise urged self-control; their reaction shouldn't be governed by hatred.

It was a long night. Bibiana stayed up with the lamp still lit in the living room. Later, she would let the house go dark when everyone had gone to sleep. Inácio tucked his sisters into bed. Ana was asking about her father. Where is he? If he's under the ground, will he feel cold and wet when it rains? Will he get hot beneath the noon sun? Inácio didn't have many answers to his sister's worries. Everything he knew about such things stemmed from Salu and Hermelina's beliefs in the encantados, beliefs reinforced by his parents, Bibiana and Severo. Salu's instruction was an especially powerful influence on Inácio, as was his closeness to the world of the encantados, for he'd spent much of his young life beside a Jarê healer. Inácio said something or other to his sister, without thinking much about what he truly believed, and eventually she gave in to her exhaustion. Inácio went back into the living room and asked his mother if she was going to bed. She said she would when she felt tired. He drew close and put his arms around her as she sat in the chair. He kissed her forehead. Bibiana felt her son's tears falling on her own hot tears that wouldn't stop trickling from her eyes. He begged her not to worry; he'd take care of her. His words demolished what was left of Bibiana's composure. Inácio was already a young man, a bit older, in fact, than Severo was when he'd left Água Negra with her.

And so the day she and Severo ran away from home came alive again in Bibiana's memory as she embraced her son and surrendered to weeping, easing her agony a little. She'd accompanied her husband's lifeless body to the hospital with his head resting on her lap. The smell of blood seemed to have penetrated her flesh, even after she'd washed and changed her clothes. She thought about the mourners smashing the gate to the cemetery where their ancestors were buried. And about their decision not to set fire to Salomão's house. Scarcely more than a day had passed and already so much had changed, and so abruptly, that it was impossible to process it all. When her son went to bed, Bibiana remained in the dark, hoping some sign might appear to her and offer direction. She leaned on her memories, on the struggles she and Severo had experienced after leaving Água Negra. She remembered the various jobs she'd taken as they tried to make a life for themselves far from the plantation: cook's assistant at a roadside restaurant, cleaning lady, babysitter. In the meantime, she'd borne her children. She even got her teacher's certificate, which was one of her objectives. She discovered, however, that life beyond Água Negra wasn't so very different after all; she was still being exploited. But she had Severo, and the dreams they shared, and everything they'd already built together. They had their rough patches, their quarrels, but above all else was an intimacy even she couldn't fully explain. An intimacy that grew from their shared histories, from what they'd learned about themselves, about their people. How that journey had made them both fall in love with the place they'd left behind! The desire to return grew stronger as they understood more and more what it meant to belong to a community of people out there in the country, people invisible to the rest of the world.

Before sleep could claim her, Bibiana rose from her chair. The sun was peeking through the doorway and windows. She opened the door and felt the fresh air touch her skin. What would happen next, now that Severo was gone? What would happen to her, now that she carried this emptiness inside? She had her children to raise. Before she had a chance to really think about the days ahead, her mother and sisters arrived. Salu began preparing coffee. Belonísia and Domingas sat with Bibiana, the three of them gazing through the doorway at the landscape, and the singing of birds seemed like the song of an entire life. The song of a past that was as close as it was distant. The song that accompanied those girls when they'd head out with their father in the early morning to scare the cowbirds from the rice paddies.

Later, the police showed up at the door. Even though Inácio and Domingas exhorted her to stay inside, Bibiana refused and went out to speak to the officers, to answer their questions regarding the murder. She alternated between moments of numbness, when the officers had to keep repeating the same questions for Bibiana to comprehend, and moments of sudden outrage and agitation, apparent in her gestures and the tone of her voice. She strove to recollect each fraction of a second, each step, each thought and gesture, even what was written, word for word, on that piece of paper she'd gone back for when Severo was riddled with bullets. But she had nothing else to add. Only that a car had sped off toward the highway, at least that's what some of the neighbors had told her. The officers spoke to them, too, taking note of the color of the car. The tinted windows, the neighbors explained, made it impossible to see how many people were in the car or who they were. The officers asked if they'd noticed anything unusual during the days preceding the crime, or if Severo had gotten into any heated arguments with anyone. After the tenants explained that there had been animosity between Severo and the owner of the plantation, the officers seemed satisfied. They stopped asking questions. They invited Bibiana and the other witnesses to drop by the station if they had any more information.

For a brief period it seemed that maybe things were truly going to change, that there would be some justice. A worker had been murdered and the police were getting to the bottom of it, just as they would had it been a landowner or some big shot from the city. A few weeks later, word arrived that the investigation had been concluded: the officers had discovered marijuana being cultivated out near the marsh. Severo had been killed in a dispute between drug traffickers.

5.

That same day, Bibiana decided to call the community together. Caught in the nets of grief, she nevertheless felt compelled to share what was on her mind. Things couldn't continue as they were, or they'd all be in danger. Though she still felt an emptiness inside, she wouldn't let Severo's memory be sullied by a lie. That lie would multiply and become a narrative, and her husband could no longer defend himself. And what about the children, having to listen as their father was being maligned? Bibiana wouldn't allow his legacy to be ruined by a fabrication the authorities seemed intent on spreading. Out of respect for her, folks stepped away from their chores and gathered to hear what she had to say. Salu made her way out slowly, leaning on Domingas, now married, and her son-in-law. Belonísia, limping, accompanied Bibiana's children, though she was uncertain at first if her sister wanted them to be present. "There's nothing to hide," Bibiana responded, with a firmness she'd been lacking in the weeks after the murder. "As much as the truth hurts, it's better to get it from one of us. I want my children to hear this, so they'll be able to stand up for their father with the same arguments."

Belonísia felt like her sister's shadow. She'd tried to avoid that feeling, that role, ever since Bibiana, almost instinctively, started speaking for her. Ever since Belonísia began sharing her most intimate feelings with Bibiana. At the same time, she'd gained access to the ferocious movements of her sister's mind. She felt, more than ever before, that they'd been united by an inexorable destiny, mapped out by the trails they were walking. After all this time they no longer needed to communicate in any visible way, whether by an exchange of glances or by reading the other's gestures. The air around them, she felt, would simply vibrate to transmit the discomfort, mental or physical, emanated by the other. It would transmit the other's excitements and desires. Those days revealed to Belonísia the degree to which they understood each other. She'd developed an acute perception in relation to people generally, but her ability was magnified when the person was Bibiana, her voice in a world she navigated in silence. The silence in the fields and in the house where she'd lived for a time with Tobias, that silence was conducive to enhancing the fierce power of her senses, connecting her to whatever was around her. Life was simply confirming what had remained hidden to the eyes of strangers, perhaps even concealed, at least initially, from her own sister; the bond between them had only strengthened, and it was something powerful and inescapable.

For much of her life, Bibiana had watched her father organize teams of workers on the plantation or guide participants during the Jarê rituals. She never imagined, however, that the need to address the community might fall on her own shoulders. Though she'd been active in the movement, Severo was the center of attention, rallying the resistance against Salomão and his men. She understood she was now vulnerable to the same violence, given the lies being spread to demoralize the workers of Água Negra. She felt as though the bullets were homing in on her and her family even after they'd found their target in Severo.

As she was about to address her neighbors and relatives, Bibiana began to tremble. She noticed Salomão watching from a distance, mounted on his horse and accompanied by the new manager. He then dismounted, and moved to the shade of a jatoba. He was there to intimidate her. His presence was clearly intended to silence her and the others, or at the very least to make sure they measured their words. This was his property, and he wouldn't tolerate folks sowing chaos, spreading more of Severo's ideas, ideas designed to undermine him. "There've never been no quilombolas around here": Bibiana could hear that old refrain even before he said anything. But there was no turning back. She was possessed with rage. She looked at her people. They were waiting for her to say something.

Bibiana was visibly shaking when she asked everyone to please be quiet so she could speak. Belonísia looked away, afraid to be possessed by the same fear her sister was emanating, but Bibiana's confidence grew as she began speaking. The shaking gave way to a voice that was strong and self-assured, a voice that could change minds.

"Our people made their way to this plantation long ago. Each of us knows the story; it's been repeated many times, a thousand times. Many of us, most of us, in fact, were born on this land. And what did our people find here? Nothing but hard work. Everything you see around you exists because of your hard work. I was born here. My brother, too, and my sisters. And Crispina, Crispiniana, their kids. And those who arrived from somewhere else have already spent most of their lives here at Água Negra. The Peixotos never set foot in these fields, but they got rich from what we planted here. You know the story of Damião and Saturnino and Zeca, my father. You know all about Jarê, and you know what we've lived through. No one knows better than you do how many times this land has been blighted by drought, how many times our crops have been swallowed up by the Utinga and the Santo Antônio."

She paused to catch her breath. She felt overwhelmed by these memories, by the need to defend her people. She looked at her own children. They were paying close attention standing beside Belonísia, whose body pressed against the girls like an animal protecting her young. Her mind was flooded by disjointed memories, and they all led to Severo.

"Everyone knows what Severo did for our community. He arrived here as a young man, and later we departed together to make our own way because things here got too difficult. But Severo loved and respected this community. He was conscious of our history. He knew full well what our people had endured long before coming to Água Negra. Back when Horácio de Matos sent ten thousand of his slaves to find diamonds for him, to wage war on his enemies. And even when Black folks were given freedom, still we were bereft. Our people wandered from place to place, asking for shelter, suffering hunger, working without ever getting paid. Working just to be allowed to live on this land. The same slavery as before, but dressed up as freedom. What freedom is that? We can't build brick houses, we can't plant the crops we need. They take everything they can get from our labor. We work from Sunday to Sunday, without seeing a penny in return. What free time we have we use to grow our own food, because if we don't, there'll be nothing to eat. It's been this way for too long: the men out in the boss's fields, the women and children in their small gardens making sure the family doesn't starve. So many of those men have died of exhaustion. Some make it to old age, but their bodies are broken."

Salomão was grinding the heel of his boot in the dirt, and the sound could be heard during the brief pauses between Bibiana's sentences. Every now and then, someone— Crispina, Crispiniana, Isidoro or Saturnino—would glance back at him. Some of the locals were whispering among themselves about his presence. Maria Cabocla was there, too, staring attentively at Bibiana; she wore a faded kerchief wrapped around her head of gray hair, with five of her ten children beside her, the ones who still lived on the plantation.

"But we won't stop fighting for our liberty, for our rights. The seed that Severo planted will not die. One of us is gone; he was my companion, the father of my children. But there are many more of us on this plantation. They plucked one fruit from the branch, but the tree remains. With roots too deep to be wrenched from the soil. The lie they're spreading, that Severo was growing marijuana, doesn't convince anyone. We know who plants the marijuana in those fields." Bibiana spoke without taking her eyes off the crowd assembled before her. "Severo and I lived in the city for a while, on the outskirts, where the police used the same excuse to break into homes and kill Black folks. Those cases never even went to court. The cops can kill anyone they like, they just say it was in self-defense. It wasn't self-defense, it was murder."

Other voices, voices of people who'd always kept mum in Salomão's presence, started joining in. It upset them to see Bibiana so distraught, and suddenly relatives and neighbors and former students felt inspired to speak up. Salomão's eyes betrayed fear; he understood he had to watch his step. Bibiana's speech had attracted a considerable audience, many of the local families, all of them fired up by recent events. Any false move on his part might provoke a response. If he ignited the mob, he'd be at a disadvantage.

"They want to dishonor Severo, because to dishonor his name undermines our struggle. They want to protect the powerful. They want to silence us, expel us from this land at any cost, bend us to their will, but we won't budge. They want us to pack up and leave. Where would we go? They don't care. They set fire to our chicken coops, set their animals loose to destroy our crops, they even forbid us from fishing, with the excuse of protecting the rivers—but we are the protectors. We're a part of this land. If all this were left in the hands of the rich men who own the fields and the mines, it would go to rack and ruin. They even tried to stop us from burying our dead in Viração. But they won't get their way. We're not leaving Água Negra."

Cheers and applause erupted from the crowd. Rather surprisingly, Salomão kept quiet, though he looked restless, still grinding his heel in the dirt. Everyone present understood how bad things had gotten since the plantation was sold. Folks had been living in fear, but Severo had motivated and mobilized them, and in his death they saw the opportunity to make their voices heard. It was now or never.

Salomão didn't wait for the crowd to disperse before approaching Bibiana. He was making an effort, no doubt, to act conciliatory in the wake of Severo's death, but his mere presence was a provocation. Nothing he could say would ease the tension. "I'm sorry about the death of your husband. I was away when it happened, but I heard about it." Then he dispensed with niceties to deliver the real message. "But, ma'am, you can't go around making accusations. The investigation, from what I understand, has been completed. The police handled it very seriously and filed a report." He stood in front of Bibiana and reached out to touch her shoulder, but she took a step back and began walking away. Then she abruptly turned to look Salomão in the eye. "Sir, I'm going to tell you something, just between us. Whoever did this to Severo is going to pay. The justice of men might fail, but no one escapes the justice of God."

Bibiana had already strode off, and her children were trying to catch up to her, when Salomão noticed Belonísia standing beside him. Her eyes were shining, transfixed, making the hair on the man's arms stand on end. Inácio slowed down, waiting for his aunt. Belonísia walked around Salomão's shadow in the dirt and spat into it the venom she'd been holding in her mouth.

6.

Miúda was still so young when I found her. As she turned into a woman, I got used to the layers of long skirts she'd wear. Miúda was like other folks in these parts who didn't call themselves Black. Black folks were disliked; they were pushed off their land. So she called herself an Indian. A lot of Black folks did the same. Indians were tolerated because they had a legal right to their land. Some people weren't happy about that, but the law was on the Indians' side, so the Black folks got wise. Now, there were plenty who'd make a wry face, since it was obvious those so-called Indians were Black. But they'd claim to have a native grandmother or great-grandmother who'd been abducted from her tribe, caught in the jaws of the White man's dogs, as the saying goes. It was difficult to say outright that someone wasn't an Indian, maybe mixed with Black ancestry. Miúda was no dummy; she'd tell folks she was an Indian, just like her mother. And if she said that's how it was, then that was good enough for most folks. Maybe that story helped her survive her journey.

Miúda wasn't one for staying put. Before she arrived at Água Negra, she'd been wandering from place to place. She roamed so much and so far that when she described her experiences, folks would just laugh in disbelief, thinking it was a lie or that she'd lost her wits. She'd cut them off by grabbing the hem of her skirt, shaking the many folds and lifting dust off the ground, then march down to the river. Miúda was part woman, part fish. She liked fishing and swimming in those waters. Mornings would find her asleep on the riverbank. She'd imitate the subtle sounds fish make. She could mimic the songs of birds. Her eyes would sometimes come alive like bright-red tanagers, the birds we call sangue-de-boi; her eyes seemed to want to take off and flutter about. Tanagers like to admire their own reflection on the calm surface of rivers and ponds, but Miúda didn't have the time, the taste, or the inclination for such frivolity. The river was an open vein of her body coursing through the woods. She wept day and night, because her children had been taken from her. During one of the really bad droughts, her compadres back in the city noticed the hunger and desperation that had befallen her family. They explained that taking the children away would make her life easier, since she didn't have a man. Her children would study in the city, learn a profession, they'd be able to help her later. The fish-woman resisted. She prowled up and down the riverbank, day and night, to find fish for her children. She'd make a fire to warm herself and illuminate the darkness. But the mining operations had choked the river with sediment, driving the larger fish away. She caught the piaba that would congregate in the shallows to nibble on the thick skin of her toes, like tree bark. But the piaba were so small they didn't even add flavor to the mush she made with manioc flour. And so she turned to planting, all by herself, and produced quite a lot. But when floods came, or drought, there was nothing to be done. When the crops had been lost, or taken from her by the landowners, she could only try to fool the children's hunger. Someone came and removed one of her boys. Then it happened again. And then someone came and removed two of her boys at once. Now Miúda was alone. In her solitude, the nights grew longer. One day, before the sun came up, she started walking down the road, amid the sound of insects, toward the city, where she asked for her children back. Her compadres replied that it would be better for the boys to stay in school, life was more pleasant there, there was plenty to eat, they had everything they needed. Miúda the fish-woman walked away, devastated. She returned to her shack by the river. She wasn't afraid of snakes or peccaries. She'd fish for piaba, and when it rained, the headwaters brought much bigger fish to her table. Miúda's hands were enchanted; they cast a spell on the fish. She'd reach into the river without disturbing the water. You only needed to watch her on the riverbank to see how cunning she was. The fish wouldn't even struggle to get free; they surrendered to her hands.

Santa Rita the Fisherwoman wandered alone, witnessing the history of an entire people who wandered, like her, from one place to another, looking for a home. For so long. She watched as battles raged over diamonds, and later over the land itself. She saw plenty of folks being murdered. When Santa Rita the Fisherwoman mounted the body of Miúda, it gave a purpose to that woman's power, the power that had begun draining away in the absence of her children. When she danced in the house of the healer, Miúda's long skirts spun round and round. Her arms undulated like the river currents of the soul. She cast her net around the sorrows of the congregation, carrying them deep into the waters. During those hours, we were one entity. I felt the comfort of being sheltered in the body of a strong woman. I was a fish-woman, too. I was a fish-woman inside another fish-woman. She moved as if she had fins, and the fox barked in the night as she danced. The onlookers would mock her, having forgotten all about Santa Rita. Having forgotten that I was the lullaby in the night when their ancestors fled from ruin. But Miúda paid them no mind and danced, casting her net, arms rising and falling, a wild river overflowing. My powers reached whoever was in need of them. The father of her father's father once lit a candle to cure the fever of his master's son beneath the waning moon. The mother of her mother's mother, on the run and desperate, sang one of Santa Rita's songs. That old dance makes me happy, and it makes me sad.

I've stopped dancing because no one remembers Santa Rita the Fisherwoman. Because the healer of this land is dead, his powers gone, his house demolished by time. I rise like air, I come down like rain on the land. I come down to wash away the blood that has been mercilessly shed. The blood of history flows like a river. First, it flows through dreams. Then it comes galloping as if on a horse.

7.

Days later, a minister of the church was brought in to hold a worship service. The intention was to assemble those few residents of Água Negra who'd go to church on market day with lists of prayers and sins. Most folks participated in ceremonies or pilgrimages, but this was the first religious celebration on the plantation that had nothing to do with Jarê. After the death of Zeca Chapéu Grande, folks went looking for other houses of Jarê, other healers to take away the old man's hand and place a different hand on their heads. Several years had passed at Água Negra without a Jarê celebration, and during that time two families had converted to the Evangelical faith, living more or less harmoniously alongside the others, even if they denounced the old ways in private.

Before the service, Salomão's wife Estela and the minister toured the plantation, inviting folks to attend, their car stopping at each and every house. Estela was wearing a white dress with a floral print. Her skin was red, but not from too much sun; it was like she'd eaten something that had caused an allergic reaction, leaving blotches on her neck and arms. The minister was well known to everyone in the region; in fact, he was planning to run for councilman, so he'd been visiting plantations and villages to ask for votes in the October election.

"They act like good Christians now, but it was always just an act," Bibiana remarked, after Dona Tonha told her about the service.

"You know, it's funny about the minister's visit," Salustiana said to Bibiana as they sat outside. Belonísia was nearby in the garden, watering the plants. "Because today I woke up thinking about Bom Jesus, all those stories I heard when I was a girl, stories I've shared with you many times. But, Inácio, I don't think I've told you this one, or perhaps your mother has."

"What story, Mama?"

"It's a story about the area called Lagoa Funda," she replied, shelling beans while her grandson spread a fishing net for mending between the door and a fence post. "My grandmother told me that the Black folks showed up in Lagoa Funda, who knows when, and each family had their little house and their plot to cultivate. They planted in the floodplain of the São Francisco River. They had children, who grew up and built their own houses and farmed their own plots near those of their parents. For a long time, there was nothing and no one else in those parts. Just them and God. But one day, the Church started claiming great tracts of land all around the city. It didn't take long for them to reach the surrounding areas, including Lagoa Funda. They said our land belonged to the Church as well."

"So the people had to leave?" Inácio asked, taking a break from his mending to hear the rest of the story.

"No. But the Church put a branding iron to all the trees around there, burning the letters B and J into the bark, for Bom Jesus. They went around marking everything. They said that all of it belonged to the Church, and that we were the slaves of Bom Jesus. Well, folks didn't take it very well. What did slavery have to do with them? My grandmother said she'd heard of slaves living in other parts, but there were no slaves in Lagoa Funda. Everyone thought of themselves as free. And today, Inácio, I'm remembering what your late father used to say: Black folks came to Brazil already enslaved. So Lagoa Funda must have been founded by folks who'd escaped from a plantation or been freed by their masters. But nobody there wanted to bring up the past. In Lagoa Funda, everyone was born free, there were no masters. They had erased the memory of captivity."

"Maybe it was too hard to talk about, Mama," Bibiana said as she filled up the sack she'd be lugging to town. "What they suffered was so awful, they didn't want to speak of it."

"Could be. And after they'd marked everything with the initials of Bom Jesus — I saw so many trees there, from jatoba to oitizeiro, with those letters burned into them — after they'd explained that the people of Lagoa Funda were now the slaves of Bom Jesus, for many years folks just went on living their lives as they'd done before. But later, the big-shot ranchers and farmers showed up, documents in hand, and they started putting up fences, so then folks fought back, and a lot of them were killed, and the ones who survived were pushed onto a much smaller piece of land. My mother and father escaped to the Fazenda Caxangá, and that's where I met Zeca." She wiped the sweat from her face with a rag. "If we still had that land, the great big world that our elders told us had once been ours before the fences went up, maybe I wouldn't be here at Água Negra, and neither would any of you. Your father's parents wouldn't be here either, Inácio."

Bibiana and her girls headed to town, while Salustiana and Belonísia stayed behind. Inácio didn't go with his mother but walked over to the floodplain. Estela and the minister finally arrived at Salustiana's door, inviting her to join them at a service to be held "for the souls who have departed," which Salustiana promptly turned down. "Thank you, but I'm busy." The minister, a man who spoke loudly as if he were always preaching to the multitude, began expounding on the lives of the saints; from the doorway, he'd noticed their portraits on Salustiana's altar. Belonísia was stomping her feet impatiently, her expression clearly indicating she wanted them gone. She was standing partially hidden by the door, ready to slam it shut at the first offense. The man went on talking as Estela forced a smile, foreseeing the failure of the minister's intervention. She finally interrupted to explain that Jarê had been practiced here for years, that Dona Salu had even played the drums during the ceremonies. But the time had come for everyone to hear the word of God.

Belonísia was about to slam the door on her right then and there, but her mother held it open. They were talking about religion, but Salu couldn't stop thinking about the struggle for the land and Severo's murder and the threats and prohibitions designed to push them off the plantation. The minister's visit was one more assault, one more attempt to dominate them. She drew herself up authoritatively before her two visitors, to say something that had been suffocating her for a very long time.

"Look here, ma'am," Salu interrupted the woman before she could go on pontificating. "I can't read well, I haven't got much learning, but I want you to understand something. I'm just one of many who live here. A lot of the folks you're trying to kick off this land got here long before you did. You and your husband weren't even born yet. And a lot of these folks were actually born here. I've got children, all of them born at Água Negra, and I've got grandchildren, too. Now, I can't tell you every little thing that passes through people's heads, 'cause I don't know what folks are thinking, so I'll speak for myself. I was born in Bom Jesus, but my home is here. I came here as a young woman. I lived here, raised my children here, toiled in these fields with my husband, saw many of my neighbors and compadres get buried right over there in that cemetery you locked up. I gave birth to this land. You know what it means to give birth? You've got children, but do you know what it means to give birth? To feed new life, to bring it out from inside of you? A life that goes on even when you're no longer on God's good earth? Maybe you're not aware, but most of these folks you see around here were born into my hands. I'm the mother who catches them from the womb. And just like I welcomed each one into my

241

hands, I birthed this land. You understand what I'm saying? This land lives in me," she pounded her chest, "it sprouted within me and took root. Right here," she pounded her chest again, "right here is where the land lives. I'm part of this land, with all my people. Água Negra lives in my heart, not on that piece of paper that belongs to you and your husband. You can yank me from this land like a weed, but you'll never take the land from me."

Estela's face grew pale. She tried to interrupt Salu, without success.

"One more thing. Maybe I'm not a healer, but I know how to put a hex on somebody. I know what food and drink to offer my guides, so they'll fix a few things around here that just ain't right." Salu turned her back to them and shut the door.

8.

There it was, the knife, luminous, among some other items in Belonísia's straw bag. Bibiana couldn't believe she was looking at it—the knife that had vanished from the old house. She thought Donana had gotten rid of it. Bibiana walked out of her mother's place, out to the front yard where her daughters were calling her to witness the baptism of Ana's dolls. She went over, in silence, then walked back inside toward the old chair where the blade was protruding from the open bag. She wanted to confirm that it was, indeed, the same knife. She reached out to it. The blade was hot to the touch, almost burning. She felt ashamed to be nosing through her sister's things, but she couldn't help herself, surprised to encounter something so deeply buried in memory. The scar on her tongue began aching from the recollection, even tingling, returning Bibiana to the day of the accident. Her grandmother's hand once again struck the side of her head, racked with questions as she stood before that object. She drew the knife out by the tip until it was entirely revealed: the beautifully worked ivory handle, the pommel and guard of duller metal, and the brilliant blade, untouched by time. The edge of the blade seemed to vibrate, eager to rip through the surrounding atmosphere as if splitting a silk scarf with one slice.

Her sister walked into the room and stopped dead, suddenly thrown back thirty years to find Bibiana once again removing the knife from the bloodstained rag. The rag, in fact, was long gone, but the silence in which Bibiana held Belonísia's gaze left her suspended in time, as if nothing could move forward until she offered some explanation.

Belonísia had grown into the habit of taking the knife with her everywhere she went, so her expression could only stand in stark contrast to the deep perplexity on Bibiana's face. The blade was shining even more brilliantly, and the sisters felt the chill of a shadow from a cloud passing over the house. Belonísia gave two light slaps to her jaw, then ran her thumb down her face to say, yes, it's Grandma's. She put her index and middle fingers together, then moved them back and forth over the fingers of her other hand, as though cutting them, to indicate, yes, it's the knife. She repeated

243

the gesture of the light slaps to the jaw and her thumb coming down her face. She didn't need to; Bibiana had understood. Bibiana asked if Salu knew about the knife. She indicated no. Why not? Salu would get needlessly worried; Belonísia didn't want to go back to being treated like the problem child, the one who'd mutilated herself. But why was she carrying that thing around with her? For work, of course, and for protection; look what happened to Severo— Belonísia's index fingers went gliding through the air, pointing toward her sister—and because she'd lost her tongue. The knife had returned to her; it was some sort of sign. She kept it for reasons she couldn't fully explain. Bibiana asked where the knife had been all that time. You wouldn't believe it, Belonísia responded, shaking her head, placing one hand over the other with palms turned upward.

When she left home to move in with Tobias, bundling up her few possessions, traveling to the banks of the Santo Antônio on the rump of his horse—that morning when she felt her womb tremble as she was taken to her future home—she could never have imagined the shocking amount of filth that awaited her, the piles of rubbish scattered throughout Tobias's house. That first glimpse caused her spirits to slump as she wondered what it would take to make the place habitable, how difficult it would be, now that she'd traded her parents' home for that barren dwelling. She wasn't able to clean up the house immediately; the first day's start was followed by many more days of hard work, tossing out garbage and empty bottles and whatever else was strewn around that pigsty.

Amid clods of dirt, she noticed a ceramic container—like one of those old-style beanpots—forgotten in a corner of the kitchen. Belonísia held off opening it, afraid she'd find a rat or a spider or even, recollecting the tales she'd heard, someone's bones. There was a piece missing from the mouth of the pot. Later, she accidentally bumped against it, breaking off another large piece from its mouth. When she lifted the vessel to set it down in a different spot, she heard something clatter inside. Still she would've turned away from it, but a beam of sunlight fell in such a way that it bounced off whatever was in there, catching her eye. A diamond. It's the first thing anyone in the Chapada region would think of. Everyone hopes to find—or be found by—the radiance of that stone someday. She removed the lid. The point of a knife was gleaming with more intensity, now that it was exposed to the light. Not yet recognizing what it was, Belonísia took it out: one more item to either throw in the trash or keep, if still useful.

The ivory handle touched her palm. Like the ceramic pot, it was warm from the sun. She felt a tingling in her mouth, just like the time she found her grandmother's knife. The intense brilliance, the mystery surrounding it, her desire to discover what it tasted like and her constant bickering with her sister, all had led to the outcome that silenced her to the world. The memory of Donana after the accident came alive in her mind: wandering around the backyard, calling to the daughter who had disappeared, warning her grandchildren to watch out for that jaguar, and Tonha telling them, when they got back from the hospital, that Donana had gone down

245

to the river carrying a small bundle. The bundle, the blade, the pot she'd bumped against. Here it was, the same knife, warmed by the sun, but cool beneath Donana's bed, hidden in her suitcase. Here was the edge of the blade, tearing the veil of the past, irrupting into the present, making Belonísia confront that terrible day.

Tobias walked in and noticed the look on her face— stunned, lost in time. Belonísia threw a dishtowel over the knife on the table. Tobias had forgotten his fishing pole. He'd catch something for dinner when he was done with work.

"I won't give him back the knife," she thought to herself. "It belongs to my family." She found a safe place to hide it, between Tobias's wardrobe, old and warped, and the wall, where only her hand and the object could fit. After she became a widow, she removed the knife from its hiding place. She started taking it with her to the fields and to the river. She used it to defend Maria Cabocla, to break the will of Maria's husband, who lost his swagger when he saw the blade and the fury in Belonísia's eyes. But Bibiana would know nothing about all that. Belonísia brought the story to an abrupt end before the memories started flooding back. She heard her sister say that even after so many years, the knife looked like it had just been taken from Donana's suitcase. The suitcase with which Bibiana had left home, and with which she'd returned. "Watch out for Ana, don't let her near that thing," Bibiana said, handing the knife back to her sister. "She's curious, like we were."

Bibiana headed out, but then turned back.

"Belô, why do you think Grandma kept this knife hidden like a treasure?" Belonísia's bottom lip curved downward into the shape of an archer's bow. "Maybe you don't remember, but there was something that puzzled me, not back then, we were still so young, but years later when I'd think back to what happened." She said this as Belonísia placed the knife in her bag. Bibiana pointed her finger at her sister. "Why was the knife wrapped in that filthy rag? It was stained with dried blood." Now she was whispering. "And why did Grandma keep the knife, if she felt such fear? She never worried about other things that were dangerous to us, like that shard of mirror or whatever."

Belonísia pressed her thumb and middle finger to her heart. "Fear?" She sought to understand what her sister was driving at.

"It was never the knife hurting us that worried Grandma. She was afraid of some secret she was hiding."

9.

Donana stole the knife from a sheath left forgotten that afternoon on the porch of the big house at the Fazenda Caxangá. Some visitors had just arrived. She took advantage of the sudden bustle and distraction when the menfolk took their horses for a ride, and she swiped the knife. She took advantage of the fact that the cowhands accompanying those important men had let down their guard. She took advantage of being at the right place at the right time, having walked

247

down the road to the big house. She'd just been looking for a bit of shade from the harsh sun addling her mind, when she came across the sheath slung from the railing. She removed her big hat, pressing it between her hands. She thought the knife was very beautiful, one of those precious items belonging to the big house she was strictly forbidden from entering. The handle was made of something like marble, she had no idea what. The blade itself was radiant. It looked like silver, probably worth a lot of money. All in all, the kind of splendid object only bosses carried with them. She started thinking about her children, who needed shoes and clothes; it was getting hard to mend their threadbare garments. A thought went through her mind: "They take from us, so we'll take from them." She'd ask God and her encantados to pardon her. She put the knife in her straw basket under the manioc she'd gathered that morning, feeling tired and gloomy. "May God forgive me," she whispered and stepped out of the cool shade, taking the treasure with her, unnoticed by anyone.

On the way home, she grew more certain that God would forgive her. After all, those people owed her a lot. The work that went unpaid. The merciless sun punishing her while she toiled in the fields. She was thankful for her wide-brimmed hat, but it wasn't enough to protect her during those long hours of exposure. In that hell called Caxangá, the hell of slavery into which she'd been born, she wasn't even allowed to give birth at home. She gave birth to Zeca out in the fields, in the marsh, with the help of the women who worked beside her, beneath that same sun currently befuddling her mind. The knife was hers now; she deserved it. God would surely forgive her.

But her initial plans for the fruits of this small crime were never realized. Donana grew so attached to the knife that she concealed it in a hole she dug beneath her bed. She felt nervous when she heard the other workers talk about a knife that had gone missing, that belonged to a guest of the plantation owner. Donana hid her fear inside of her, not breathing a word to anyone. One false step, and she'd be turned in. She heard that they were threatening to send the foremen into every single house to search for that knife. They might make an example of her by cutting off her hands, then kicking her off the plantation. But later, word went round that the knife had been lost somehow when the men went riding that afternoon, an afternoon that would remain vivid in Donana's memory. The workers were deployed to search the fields of corn and manioc, sugarcane and castor beans, but they found nothing. In time, the lost knife was forgotten.

While the search was still ongoing, Donana mulled over where she could sell her newfound treasure. Not in town, where everyone knew everyone else. They'd ask what a woman without a pot to piss in was doing with such an expensive, expertly wrought tool. It wouldn't take long for the accusations to fly. She thought about selling it cheap to any passing peddler or gypsy, so long as they were strangers to the big house, so long as she made a little money from it to spend on her children. But she kept putting it off, for Donana was in no hurry to part with that knife, and didn't trust the peddlers who'd show up at her door. In the end, she figured she'd leave the knife to one of her children as an inheritance.

When folks had stopped asking questions and the workers had quit searching the thickets and fields, Donana exhumed the knife from under her bed, away from curious eyes. She wiped the blade, polishing the metal with an old rag which she then wrapped around the object. It was so beautiful. What she felt, as she admired the pilfered knife, was that it was the most splendid thing her hands had ever held. She was keeping it for herself. She'd take the knife out, wipe and polish it, then bury it back in the hole in the ground beneath her bed. It was a nuisance to bury and then unbury the knife every time she wanted to admire it, so she covered the hole with a rug made from the hide of a peccary.

She would never give that knife to anyone. Not to any peddler, not to her own family as an inheritance. That's the decision Donana reached after seeing one of her grand-daughters lose her tongue. God had not forgiven her. Worse, God had wounded the flesh of her flesh, a granddaughter she'd watched over and prayed for, protecting her from curses and the evil eye. She'd meant to teach the secrets of the encantados to her granddaughters, just as she'd taught her eldest son. Not so they'd become healers, but so they'd be free, free even from those obligations that had dogged her all her life. She wanted to teach them the mysteries of the spells and of the encantados to help them with the challenges they'd face. She wanted to teach them so that they could become women on their own terms, so that they could help others who needed it, but, more than that, so they could find the freedom denied them since the time of their ancestors. From plantation to plantation, from Caxangá to Água Negra, Donana had lived as a captive. She wanted those girls to grow into women in charge of their own destinies.

When the knife came to serve its ultimate purpose in her hands, a purpose she never could have predicted, Donana found herself entangled, for the rest of her days, in a fatal web. It all started after her eldest son left the Fazenda Caxangá to find work and a place to live on another plantation. Without Zeca, her mainstay, Donana felt alone, raising her younger children by herself. Then, a new worker arrived at Caxangá. A generous man, who shared his strength with Donana as she worked in the fields. He'd finish his tasks and then help her with hers, when her body ached from toil. The lonely Donana let him get close to her, take shelter in her modest home, join her in her daily struggle and bring warmth to her bed, making her feel, despite so much fatigue, alive again. And so she found herself living with him, this man whose name Donana would erase from her memory, rendering it unspeakable. A man no one outside the household, not even her own son, would ever know anything about. A man who arrived from who knows where. And where he ended up, only Donana knew.

When she came home to find her daughter Carmelita, still so young, underneath that man, his pants pulled down, right there in Donana's bed where she'd find some solace from endless toil, Donana collapsed to the ground like a broken-down donkey. Her body stiffened as though she'd never rise again. Then she howled with rage and gathered up her children, furious with herself. For some time, Carmelita had been keeping a certain distance, whimpering in the corners of the house. Donana knew something was wrong, but would never have suspected what she'd just witnessed. Carmelita had been avoiding her eyes, but Donana just thought her daughter was unhappy with her for bringing a man into their home. A whole year had gone by like that, then two, and this was the third. The bruises her daughter couldn't hide, as though she'd become clumsy, bumping into furniture, tripping over things, they all made sense now. Donana's man had been hitting Carmelita, abusing her, threatening and raping her under Donana's own roof, and she let that happen? Carmelita begged her mother for forgiveness, the mother who now couldn't look her daughter in the eye; the daughter who wanted to run away from home. Carmelita was planning to strike out on her own, just like her brother did. And that man who lived with them made no amends. In fact, he grew cockier, ordering Donana around, because he was the man of the house. He'd put a bridle and reins on his woman.

She made the decision one night when the moon was hidden behind the clouds that later would wash the land clean. There was still no sign of rain, but she knew it was coming. There'd be no traces. He went off to fish, taking a bottle of cachaça, as he liked to do. Donana used to keep him company; now, she no longer fished beside him. She stayed home, her mind corroded by anger, by what she'd seen, by the enduring pain, by her daughter's ruin. When

Donana arrived at the spot, she found him asleep on the bank. He looked dead even before being sliced open. There was no light; Donana wasn't carrying a lamp. She didn't want to attract attention or leave evidence behind. No one would know. If anyone asked, she'd say he left home without telling her where he was going. Before working out such details, she bled the man the way you bleed a pig. Then she filled his pockets with stones and dragged his body into the river. Nobody was likely to pay her a visit and ask a bunch of questions anytime soon. She walked home dripping with sweat from the exertion. But those few hours when Donana was out of the house, repairing her last mistake in the lands of Caxangá, gave Carmelita enough time to run away, leaving no message. The rest of the story is this: Donana would spend the final years of her life seeing Carmelita's face in the faces of her grandchildren.

When morning arrived, she was certain of one thing: God would never forgive her wickedness. Worse, he'd pay her back twofold.

She could smell the rain that soon would fall.

10.

Salustiana, your mother, always said that her hair started going gray when she was just eighteen. She stopped straightening it with an iron and began tucking it under a kerchief like the other country girls. You look at yourself in the mirror that's leaning against the wall—the dried mud would crumble if you nailed anything to it—and pull the pins from your mouth and fix your hair, noticing how gray it, too, has become. Something you inherited from Salu. Maybe it's become even grayer in recent weeks as you try to make sense of everything that's happened. As you get through these nights of watchfulness and fear, ever since your husband was taken from you, the companion who'd given you so much of himself.

You move through the house like a ghost. Sometimes you don't hear people when they talk to you. You stay awake deep into the night, tossing and turning beside your daughter, Ana, whom you've brought to your bed because you can't bear the emptiness of your room. You watch her sleeping, the flutter of her eyelids, maybe she's dreaming, but then your mind returns to your husband. When you give up trying to sleep, you rise and open the door to feel the night air. You leave the door ajar, even though the memory of what happened to him returns with every noise in the night. You remember the violence every time you glance at the motorcycle parked in back of the house, every time a car goes by. Your mind, confused by his abrupt absence, keeps returning to those fateful moments. When a cloud hides the sun, the shadow is like a figure passing through the room. You hear the horn of a motorcycle, and your throat tightens as though a hand were squeezing it, but how would you explain this to your students? You hear those particular noises and mistakenly think it's your husband coming home. The places he frequented are charged with an electricity only you can feel. And there's the smell of his clothes, untouched in the closet.

His pillow, now your pillow, infused with the scent of his body. When you manage to sleep, you awaken slowly as if coming out of a long dream and hesitate to reach your hand over to his side of the bed. You're reassured by a familiar smell, by the soft gust of breath, by the warmth emanating from the person beside you. You reach out your hand, not daring to open your eyes, and find your sleeping daughter. But whenever you're startled awake, your eyes open wide with terror, and grief, and you're instantly aware that he's gone. That's when the tears come, uncontrollably.

Your youngest daughter asks when her father is coming back. You tell her he's not coming back. She starts crying, and yet you don't comfort her. If you had been the one to go, your husband wouldn't let the children become weak. He'd teach them to move forward by finding a purpose in their work, in the unending struggle. Then you stroke your girl's head, you lift her to your lap and promise her something that's within reach, maybe an ice cream or a bag of popcorn next time you go to town. But you won't tell her that he'll come back; it would be too cruel. Even a girl that young shouldn't cling to a promise that can never be kept.

In the morning you drag yourself to the backyard. You light the wood in the outdoor stove, and you think about the enamel mug that will remain on the shelf because you're not capable of drinking from it, not even your children dare touch it. You don't know what to do with the questions that haunt you: what if you hadn't forgotten that piece of paper? If both of you had headed off together to the city, would that car have caught up to you on the road? What if you hadn't come back to Água Negra ten years ago? Or if the two of you hadn't spoken up against the injustices? The many ifs ambush and ensnare you in invisible lianas from which you can't easily extricate yourself.

You went back to teaching, but something was ruptured forever inside of you. The children grow wild in the face of your indifference. Not even from a distance do you resemble the teacher you used to be, the one who taught math and science along with the history of Black folks, making those children feel proud of being quilombolas. Telling and retelling the history of Água Negra and of the times long before the diamond mines and sugarcane, before the whippings, before the abductions from their original homeland to be shipped across the ocean to a new continent. The children would listen with rapt attention; they hadn't known there was such an ancient history behind those forgotten lives. A sad history, but a beautiful one. And they began to understand why they continued to encounter prejudice at the clinic, at the market, or at the notary's whenever they went into town. Where people would point and sneer, "look at those hillbillies," and call them "backcountry Blacks." They understood how history repeated itself. You instilled in them a sense of respect for their own stories; but now, even you seem uninspired by the possibility of change. You've stopped believing that what those children learned in school could make any real difference. Nothing pacifies the rage within you.

A few weeks ago, you began leaving the house in the darkness of the early hours. Carrying your hoe. You wouldn't tell anyone where you were going, what you were doing.

Maybe you wandered down trails and followed the river as a way of assuaging the pain that never diminishes, the pain eating away at you. You'd return home before sunrise, oblivious as to whether your children were still asleep in their beds. You'd sit in your chair, your hair covered with grass and dirt, your hands knobby and thick like your father's, the hands of a farmer. You'd fall asleep in your chair, and for that brief period you seemed to be at peace with the world. You'd wake up when Inácio or one of the girls came in and asked why you were so filthy. Mud on your face, your neck, your hands, your clothes. "I was working in the backyard," you'd say. But in the backyard, there was no sign of your labor, nothing new had been planted. In fact, some of the plants had withered for lack of water and attention.

Your hands ached. They throbbed all day long. You'd immerse them in a pot of ice-cold water and leave them there for a while, palms scratched and swollen, covered with calluses. Your hands, in fact, would bleed. You'd hide them from view and not explain. They resembled the wounded hands of Christ. The hands of your people, your ancestors. Hands that helped them survive, that brought forth food as well as enchantments, working with powerful herbs, moving them over sick bodies. Hands that built defenses and, when possible, meted out justice. The healer's hand, which he placed on the heads of his children.

With the strength of those lacerated hands, you were simply opening a path.

11.

After you were silenced, you missed being able to sing. When you were still very small, on those nights of Jarê, you'd sit in the center room on your mother's or grandmother's lap, and sing invocations to Saint Barbara and Velho Nagô. But your singing was spoiled too soon. You couldn't make the songs echo even inside of you. When you were able to make sense of what had happened, you asked yourself, why do we want the things that are most unattainable?

You remained attentive to the subtlest sounds. You knew when the xanã was making its nest, or when the fox was approaching to steal eggs from the coop. You could hear the rattlesnake's warning from afar. Or the monotonous song of the finch, the one called rabo-mole-da-serra, or the long claws of the armadillo digging a burrow, when no one else could hear them. You'd stop what you were doing to listen to the warble of the tapaculo, and you'd feel it resonate, vibrating in your body. That's how you allayed the silence in the solitude of your backyard after your sister left home, or in the house by the Santo Antônio after Tobias had died, or when you could no longer stand beside the man who was your father and teacher. The woods made you strong and perceptive, even when you were still a young girl, allowing you to see the movement of the world. You once heard someone say, "the wind doesn't blow, the wind is the blowing."

Shortly before you were silenced forever, your mother came back from the fields to find a plate of couscous prepared for her. It took her aback. She asked who'd brought

258

it over. Nobody. "Who made this?" "I did." "But you could have burned yourself." That offering of food touched your parents, exhausted from their labor, and they were grateful. The land was your treasure, part of your body, something very intimate. Whenever you went to the public market, walking to town with your limbs made coppery by the buriti pulp dripping down your dark skin, you couldn't wait to get back to the plantation. You never understood how your sister could live in that chaos of motor cars and buildings and people. Any little thing required money there, the slightest thing. But out in the country, the food was right within reach. If the drought or the floods wrecked your crops, you could eat whatever was spared. You could make food from manioc flour or gather jatoba seeds to make crêpes. In the city there was no land to dig into, nowhere to experience that lucky omen of humid air foretelling rain.

You've been recollecting, especially lately, the brief period when you lived with Tobias. The unpleasantness you experienced in his bed. Your relief when you learned he'd died. His grave, untended, overgrown with weeds, you never visited it, not once. Not due to rancor or even negligence, but because you came to understand that time in your life as a mistake that needed to be erased from your mind, even though the persistence of memory frustrated that wish.

The best thing Tobias ever did was unintentional: he returned your grandmother's knife to you. Perhaps that was the purpose behind your mistake. No matter how many years had passed, you remained just as fascinated by the radiant blade. When you were able to hold it in your hands again, you saw yourself reflected with that same radiance in your eyes, both the girl and the woman, the innocent and the guilty. The edge of the blade had split your life from that point onward. And each time you polished the blade and saw yourself in that mirror, you knew your life could be split again. Like the umbu tree, either leafy or barren, in the fleeting rainy season or during the rest of the year. The day when, filled with rage, you pressed that blade against Aparecido's neck, your life almost split again. You wanted to protect Maria Cabocla, who had touched you with her fingertips, braided your hair and laid you down in her bed to rest as though you were her beloved warrior returning from battle.

Suffering: it's something difficult to express, a feeling shunned by everyone, but it tied you, irreversibly, to your people. Suffering was the secret blood running through the veins of Água Negra. And how you suffered when you climbed the trunks of buriti and palm fruit, your feet maimed by the spines. Your arms too were a source of suffering, the muscular arms of a soldier, tilling the land to sow, then to reap, despite knowing that sometimes there'd be nothing to reap, or that what you brought home could be taken from you by the owners of the fields. Limping along, watching over your house and crops, watching out for animals and misfortune. Caring for your father who was preparing to die. The heartache that wouldn't let you forgive your sister completely, just like when you'd quarrel as children. The recurring nightmare in which you were pursued and cornered, in which Donana's knife was the blade that once again opened the flesh, the world, the ground itself, from which a river of blood began flowing.

You recall your father driving that heavy, ancient plow, its bent iron tearing the earth in crooked lines. Those furrows into which he'd cast kernels of corn. And that plow, it was something no one bothered to mention: it just belonged to the landscape. It had been there since before folks had started pouring in, no one knew where it had come from. That plow had been guided by the hands of workers arriving from distant places, workers long since forgotten. The ones who cleared the forest and whose hands then drove that plow to prepare the fields for planting. The same knobby, wounded hands that the workers of Água Negra tried to hide from view. Hands that dug with a hoe, breaking up clods of soil and weeds to help the manioc flourish in that ground, or to bury their dead. Hands sorting herbs for prayers and medicines. The incantations, the candles, the rhythms of the encantados churning the air, the fish swimming against the current.

That's when you sense, and come to accept, that your hands, those same hands that cultivate the land from which life itself is harvested, those hands could boost, or fail, the struggle of an entire people. You've been digging within yourself now that Severo has been taken, robbed from your nephew and nieces and your parents, from your sister, from you. He taught you about the rights that were yours but were being denied, and, like your father, he shared with you a forgotten history. It was eating away at you, what they did to him and what they could still do, what they wanted to take from your people.

261

You've been roaming all over Água Negra. Through woods and marshes, along rivers, across every acre of the plantation, trying to identify and commit to memory each single tree. Your knowledge of those trails and paths has formed a precise map in your mind. You needed to become familiar with every slope, every ditch that had been filled in or left open, every movement of the landscape, every departure and every arrival, every captive animal, every animal that was wild. You'd leave in the early morning and lose yourself exploring each nook and cranny of the forest. You'd return filthy, exhausted, your clothes increasingly tattered. No one ever asked where you'd been; what for? They knew you wouldn't respond.

And the sounds, the sounds of animals, of rustling leaves, of flowing water, those sounds kept reverberating inside of you. During your daytime duties. During your light sleep at night.

You felt that the sound of the world had always been your voice.

12.

Estela came running down the road from her house on the edge of the marsh, out of her mind, as though fleeing from a fire. Her tearful children were being reassured by Santa and her daughter, who'd been passing by with their loads of laundry and fresh fish. Estela's screams were enough to draw folks out from their homes. She was wearing a white night-gown of delicate and almost transparent fabric. Her youthful breasts swung this way and that in her frenzy, her firm nipples visible through the nightgown. No one could make sense of what she was saying, while her children's cries grew shriller; they were calling on their mother to come back and comfort them. The women heard from the men what had happened, and, with the usual speed of bad news, word spread quickly down the street and to every house. Salomão was dead.

Salu traveled the short distance between her house and Bibiana's to tell her daughter what she'd heard. Bibiana, busy grading her students' workbooks, didn't look up. After a moment, she took off her glasses and invited her mother to sit down. "Are you upset, Mama? You should rest a little." She poured a cup of coffee, then carried it to her mother in the living room. "Salomão had a lot of enemies," she said, returning to her workbooks, lowering her eyes once more. "Sooner or later, this was bound to happen."

Her mother sipped the coffee. "But it could have happened anywhere. Why here? Salomão owned other plantations, even other houses." "When these things occur, Mama, they occur where they must." Bibiana had the resigned voice of a widow still in her first year of mourning. "It's only right for Estela to feel in her bones what I'm going through." She said it without looking at her mother.

"What's this, Bibiana? Is this how your father and I raised you? You should never wish ill on anybody, no matter what you think of them."

"The workers should've burned down that house with her and her children inside. Then there wouldn't be anyone to inherit this land and expel us . . ."

Salu jumped up, knocking over the chair in her agitation. Bibiana glanced up at her mother and told her to leave the chair as it was, she'd pick it back up for her. But the old lady, having already suffered so much hardship, was appalled by the violence of Bibiana's words. She struck her daughter across the face. It was the second time she had ever hit one her daughters. She remembered the first time, the beating she'd given Belonísia because of a kiss, the kiss Bibiana said she'd seen her sister give her cousin. Now Bibiana was touching her face, burning from the slap, as she held back her tears.

"I never thought that, in my old age, I'd have to do that to you, Bibiana, after you'd already given me grandchildren. But I didn't raise my children to go around causing harm to anyone. Don't ever wish for somebody's death. Isn't it enough, the misfortune that's befallen our home? You want more punishment to come to us?" Salu moved toward the door, drying her tears with the back of her hands. "I'm tired, Bibiana. This is not the life I wanted, and I'm afraid for my grandchildren." As she left, she asked, "What kind of a world are we leaving to them?"

Bibiana remained standing. She didn't pick up the fallen chair. When her mother was far enough away, she surrendered to a weeping she'd only allowed herself the night her boy had said to her, after Severo's murder, that he'd take care of her. Her hands were aching and wounded. She started shaking them in the air as if that gesture could alleviate her pain. Not even this news—that the man she held responsible for her husband's murder was dead—brought her any peace. The emptiness she was feeling seemed to expand with time, opening a pit inside of her that only got deeper. The hardest truth for her to face was that nothing, not even winning the dispute for the land, would bring her husband back.

Belonísia, who'd gone out before daybreak, returned home at noon. She brought some manioc, sweet potato, and a large squash. She put it all on the kitchen table. Domingas and her husband as well as Zezé were in the living room, sitting beside Salu. When Belonísia heard her mother explain what had happened to Salomão, she stood stock-still, her face expressing astonishment. She lifted her chin toward her brother, asking, through the movement of her lips and hands, for more information. Salomão's body had been found nearly decapitated, lying by a forest path not far from the banks of the Santo Antônio River. The horse he'd been riding showed up near his house, that box of wood and glass. It was alone, grazing on the edge of the marsh. Apparently his wife, on her way out, noticed the horse and thought it strange. Tião and Isidoro were going down that same path to the river to fish when they discovered the body, next to a large pit. The real mystery, which Zezé had been discussing with the others when Belonísia entered the house, was the pit. Some folks said it appeared out of nowhere, others said it had been getting larger and larger over time. But that pit didn't seem to be the work of any man. It was as if the land had been opening up by itself, making a well, wide and deep.

Belonísia noticed that her sister wasn't there. Had she heard the news? Yes, they answered. Salu, though upset by

Bibiana's attitude, didn't want to tell Belonísia about it. She was ashamed of her daughter's hatred. Belonísia could imagine how painful it must have been for her sister to hear about Salomão while still seeking answers regarding her husband's murder. She decided not to go looking for Bibiana just yet.

When Belonísia went back to empty the bag she'd left in the kitchen, she fell hard to the floor and blacked out, like a bird struck down in flight. Everyone rushed over to her, and amid the commotion Zezé and Domingas's husband carried her into Salu's room. Salu immediately started praying as she removed the scarf wrapped around Belonísia's hair. Domingas pulled off her boots and unbuttoned her pants and long-sleeved shirt, both caked with dirt. When she awoke, Belonísia didn't remember a thing. She didn't recall that Salomão was dead. She had no idea what she was doing in Salu's room. She didn't remember her own exhaustion from work. It was as if the entire day had vanished from the calendar. She grew agitated and tried to get out of bed. Salu told her to stay put, she needed rest. "It must've been the heat," her mother said, handing her a cup of water, trying to understand what had just happened to her daughter. "Did you eat before you left this morning, Belô?" But she didn't get an answer. Belonísia seemed distant and tired. She drank half the cup of water, then leaned back against the pillow, staring up at the thatched roof. She fell into a deep sleep and didn't wake until the next day.

It didn't take long before the detectives arrived, in two separate vehicles. The plantation was suddenly besieged by armed men. They interrogated everyone who'd seen

Salomão's body and everyone residing along the main road, although Salomão had been found deep in the undergrowth. The rain over those last few months had put more leaves on the branches, casting shadows across the paths. Withered trees and open clearings had been transformed into a dark wood where someone might easily lose his way. The interrogations were relentless. The detectives wanted to know if Salomão or anyone else had mentioned any threats against him. If he had enemies, if there'd been any suspicious activities or unfamiliar cars or motorcycles; if any strangers had recently passed through who might have been studying Salomão's habits, so as to know the most advantageous moment to commit the crime. The tenants of Água Negra grew nervous. But they didn't believe that one of their own could have acted with such savagery.

13.

A kernel of corn slid from Belonísia's hand into the plowed earth. With her feet, she gently loosened the soil to cover the seed. The movement of the world would handle the rest. There was more land to farm now. Her feet were once again on the floodplain of the Utinga, shaping the damp, dark earth nourished by the overflowing river. The rain had been generous over the last few weeks, falling abundantly, inviting the workers to cultivate their plots with whatever they had to plant. There were fish in the ponds that had suddenly appeared in once arid places. Another kernel dropped from her hand into the earth, forming a subterranean trail of golden seeds.

Many years before, she'd often felt her body tremble like the damp earth of those fields. Living among the young women of the plantation, she thought that her destiny to be a mother was also being mapped out. But, like the rain, that desire vanished without explanation. Years later, whenever she was seeding the fields, she could feel nature quiver all around her, just like before. When she was alone and knew that no one would be watching or judging her, she would lie down right there in the field, the way she'd seen her father do innumerable times. She'd listen for the most intimate sounds coming from the most secretive places inside the earth; this would help her free the crops of pests, find solutions to all kinds of problems, and boost the harvest.

The workers had already begun building houses with more durable materials, even before Salomão's murder. They wanted dwellings that wouldn't crumble so quickly and would mark, in an enduring way, their relationship with Água Negra. The children who'd gone off to work in the city sent money home to pay for the new construction. Those tenant farmers who managed to retire with a pension began purchasing building materials on loan. They'd return in the quiet of the night with loaded wheelbarrows and wagons, so as not to draw attention. Saturnino, with the help of his children and grandchildren, was the first to lay down brick. Another resident passed by those walls going up and decided to do the same thing. The managers, following Salomão's orders, rushed over to give them a hard time, but it was too late. The landscape had already begun its transformation. Salu mentioned to Zezé and Belonísia that she, too, wanted a brick house, but she needn't have: her children had already guessed. She was an old woman, and she wanted to live comfortably, without worrying about the walls crumbling around her. The rainfall was usually sparse, but when it did rain, it rained violently, damaging those mud houses. Salu, who had never truly owned anything, never gave up on the dream of having a proper house, a dream she'd cherished with her husband. She wanted one with whitewashed walls and a tile roof. Zezé, Inácio, and Belonísia devoted their weekends to building the family home. Bibiana and Salu pitched in by making lunch for everyone. There was a sense in the air of new beginnings, like the feeling of planting in the fields after a drought or flood had come to an end.

No doubt perceiving that the workers' disobedience was growing into an unstoppable movement, Salomão petitioned the courts to rule that any part of the plantation occupied by tenant farmers was still, in fact, his property. It caused an uproar among the workers. They had no idea what they'd do if the tractors knocked down their houses and forced them off the plantation. Genivaldo was the first to speak up loud and clear: he wasn't about to move to the city just to "pace the sidewalk," as folks around the plantation liked to say. "I was born here. Working the land is all I know. I'm not leaving." Others felt the same way. They all met with Bibiana and decided that if an order came from a judge—entirely possible, given Salomão's connections—they'd lie down right there on the ground in front of their houses to stop the tractors from demolishing their homes. No family would abandon the family next door, no matter what disputes they might have had in the past. Together they'd resist to the end.

They prepared themselves for war, just as those powerful coronéis used to do when they were fighting over the mines. But these folks were fighting for the right to live on the land. The courts were taking their time, and while everyone awaited the decision, someone went and killed Salomão. Suspicion fell immediately on the workers. Many were taken to the police station for questioning, including Bibiana, as well as her son. Being there reminded Bibiana of her husband's murder; not a full year had passed. The police pressed her on her role in the unrest they'd heard about on the plantation. Bibiana explained that she was a teacher, and for many years she'd been married to an activist. She declared she was a quilombola. They responded by telling her there were no quilombos in that region. She said calmly to the police chief and to the clerk taking notes: "Look at our suffering, look at our struggle. Of course we're quilombolas."

The folks at Água Negra were worried that Salomão's death would mean trouble, that his assassin lived among them. At the same time they began hearing talk from Salomão's other plantations, tales of similar discord between Salomão and his workers and neighbors. Wherever he went he left a trail of discontent, a desire for revenge. It made the detectives' work more difficult. They collected testimonies and followed every lead, but the investigation led nowhere.

Estela had moved to the capital, but she continued to manage the plantations from there. Acquaintances reported that the woman had gone crazy. Everywhere she looked, she saw people conspiring against her, plotting to kill her. She wouldn't leave the house and imposed ruthless discipline on her children, worried that the retaliation that had felled their father would eventually find them.

News of the two murders brought public officials to the area months later. They interviewed the tenants as part of a land redistribution process. Among the workers, the arrival of those officials was celebrated with sighs of relief. Everything would remain somewhat vague; there was no deadline for a definitive solution to the problem, but all this bureaucratic activity meant that the existence of their community was a public fact. The workers were no longer invisible. They couldn't be ignored.

It was a time of great upheaval. Inácio was about to leave his mother's house, moving to the city to prepare for university entrance exams. He wanted to become a teacher, and participate in the same social movement as his father. Bibiana supported his decision; she never let her son see that his absence would make life harder for her. She put on a brave face, unlike Belonísia, who gave in to melancholy. She loved her nephew and nieces as if they were her own children. She was always near them, ever since Bibiana had come back home. Domingas would soon have her first child, but Belonísia had no intention of letting anyone else drift away. She was done with goodbyes.

She imagined that, on the day of Inácio's departure, she'd have to console Bibiana. Before Inácio left, Salu, Bibiana, Belonísia, and his sisters all lined up for farewell embraces.

271

Flora and Maria had written letters for him to take with him, saying that they'd miss their brother, and, should he find work, they expected gifts from the city. Ana gave him a picture she'd drawn of the entire family, including their late father. Inácio hugged each of them, with a longer embrace for his mother, but it was Aunt Belonísia who wept so much that he had to wipe away her tears, begging her not to cry. He'd always return at the end of the year. He'd remember everything she taught him. Belonísia gave him a bottle of honey and a chaplet with an image of Christ carrying the cross. It would be his amulet.

Long after the car had driven off and the family had returned to their various tasks, Belonísia remained by the door, looking down that road and at everything else she couldn't quite see from where she stood. Bibiana was about to start grading students' work, but she got up from the table and stood behind her. She wrapped her arms around her sister's waist and nestled her face against her neck. Belonísia held her sister's hands in hers. They both closed their eyes and shared the moment, surrendering to that gesture and experiencing something that might be called forgiveness.

14.

I could no longer restrain my longing to ride, to gallop over fields, to swim in rivers and sprint across this earth with two feet and a body. From the other side of the road, I'd stare at the ruined house, the image of Saint Peter carved into the wall, holding the keys to heaven. Then one day the house was gone, demolished by the softly falling rain. I longed for a body that would move among the devotees on festive nights that were celebrated no longer. There was something profound in those eyes and in those prayers, in the encantados, the Indians, Blacks and Whites, the Catholic saints and spirits of the forest, one after the other pouring into the emptiness of that expanse of parched scrub; without God, without medicine, without justice, without a piece of land to call home. But the people have forgotten their encantada, her name is no longer spoken, and so she begins to forget who she is, and the fateful hour approaches.

I glided over to Bibiana's bed like a gust of air. At first, I wanted to comfort her in her pain, which grew like a weed in an abandoned field. I slipped in as she inhaled, occupying the emptiness in her eyes, taking hold of her so completely, it was as if she'd been enveloped by embraces. I'd forgotten the power of riding a body; how good it was to immerse myself again in the rivers of blood, in the fire of a bosom pulsating with life, in clouded eyes, in desires and freedom I lifted Bibiana from her bed, then walked her here and there, raising her arms and letting them fall with every turn around the living room, and with the tips of my fingers I venerated each fraction of her dark skin.

Wandering her house in the night was not enough for me as I gazed out at the vastness of the world, knowing what the two of us could accomplish together. Every woman feels the strength of nature her body houses in the vital torrent of her life. I headed out to do what I most enjoyed, to get my feet wet in the shallows of the river. I took Bibiana out walking in blackest night, under the call of the owl. Her body would be soaked in dew when the first light of morning appeared. Her strong arms were ready to take down her prey. I raised the heavy hoe, then buried it in the rough earth to dig a trapping pit, tearing out the first clod of soil. Bibiana's eyes were two searchlights scanning the horizon. I'd brought her to one of the many hidden corners of Água Negra. Her body carried within it the maelstrom of those who survive. With each swing of the hoe, she split the air and blew out an evil she'd witnessed. A woman who killed her son so he wouldn't be enslaved. The tortured body of a man hanged from a branch of jatoba. Each strike of the hoe lifted a clump of damp earth from the riverbank. Another strike. And another. The loosened earth flies through the air like sand, blows toward the river, buries a bush of bitter melon.

Every night when I tread those paths, I see the ruined house where the encantados once reigned. Like a seed dropping into plowed earth, I slip into Bibiana's body. Every night, I breathe her breath. And I return to the spot where a trapping pit slowly takes shape. The darkest place of our nights. The hoe comes down, and the pit grows more defined. The land itself can be a trap. We will trap a wild beast that's on the rampage, terrorizing the people of Água Negra: the jaguar Bibiana's grandmother had seen. She was the only one who saw it. She'd warned folks to be careful. The jaguar was a memory of the distant past. Now it had returned to terrify the tenants of the land. This wasn't the same jaguar that had once protected Bibiana's father when he was a boy, when he'd gone crazy in the woods. No, the jaguar we were hunting had tasted blood, and it was keen to kill again until it got what it wanted.

We've spent so many nights digging out the earth, making the pit, that Bibiana's hands are covered with lacerations. In the morning, when I leave her body, she tends her wounded palms, worked numb, punished with blisters and welts from making war.

Then, late one ordinary night, I crossed the yard and approached Belonísia. She was alone, like Miúda. Wild. She knew the land better than anyone. I became one with her flesh and off we went, racing across wetlands, jumping over fences, past rivers and houses and dead trees. Her name was courage. She took after Donana, the woman who gave birth in the sugarcane, who raised her house and her crops with the strength of her own body. The woman who felt the pains of labor and lay down in silence, biting her lip, giving birth to yet another child. The woman who buried two husbands, and didn't bury the third only because she'd bled him the way you bleed an animal. Riding Belonísia's body, I could feel that the past never deserts us. Belonísia was the fury that had traveled through time. She was the daughter of a strong people who'd been wrested from their land, who'd crossed an ocean, who'd left their dreams behind and forged in exile a life that was new and luminous. The people who made it through, withstanding the cruelty of their treatment.

In the chilly early morning, before folks had bundled up and headed off to work, Belonísia's body was a burning flame. She knew the jaguar was making its rounds. But what if someone were to challenge the beast, provoke it, lure it into the woods? What if it were to fall into the trapping pit we'd made with our hands and our ancestral strength? And what if someone were to bleed it to find peace, dispelling the fear caused by its very presence? The sound of a machete hacking down a tree echoed through the woods, but there was no machete. The sound of a plow tearing through flesh. The sounds Belonísia's mouth couldn't turn into words, they reverberated now like thunder.

I see from inside her eyes.

The jaguar fell into the pit but was holding on, clawing at the edge. The trap, hidden deep in the woods and covered by a mat woven of buriti fibers and dried cattails, filled it with terror. Some people swear that overseers used this kind of trap long ago to capture runaway slaves. The jaguar hit the bottom of the pit, its fangs driven into the ground. It wiped the dirt from its mouth. No, it was foolish to think the pit could hold the prey. But as it made to escape, a blade slashed its neck with a rage the beast had never before confronted.

On this land, it's the strongest who survive.